LEGACY

LEGACY

A POLITICAL THRILLER

C. A. SACHA

Matador
9 Priory Business Park,
Wistow Road, Kibworth Beauchamp,
Leicestershire. LE8 0RX
Tel: 0116 279 2299
Email: books@troubador.co.uk
Web: www.troubador.co.uk/matador
Twitter: @matadorbooks

ISBN 978 1800461 970

British Library Cataloguing in Publication Data.
A catalogue record for this book is available from the British Library.

Printed and bound in Great Britain by 4edge Limited
Typeset in 11pt Adobe Garamond Pro by Troubador Publishing Ltd, Leicester, UK

Matador is an imprint of Troubador Publishing Ltd

This book would not have happened without the following people: Katrin and Richard Laurence, Sam Barnes, Nikhilesh Dasgupta, Chris Curry, Wendy and David Price, Gwyneth Olofsson, Karen Dennison, Denny Denham, Christina Malone and Christine Singleton.

Daniel Blythe read it and suggested there was a kernel of a good story and I should rewrite it. I did twice. It has meant my husband Paul putting up with the loss of his wife for more than a decade.

I'd like to thank all my friends who stuck with it and asked on a regular basis, 'How's the book going?' Well it is here, done, finished.

It wouldn't have happened without the team at Troubador.

If you like it, tell your friends about Legacy; who knows perhaps one day someone will turn it into a film!

CONTENTS

PART THREE

GATHERING EVIDENCE

PART FOUR

ATTACKS ON US SOIL

PROLOGUE

Light from the window shone across an exquisite vermillion lacquer screen. On it the life-size tiger shimmered, the gold's intensity reinforcing the sense of living flesh. The powerful creature, rather than leaping forward, lay beside the river intent on licking one of its paws. Looking more closely he saw the embedded jade thorn. He flipped his own talisman; a movement so familiar he barely registered the movement. He looked to the other side of the screen. A large mother-of-pearl horse, its head down, was drinking calmly from the lapis lazuli river, unconcerned by the proximity of the tiger. Above these symbols of good fortune and intelligence swooped iridescent long-tailed birds.

'Do you remember the story?' A thin, high voice broke the silence.

He nodded.

PART ONE

WHEELS SET IN MOTION

CHAPTER 1
BUCEPHALUS

Dr Tomas Olofsson watched fixated as the liquid dripped down the pipette into the flask, unaware Professor Li had come into the lab and was standing close behind him.

'How is it progressing?' Professor Li asked.

Tomas looked up and stepped to one side. The professor picked up the handwritten notes and gave them a cursory glance, before putting his glasses back into his top pocket.

'It's too early to say,' the black chemist said; his lilting voice had an echo of his Swedish upbringing.

The professor didn't ask for more details. It wasn't why he'd come. 'Good – are you coming to our Christmas party tonight?'

'No, I need to be here.'

'Now, now Tomas, I insist. The others will probably go on to a nightclub but you and I,' his hand firmly resting on Tomas's forearm, 'can slip away and celebrate in a more intimate way.' He leaned in conspiratorially close, his aftershave bridging the gap between them.

Tomas stiffened, staring ahead. Suddenly he swept his arm across the bench, freeing himself from the professor's grip; shattering glass as the colourless liquid dropped bead by bead onto the floor.

Fastidiously the professor stepped away, his silk handkerchief quickly to his nose. 'You are an expensive toy,' he looked amused, 'your colleagues think I indulge you. But you and I are more alike than you realise.' The professor turned around and opened the door. Looking down the corridor he called out, 'Maguire, clean up this mess.'

Tomas pushed past the technician, offering no apology. The professor watched him stride away. He caught sight of the coterie of females by the water cooler; everyone within hearing distance an interested bystander. They melted away with smirking glances. He knew the gossip. Tomas was too attractive to be ignored. It made him a target for their wiles and scheming. Yet he seemed impervious to them. It reassured the professor and gave him hope.

Professor Li ran the research facility at LCC. His laboratory kept Finnegan's car empire at the forefront of the industry. He worked tirelessly until he was indispensable. Everyone assumed he took Finnegan's generous package because it paid for his expensive tastes, they even suggested in some way it made it possible for him to swallow Finnegan's homophobic taunts; what no one knew was Professor Li had a very different reason for working at LCC.

♦

'What the hell do you want? It's five o'clock in the morning.'

‘I’m sorry, but this is delicate.’

He’d recognised the caller. ‘Delicate,’ Finnegan repeated the word, making it sound unsavoury.

‘One of my chemists is in trouble with the police. There was a fight and now they want to charge him with an assault.’

‘Why the hell should I care if one of your catamites is in trouble.’ He heard the smothered cough.

‘Dr Olofsson has an idea that will transform your company.’

Finnegan’s attitude changed immediately, ‘How exactly?’

Both men (and for different reasons) were aware of the significance of the next moment. ‘It’s a formula for a new fuel, one that has the potential to deliver an emission-free vehicle.’

Finnegan felt his pulse quicken, his heart thumped, blurring his vision for a moment before clearing. His hand involuntarily went to his chest. He realised the impact such a fuel would have. A world of opportunities opened up; his brain plotting out the critical decisions and investment needed. As the adrenalin coursed through his body he recalled every merger, takeover and accolade. They all seemed like flimflam compared to this. This offered him immortality; the man who changed the world. It would require the utmost secrecy if he was to succeed and make another fortune. He paused, a moment of doubt made him hesitate. He controlled his breathing, recalling the professor’s words – making sure he’d heard the professor correctly, before deciding no one lied to him. They knew what he was capable of.

‘Do whatever is necessary.’

♦

'Mr Finnegan wants you in his office, immediately.'

Josie Ryland put down the telephone, staring blankly at the computer screen unable to move, before a voice in her head screamed, *Don't keep Finnegan waiting*. She entered his private elevator, ironing her clammy hands on her black trousers, hoping her white shirt still looked crisp underneath the boxy business suit jacket.

Eliot, Finnegan's assistant, looked up. There was no smile. 'Leave your phone with me.'

Josie placed it on the outstretched hand. The thick twisted coils of Eliot's gold bracelet reminded her of a shackle. She heard a buzz and Finnegan's door opened. Josie tried to take in her surroundings; get a sense of the man without appearing overawed. Until now she'd only ever seen photographs of him.

He sat underneath a huge Jasper Johns painting. Its surface rippled with thick lumps and smears of pigment and wax; the iconic image of the stars and stripes leaving no doubt as to Finnegan's patriotism. Number four on Forbes list of billionaires, Gene Finnegan had the reputation of a high-functioning psychopath, a businessman with a killer instinct. He was seventy-two.

There was no preamble, no attempt to make her feel comfortable. 'I've got a job for you.'

Josie tensed her knees to stop herself from swaying and straightened her spine. It had the effect of pushing her breasts forward. She noticed Finnegan's pupils react momentarily.

'It's a top secret project I've named Bucephalus.'

On the outside she tried to appear unfazed by the words. Inside she tried to control the rising nausea. Her mouth was dry. She could feel her philtrum glisten with perspiration. The phrase lingered like the smell of cigarettes.

Finnegan rose and crossed to the green tinted glass window. Her grey eyes, framed by her long black lashes and thick hair, followed him. He stared at the city beneath his feet, a dark, brooding presence that blocked the dazzling light; surrounding his profile were millions of dancing motes. As the air conditioning gave out a blast of cold air, Josie's imagination conjured up Alexander astride his horse Bucephalus; the hairs on her arms rose. She shivered.

He turned slowly. 'No one is to know what you are doing.' The silence that followed underlined the unspoken words, "*or else*". The threat felt tangible. 'Eliot has the Bucephalus file.' He sat down. 'I understand you're smart – prove it.' His challenge didn't allow for failure. Finnegan got what he wanted.

'I'm good at keeping a secret.' She cringed. A pink flush coloured her neck. Momentarily she wondered, *Does he know who I am?* Josie looked for any signs of recognition. 'You won't regret your decision.' This time she managed a brief smile.

Finnegan pressed his buzzer. Clearly the meeting was over. As she left, one thought reassured her, she had seen his reaction to her body. It made him surprisingly human.

'Is he always so charming?' Josie asked Eliot, hoping to illicit a reassuring comment.

'Never underestimate him.' It was a stark reminder and a warning to Josie. Eliot returned Josie's phone. 'I've added the number you should use.' She unlocked a drawer and passed over the Bucephalus file along with an LCC credit card.

Josie's right eyebrow rose, inviting more detail.

'No limit,' was the answer.

CHAPTER 2

LUCKY

'Lucky!' Finnegan held his arms wide open in welcome. Andy 'Lucky' Malone owned AMOIL.

'You're the only person who calls me that to my face. Though the way things are at the moment, I'd say you're being ironic. Hell Gene, Lulu persuaded the divorce lawyers to get the case heard in London. It cost me an oil well.'

Old friends, they laughed and embraced. Finnegan sat down in the middle of the hide-covered sofa, inviting Andy to sit opposite him as Eliot brought over the drinks and left.

'Found any new ones recently?' Finnegan asked.

'I'm always looking for new ones.' Andy's answer was jovial.

'So where are you looking?'

Andy realised Finnegan wanted something. This wasn't a social visit. He'd play along and give him an insight. 'The Kazakhstan fields are good but the region's not stable. Brazil is a better option but opening up the fields there requires new technologies.' He paused with a smile on his suntanned face. 'Gone are the days when you could drill down in your own backyard and hit a gusher. Now it is all about tar sands and extracting bitumen from shale.'

'At least the Canadians talk our language, not like those other bastards.'

Andy ignored the remark and instead asked, 'Why the interest in my oilfields?'

'I wanted to know if you're still a gambler.'

Andy relaxed deeper into the sofa, his legs crossed, stretching his left arm along the top whilst cradling the cut-glass tumbler in his right hand. 'You son of a bitch, what are you up to?'

'Got any operations in Africa?'

'No,' he said, remembering a competitor whose Mozambique exploration had come up with dry fields; wasting millions of dollars and driving down the company's share price.

'That's a pity.' Finnegan got up and walked over to the cabinet to refill his own glass, waving the decanter in Andy's direction.

He shook his head.

'I make cheaper cars than they can in Japan, South Korea, or anywhere in Europe.' He took a large gulp, and refilled the tumbler immediately. 'I'm going to build three LCC plants in China.' He sat down, crushing the hide cushion beneath him.

Andy hid his surprise. He'd not heard about it, but if Finnegan was upping his production, it meant AMOIL selling more petroleum. *So that's why he's interested in my oil reserves*, he thought.

'I'll need a grateful Commander-in-Chief.'

He stared at Finnegan, 'Are you saying we support President Montgomery for a second term?' He knew it was always a good idea to limit your alcohol intake in Finnegan's company.

'You and I can put him there with our combined wealth.'

'It will take more than that,' he said, surprised. He never thought Finnegan had political aspirations.

'I know it will – but trust me. I've never met a politician that cannot be bought. Besides, I'll give President Montgomery something so huge, he'll give you access to explore in the most sensitive oilfields; even if they're located in the middle of Central Park!' He laughed loudly.

'What the hell are you talking about?' Finnegan was making him feel uneasy. What was the old bastard up to?

'Find me the biggest oilfield you can because I'm about to change the face of history. I'm going to wipe the smile off those OPEC bastards. I'm tired of America being kicked in the ass! All of that is about to change. I am going to sell more vehicles than even the Chinese can dream of producing. I'm talking about LCC vehicles the whole world will want to buy.' In one gulp he finished off his drink.

There was a long, uncomfortable silence.

'Have you gone mad? Oilmen aren't exactly employees of the month, especially after that incident in Alaska, but that's nothing compared to car manufacturers.' He paused. 'Even I privately accept the earth is heating up.'

Finnegan shrugged his shoulders, apparently indifferent to the impending catastrophe.

Andy sat back. He finished off the remains of the whiskey. He badly needed another. 'And you want to sell more damn cars. You'll have Green Peace barricading your factories, and the government suing you personally for destroying the ozone layer.'

'Also I want you to lease me one of your new oil refineries.' Finnegan paused, 'I know about your acquisition down in Baton Rouge.'

'How the hell did you hear about that?' He stood up, furious, on the point of leaving. 'You son of a bitch, it's meant to be secret.'

He'd often wondered how Finnegan appeared to be so well informed. Most companies had teams lobbying politicians, gathering information, feeding the media with stories but Andy suspected Finnegan had something akin to a personal black ops team. Their role was to apply pressure to reluctant competitors unwilling to sell their businesses, sort out troublesome union leaders, bribe, threaten and who knew what else; actions that were never discussed at board meetings. Ruthless, manipulative, arrogant, a strategist – he ticked off the lexicon of words defining the billionaire sat in front of him.

'Relax; I only want the petrol and diesel fractions. I'm not interested in the rest of your operation.'

Andy got up and helped himself to another drink, giving himself time to regain his composure. They were talking about a business opportunity after all.

'I need access to unadulterated petroleum and quickly and it is vital no one knows we're in this together. Are you still…' Finnegan paused, '*Lucky*?'

Clearly Finnegan was up to something and it was huge. It involved the President of the United States. Andy looked at his old friend, someone he'd known for fifty years. He weighed the risks and took a gamble. 'I'll give you what you want.'

Finnegan stood up. 'This deserves a toast.'

'I'm still not sure what this is all about?'

Finnegan's face was florid but rigid, like a poker player controlling a telltale tick. The words came out slowly. 'We're designing the world's first emissions-free vehicle, and the fuel that makes it possible.'

The magnitude of his sentence was immense. Andy tried to recall any news in the American press about a revolutionary car. Nothing came to mind. How had something this significant been kept so secret? He looked at Finnegan with awe. Everyone knew his employees were well rewarded, but it took more than money to buy this level of silence.

Andy continued to rapidly process the consequences of what he'd heard. If it was true, Finnegan had two problems. The first was the car's design. He assumed LCC had come up with some revolutionary design that allowed the car to run clean, without producing harmful emissions. To protect this change it'd require a patent, giving LCC eighteen months of legally enforced secrecy, before every other car manufacturer began stripping down the car to see how it worked. Could he dominate the world's car market in such a short space of time? If anyone could, it'd be Finnegan. Assuming of course LCC could prove it wasn't merely a clever modification or some other minor change to a pre-existing application. Patents only applied to innovative designs.

But this wasn't his biggest problem. It was the fuel. Chemical formulae could only be covered by patent in America. In the rest of the world, patents excluded scientific and chemical discoveries. They applied only to inventions: how things worked, what they did and how they did it. For the fuel LCC would have no period of secrecy. Finnegan's only hope was to register it as a trade secret. Compared to a patent, a trade secret was not time-limited and it came into immediate effect. It was enforced by non-disclosure agreements and employment law, but that made it vulnerable to a disgruntled employee leaking information, corporate espionage or reverse engineering.

In a flash Andy knew why Finnegan had invited him. *He needs me because I'm the only one he trusts.* Lucky smiled; he knew he was holding a royal flush.

'You'll have sole distribution rights,' Finnegan said as if reading his mind.

'Until the other manufacturers come up with the formula.' He was a pragmatist. He knew his competitors would look at the fuel for answers. But it would take time for them to replicate it, leaving AMOIL in an unassailable position. 'Run it past me once more.'

Finnegan repeated it. 'A car that runs clean, I've called the project Bucephalus.'

'You've found the frigging Holy Grail.' He leapt up, wrapping his arms round Finnegan. AMOIL was going to be selling huge amounts of petroleum worldwide. Suddenly he felt years younger and as his nickname suggested – very, very *Lucky.*

CHAPTER 3
HAM FARM

Josie left for Ham Farm in southern England apprehensive and excited. Her new LCC 4x4 made easy work of the farm track, bouncing in and out of the potholes. It reminded her of driving towards Tugela, her home in southern Africa. She pulled up in the middle of the rough concrete yard. Farm machinery lay rusting, partly hidden by clumps of nettles and yellow ragwort; nature quick to reclaim its tenancy rights. Josie walked towards the corrugated barn, trying several keys before rolling back one of the oversized doors. It creaked in protest at being moved. She immediately ducked, avoiding the disturbed pigeons. She found a light switch and to her surprise the fluorescent tubes flickered on one by one. It was empty apart from a few scattered straw bales. Josie didn't venture further in. There was no need; she'd seen how big it was. Closing the door she walked over to the stable block. There were no signs of recent activity, only a well-rotted manure heap and empty fields beyond. She tapped the red diesel tank, its hollow sound reverberating, answered by the caw of the crows watching from their vantage point. Josie followed the low stone wall. It led to a handsome brick house with a bloated gable-end chimney. The chimney's girth suggested a much older house, remodelled and enlarged as the farm prospered. She peered in through the windows; the chintz-covered sofa and armchairs looked shabby. She wondered how long it had been like this.

♦

Mike Evans dropped his overstuffed sports holdall, took off his full-face AGV helmet and shoulder bag, instantly creating clutter. He was a short bear of a man with an unruly brown beard. In his mid thirties, he was the oldest member of the team. An engine designer for the high-performance and exclusive Genco marque, Finnegan's privately owned company based in England.

'This is going to be more interesting than I thought,' he said with flirty eyes and a broad open grin.

She liked Mike instantly.

The kitchen door opened. A man stepped in, carefully avoiding the low doorframe. As he straightened up, Josie decided he must be six foot four. His lithe body and regular features gave him the good looks of a Hollywood film star. Josie felt disarmed. She'd found it strange. But his file (unlike Mike's) contained nothing about his background or private life, referring only to his brilliance as a research chemist at LCC. Professor Li described his work as akin to alchemy. At the time the word struck Josie as an anachronism, conjuring up a very different mental picture. It certainly didn't fit the man who stood in front of her.

'Dr Olofsson, I presume,' echoing another more famous meeting. Amused, Mike advanced towards him, his arm and large square hand outstretched.

Dr Olofsson merely nodded his head.

Mike appeared to ignore the stranger's aloofness. 'Have you ever sailed?' he asked, appraising Dr Olofsson's physique. He turned towards Josie. 'It'd be a good way to R&R, build our team spirit,' he said smiling.

Josie felt like a bystander. She couldn't decide if Mike was trying to establish his role as the alpha male or merely being friendly.

There was a long pause. 'We had a traditional wood clinker Folkboat. It was designed in Gothenburg in 1942.'

Immediately Josie heard the Scandinavian lilt. He didn't elaborate further. It appeared the subject was closed.

'Then we'll have to see how good you are.' The challenge was clear. Mike picked up his bags, waiting for Josie to show him to his room.

She felt outmanoeuvred. She hadn't expected this undercurrent of rivalry. 'I've sailed.'

Mike dropped his bags and came over to squeeze her bicep.

'I'd better be careful,' he said, amused.

'Where is my laboratory?' Dr Olofsson asked, ignoring them.

Josie realised she had to assert her position and quickly. 'Finnegan insisted this project is to be top secret. If anyone asks you what we are doing here, tell them we've rented the house to use as a base while we prepare for the Fastnet race.' She looked at Mike. '*Grey Goose*, your boat, it's a Contessa, ideal for the Fastnet.' She hoped it would explain their presence at Ham Farm.

'Great cover story,' Mike laughed, 'in my experience boats are like women – expensive and they need hours of loving maintenance.' He winked at Josie.

Josie didn't react. She hoped her first impressions of him were correct. 'If you do let something slip about Bucephalus,' she mimed firing a gun at Mike. On cue he fell to the ground writhing as if mortally wounded before expiring like an actor in a silent movie. She couldn't help herself. She giggled at his performance. But as she pulled him up, she whispered in his ear, 'Bucephalus isn't a game.'

He gave her a long stare.

She turned to Dr Olofsson, 'You and I can begin after lunch.'

♦

Dr Olofsson's laboratory became her focus. They spent hours together, Dr Olofsson specifying the latest and best technical equipment to meet his exacting standards. Josie was shocked at the number of items his laboratory required. Fortunately there were companies who installed bespoke laboratories. The five linked portacabins sat inside the cavernous barn, hidden from prying eyes. Finnegan's deep pockets and her firmness ensured they got priority on any requests. His latest was for clean, pure fuel. He explained any contamination would invalidate his results. To procure this item Josie used the phone number Eliot had given her.

Over decades of marketing the message was ingrained: if you used anything other than AMOIL in your LCC vehicle you were being un-American. Their logos were ubiquitous across the world. Ten days later an unmarked fuel tanker arrived at Ham Farm. Its contents were decanted into a new stainless chamber, hidden inside the farm's redundant diesel tank.

Dr Olofsson – Tomas – was ready to begin work.

♦

'Do you need help in the lab?' she asked.

'I always work alone.'

It didn't surprise her. She'd watched him over the last few weeks. He rose early and went to bed late. Josie realised if she didn't bring meals down he'd never eat. His excuse was always the same. The experiment was at a critical stage and he had to be there. She wondered how he had coped before. He had little conversation. Occasionally he spoke of his work as a quest – looking beyond accepted principles and orthodox combinations. Surrounded by bubbling liquids and humming machinery, she now understood Professor Li's use of the word "alchemy". Yet Tomas never explained what it was he was striving for. She was curious. There was nothing in the Bucephalus file to explain their ultimate goal.

There was an intensity about him that fascinated Josie. She found herself lingering when collecting his food tray, taking her time opening boxes of new supplies; making any excuse to visit him. His physical presence made the hairs on the back of her neck rise and her stomach flip. She felt excited by him; aware of her (inconvenient) growing physical attraction towards him.

Despite his work ethic, the days became weeks and still there was nothing. Each new combination of chemicals failed, before he'd even begun to modify the concentrations. It seemed whatever he was after was beyond his reach. His frustration grew. Josie found smashed glassware in the laboratory. He never apologised. He barely acknowledged her presence. She cleaned it up without comment. His file gave her no clues as to his past behaviour. Josie began to worry about the time it was taking and the lack of progress. The possibility that Bucephalus might never succeed began to surface. How would Finnegan react? LCC's reputation was well known. Finnegan crushed competitors with callous efficiency. What did their lives matter to him? To steady her increasing anxiety she reminded herself Finnegan wouldn't have invested in Bucephalus if he didn't believe it was possible.

However, Josie's paranoia was constant. She worried about the smallest details, innocent out-of-the-ordinary things that suggested something unusual was going on at Ham Farm. She reminded Tomas to take off his lab coat, hairnet and overshoes whenever he stepped outside. She paid the suppliers and collected the consumables herself, so no one would notice unusual liveried vans going up the lane towards Ham Farm. She varied her routines. She avoided using the village shops, choosing instead the anonymity of supermarkets on the outskirts of the town twelve miles away.

Until Tomas found whatever it was he was searching for Mike was left kicking his heels; riding his Augusta on long days out or tinkering with *Grey Goose*. He was too gregarious to be locked away with just her and Tomas for company. She hoped he was a convincing liar, and the people down at

Denny's boatyard believed their cover story. She wasn't sure how long they could maintain it because they never sailed together. Tomas insisted it was a waste of his time. It was more important for him to be in the laboratory.

♦

Josie put the cardboard box down on the workbench. She wondered how he'd fitted in at LCC, where technicians carried out routine tasks. It suggested the professor treated Tomas differently. It made her wonder about their relationship at LCC. 'Are you sure a technician wouldn't help?'

'No,' Tomas replied with his usual brevity.

'Surely something this important—'

He interrupted her, 'There's always pressure to get results. It leads to mistakes. They blame the scientists.'

She was surprised by the sharpness of his words. It sounded like an old grievance. She'd seen how he reacted when frustrated, acting like a petulant child. She hoped Professor Li would support Tomas, if Finnegan demanded that Bucephalus go into production before he was ready.

'How long do you think it'll take?' she asked, hoping he'd open up. There was so much she didn't know about him, despite their intimacy at Ham Farm.

'It might never work.'

She stopped opening the box, shocked by his answer. It didn't make sense given Finnegan's investment. Someone (she assumed the professor) had persuaded Finnegan that Tomas was on the verge of a significant breakthrough, or why else had he gone to so much trouble and expense? If only she knew what he was trying to achieve. Her ignorance was like a horsefly bite. The more she scratched it, the bigger it grew and the more irritating.

'Did Finnegan give you any time frame?'

'I never met him.'

He appeared awkward, as if he was covering up something. She became immediately suspicious. Josie believed everyone had something to hide – well, except for Mike. He was straightforward. Finnegan's secret breathed a sulphurous "or else" in her nightmares; hers remained raw and shocking.

♦

She'd grown up believing her father had died when she was only a few weeks old. Until she'd found a hidden photograph of her mother in the arms of a man. She knew the location. It was Storms River in the Tsitsikamma forest, an ideal romantic getaway. He seemed familiar. Could this be her father? She had to find out. Fortunately the national park archived its visitor registration forms and she found theirs. The moment she read his name she knew why he'd seemed familiar. He was very much alive!

Josie confronted her mother Kate. It led to a bitter row. Kate told Josie he didn't matter; one sperm didn't convey any paternal rights. Josie disagreed. How dare she lie about something so important? She wanted to meet her father. Kate told her if she did, she'd regret it. Josie didn't understand. She left home, vowing never to call her mother. She went to America secretly hoping she could engineer a meeting with her father by joining LCC.

♦

Tomas took out a bottle from the cardboard box and ticked it off against the invoice.

'That's my job!' Annoyed, Josie grabbed the paperwork. She knew her outburst had more to do with her hurt feelings than any job demarcation. Their hands brushed as they both went to pick up the next one. Her stomach flipped. She wanted to scream at him, *Don't you feel anything for me?*

'Leave me alone,' he said.

His words felt like a slap across her face. She got up abruptly, letting the stool clatter to the ground; raising her voice she shouted, 'Your idea had better work or… or else!' She stormed out. The moment she was outside she regretted her outburst. She knew she'd acted like a teenager; but she'd never fallen in love before.

Whenever he came into a room she felt her heart beating faster. She hardly dared look at him, aware her pupils exploded revealing her inner desire. His presence made her clitoris thump with excitement. She imagined his tongue exploring her labium, making her wet before his penis, thick and long, brought her to a gasping climax. She wanted to kiss him, explore his body, taste him – feel his arms grasping her to him and the weight of his body on hers. It was pure lust. She breathed in his musky body odour before washing his clothes. It reminded her of her childhood: the warm African sun and the sweating bodies of Johannes and Balipi. His smell stirred up forgotten memories of people she loved. He filled her thoughts at night. Her dreams left her frustratingly unfulfilled. He was totally different to the men she usually dated. They were more like Mike, straightforward and easy to get along with. Tomas was a challenge and that increased his attraction. She found his moody intensity deeply attractive. It hinted at a slow, attentive, sensual lover. Her burgeoning feelings added an extra unwanted twist to the household dynamics. She hoped Mike wouldn't notice. So far he'd said nothing, although he'd given her several knowing looks. She wondered if he was jealous. He certainly didn't like Tomas. He nicknamed him Eeyore, after the lugubrious donkey in A.A. Milne's book. It made her smile. Mike cast himself in the role of Pooh – ever amusing and lovable.

Shadows appeared under her eyes, made darker by the paleness of her skin. Her optimism drained away. It no longer seemed like an adventure or an opportunity. Mike and Tomas ignored each other. She did her best to remain positive but it felt like Bucephalus was slipping through her hands. Above all she feared Finnegan's reaction. It didn't help that he never replied to any of her calls. The phone number appeared to be connected to an answer phone. It left her confused. Did Eliot monitor the calls, passing on information to Finnegan, or did he sit in silence listening to her voice? This watchful, malevolent image of him reinforced her anxiety about what he would do; failure wasn't in his lexicography. He'd blame her. Her sweaty nightmares increased. They conjured up a frightening demon who whispered Finnegan's sulphurous words.

♦

Mike came into the kitchen with his usual clatter, bringing in with him the smell of diesel and sweat as he peeled off his motorbike gear. He'd spent the day down at Denny's. The

Fastnet date was approaching. Time was running out. Pride and determination stopped her from contacting Finnegan and asking him what to do. She reminded herself she needed his approval and gratitude.

Mike saw Tomas. 'Why, it's Eeyore! Still working hard?' Mike's sarcasm was fuelled by his own frustrations.

Josie intervened, 'Enough!' She wasn't in the mood.

Mike ignored her and fell to his haunches, his face inches away from Tomas's. 'Admit it – you're a bloody crap chemist.' He stood up smirking at Tomas. Then he started to jab his fists, circling round like a boxer warming up before the fight.

Stony-faced, Tomas ignored him. Josie decided not to intervene. She secretly hoped Mike's actions would provoke Tomas into showing some feelings. Irritated by Tomas blanking him, Mike grabbed Josie by the waist. She shrieked like an excited child.

'Not that I'm in a hurry,' he snuggled his bearded face into her neck, 'to say goodbye to this tasty morsel,' and growled. He swung her round and round, Josie laughing as they waltzed around the room.

Thud! Tomas's chair hit the floor. He rose up like a wakened giant. He was eight inches taller than Mike, the low ceiling further emphasising his height.

'Put her down!'

'I'm fine.' She slipped out of Mike's arms, swatting him away with a tea towel. Out of the corner of her eye she caught Tomas's reaction. His breathing was heavy, his fists clenched by his sides. Suddenly he turned and strode out of the kitchen, slamming the door behind him.

'What the hell do you see in him?'

She'd been wrong! Tomas did care for her. Her heart exploded with joy.

'Do you know what he's looking for?' she casually asked, her eyebrow rising.

'Haven't a clue. It's been a waste of my time.'

She remembered her first meeting with Finnegan, as he'd stood by the window staring down at the city beneath his feet. She shuddered, sensing his hand moving them like chess pieces; each player only knowing as much as they needed to. It reinforced her vulnerability.

Later she went down with Tomas's meal, wondering if she should say anything about what had just happened. He wasn't in the office. In the laboratory everything appeared normal. She heard the spectrometer printing out a graph of chemical elements and in the background the constant hum of the air purification system.

'I've brought you something to eat,' she called out.

There was no answer.

'Where are you?' Her voice made it sound like it was a game of hide and seek. *Surely he wasn't sulking? Annoyed that he'd finally revealed some feelings!*

'Tomas.' Her voice now had an edge to it.

In the wet lab she saw a red smear on the grey vinyl floor; walking towards it she saw Tomas lying in a pool of blood, his white lab coat stained crimson. He was motionless. For a brief second she wondered if he was dead. She fell to the floor, careful to avoid the glass fragments; turning him over she saw his hands. They were covered in blood. It looked like he'd slashed himself. Her first thought was that he'd done it deliberately. 'Tomas,' she shook him, 'Tomas, what's happened?'

His eyes fluttered. 'I crushed the beakers in my hands.'

Relieved, she nearly laughed out loud. 'We need to get you to A&E. You'll need stitches.' She leant him up against the wooden bench as she wrapped his hands in bandages, staunching the flow of blood. 'How did you end up on the floor?'

'I fainted.'

This time she did laugh out loud.

He looked ashamed. On their way to the hospital it came out: his mother's constant drinking, her increasingly violent outbursts and his father's inability to deal with her. 'I was seven when Papa lost his temper.' The home movie played in his head accompanied by the sound track of her screaming angry, bitter, taunting words.

♦

He was in the doorway watching. He saw Papa's arm swing round, his clenched fist slamming into the side of Mama's head, the force of the blow flicking her face towards him. For a split second she looked surprised then her eyes rolled back, as a glob of spittle flew out. In slow motion he watched it fly through the air, before she tumbled over the sofa like an acrobat. He heard the thump and the sound of the glass table shattering into tiny shards. He stared at the blood creeping over the blonde floor towards him. He watched it, mesmerized, unable to move; the room now unusually silent. He glanced up at Papa, seeking guidance. Papa's body crumpled. His hands covered his face, quietly weeping.

♦

'The blood – it reminded me. I thought Papa had killed her.'

The rest of the journey was awkward, the silence an unwelcome passenger.

Eventually Josie asked, 'What happened?'

'My mother got custody. We left Sweden,' his words devoid of emotion and further detail.

♦

Inside his head the movie continued. It was a different location, outside the family court. He watched like a film director through a lens as the little boy screamed, 'Papa, Papa, don't leave me,' his mother dragging him away. He struggled and writhed before collapsing to the ground – a dead weight. Briefly she let go of his hand intending to scoop him up. Free, he ran the length of the corridor, back towards Papa. A man caught him. The stranger's grip was strong. He pulled him along the corridor back towards his black mother. She grabbed his hand. He hit out pummelling her with his fists and flaying legs. 'Papa, Papa,' he screamed, the tears streaming down his face; inconsolable and confused by what was happening. Through his wet blurry eyes he saw Papa walk away, leaving him there.

♦

'I've never forgiven her.'

Josie parked the car without saying anything more. She glanced across. He was staring out of the passenger's window.

'She used to touch me in places that made me feel

uncomfortable.' The words, 'It felt sexual' were barely audible.

Her instinct was to reach out to him, but the gesture seemed too intimate to be reassuring and especially now, after what she'd just heard. Neither of them moved. Josie's mind was trying to make a coherent narrative, to understand the implications of his revelations. It began to explain so much about him but left large pieces missing. She felt his pain. It was the first time he'd spoken about his past or his feelings. It felt like a significant moment. Eventually they got out. A&E was busy. She pointed, directing him to a pair of seats. She gave him an encouraging smile as they sat waiting, both aware of a new intimacy.

Tomas continued to stare down at his white-bandaged hands. 'When I was eighteen she gave me a letter from my aunt Anna in Sweden. In it Anna wrote that Papa had burned the Folkboat on the beach at Tjorn, a month after the custody hearing.' There was a long pause. 'He died in the fire.'

This time Josie did reach out to cradle his face in her hands, as a line of tears began to run down.

'I think about him every day.' She wiped them away. 'He abandoned me.'

Josie kissed him lightly, tasting his salty cheek. He didn't pull away. He captured the closeness of her gaze in his dark eyes. She sensed her pupils reacting as they exploded into a black hole surrounded by the grey halo of her moonlit love-struck eyes.

'I never expected to fall in love,' Tomas whispered.

'Me neither.'

Tomas kissed her tentatively and she responded eagerly; oblivious to the rest of the world.

'Tomas Olofsson.' Someone called out his name.

Josie watched him walk away; he turned by the curtain. She beamed back and gave him a discreet wave. Then he was gone. She pumped her left fist and let out an audible, 'Yes.' It wasn't the setting she'd imagined for their first kiss, but it felt perfect.

Josie noticed the woman opposite watching; unable to suppress her emotions she smiled broadly. The woman turned away showing no empathy towards the young lovers; instead she took hold of the man's hand beside her. He was hunched over, breathing in shallow rasping gasps. They both looked worn out. Josie didn't care, inside she repeated over and over again – *he loves me!*

CHAPTER 4

EUREKA

Bang! Josie heard a crash. She came down the stairs two at a time. Standing in the doorway she saw Tomas dart round the kitchen table, chased by Mike.

'Bloody Meccano you said. I don't think so!' Mike grabbed hold of Tomas's empty outstretched arm, as if it were holding a trophy. The lunge sent them sprawling onto the floor, along with a second chair.

'What the hell's going on?' Josie demanded.

'Eeyore, he's a bloody genius!' Mike stood up grinning at her as Tomas, looking embarrassed, righted the chair.

'So... is someone going to tell me?' She clearly expected an answer from one of them.

Neither of them moved, instead Mike burst out laughing, 'No, it's a secret.' They tore out of the kitchen like delinquents, carrying on outside with their horseplay.

Josie followed them out and bellowed, 'Bastards,' sending the ever watchful crows nosily skyward.

Everything changed after Tomas's eureka moment.

Mike abandoned tinkering with *Grey Goose* or disappearing for hours riding his Augusta on the winding roads that crisscrossed the county. He now stayed at Ham Farm, spending time in the machine shop building and running prototype designs on the test bed or hunched over his LCC laptop working on CAD drawings; preferring to use their spare bedroom as his office. Josie didn't see that it mattered where he worked, as long as his laptop was locked up in the laboratory's safe each night. His enthusiasm for Bucephalus was in sharp contrast to Tomas's constant anxiety, as he tested and retested it.

What hurt Josie was Tomas's reaction. The joy of being lovers was short lived. Tomas returned to his old routine, working long into the night. He'd even gone back to using his own bedroom, insisting he didn't want to disturb her. It was a feeble excuse. He was obsessed by the chemical formula. He spent more time thinking and worrying about it than her. Josie felt like she had a human rival. It was ridiculous, but she was jealous! Inside she seethed. She noticed whenever she came into the laboratory, they'd stop discussing Bucephalus and wait until she'd left. It made her feel like their servant. She tried dropping the meal tray on the bench from a height, sending the cutlery clattering and the contents slopping off the plate, and still they ignored her, both men totally absorbed by their work.

How dare they keep the secret of what they were doing from her? How dare they assume she couldn't understand complex chemistry or mechanical engineering? It felt like her contribution of setting up Ham Farm, making sure everything ran smoothly, keeping them on track and hidden, counted for nothing. Of one thing she was certain –

this wasn't some new incremental development for LCC or Genco, it felt way more significant. Pride stopped her from asking them to explain. It appeared Bucephalus was men's business and she was only a pretty girl with long black hair.

Then Professor Li arrived. Neither Eliot nor Finnegan had said anything to her about his arrival. It was Tomas who'd told her to expect a visitor from LCC. She waited at Heathrow's arrivals concourse carrying her A4 card with his name on it. He was easy to pick out from Tomas's description: a short, immaculately dressed man, probably wearing his round tortoiseshell glasses. She greeted him and asked him how the flight had been. He didn't reply. They walked back to the car park in silence, she leading the way. He got into the rear passenger seat; his aftershave filling the car's interior. He didn't make eye contact or speak to her on their journey back to Ham Farm. In her increasingly irascible mood she felt like his chauffeur. She noticed he was distractedly flipping something. The action reminded her of a cat's tail.

They pulled up abruptly in the yard, Josie having driven at speed over the potholes; hoping it had been an uncomfortable experience and one he wouldn't want to repeat too often.

'Where is Dr Olofsson?' he said, clearly expecting to find Tomas waiting for him.

Josie ignored his question. 'Come up to the house,' she said, pointing the way. He had no choice but to follow her. It was a small victory, but she'd resented his attitude. She took him through to the sitting room. He looked at the sofa and chairs and remained standing, either through disgust or irritation; she didn't care.

'I need to see Dr Olofsson.'

She sensed his eager impatience.

♦

Tomas and the professor walked down past the dry stone wall and empty stable block before stopping. Josie watched Tomas point at something. She looked in the same direction. It was a bucolic view. In the foreground were the remnants of the manure heap and beyond it the fields and wooded copses; all leading the eye towards the rolling South Down hills. Yet this wasn't a sightseeing visit. Professor Li appeared to be a man more comfortable in the ordered cleanliness of a laboratory rather than the mucky haphazardness of the countryside.

Seeing the two men standing there she thought what an odd couple they made. Tomas was casually dressed in jeans, trainers and a blue cotton shirt with his sleeves rolled up. The professor was half Tomas's height, forcing him to look up, his manicured hands grasping Tomas's forearm. Suddenly the professor threw his arms round Tomas in an embrace. It was so unexpected, she laughed out loud. Immediately Tomas tried to pull away. She knew how much Tomas disliked uninvited intimacy. But the professor held on, seemingly reluctant to let him go. Tomas broke free and stepped back. As they walked down to the barn, Josie watched the professor stroking Tomas's back. The gesture seemed tender. It reminded her of a man stroking his pet. Josie wondered about the professor's sexuality. Unexpectedly Finnegan's presence rose up. Did his omnipotence blind him to the power of human love? It felt like someone had walked on her grave.

The two men disappeared into the laboratory to join Mike. Josie decided to go for a bike ride. Her presence clearly wasn't needed.

♦

Tomas waved her over. 'The professor is sending over a technician.'

'I thought you preferred to work alone,' she said, surprised, directing her remarks at Tomas.

The professor answered for him. 'Jon Maguire will assist Dr Olofsson.' He looked at her. 'Bucephalus has taken too long.'

Josie's neck reddened at his implied criticism of her handling of the project. 'Are you ready to leave now?' she asked curtly. He seemed reluctant, so she opened the 4x4's passenger door, clearly inviting him to get in. Professor Li ignored her and instead embraced Tomas once more. Josie heard Mike guffaw. Momentarily she caught his eye and immediately had to look away in case she burst out laughing (she couldn't wait to hear what Mike had to say about the strange little man). As Professor Li climbed into the vehicle, the sun caught his glasses giving him a piercing stare. He directed it towards her.

She wasn't intimidated. 'I'll let Finnegan know about your visit, shall I?' implying a working intimacy that didn't exist. She had no intention of ringing Finnegan but he didn't know that.

On their way to the airport Josie studied the professor in her rear view mirror. Their eyes met. She held his gaze before he looked away and coughed into his silk handkerchief. It was a small victory. She wondered how Finnegan, with all his testosterone-fuelled ambition, treated this effeminate man, their appetites being so clearly opposite. It made her mildly curious. Nonetheless she hoped she'd never see him again.

♦

Sat in the 4x4, Professor Li thought about Tomas. *I panicked when you stopped answering my phone calls. I know how obsessed you get. It consumes you like a new lover. Maguire will be reliable, he has no imagination. I need results and quickly.* He flipped his talisman. Next he thought about the engineer, shuddering at the memory of his fingernails. They were black! *He smelt unpleasant too and shows no respect – acting like a clown all the time. I must have his CAD designs.* Lastly he thought about the girl. *Insolent bitch, she drives too fast. Why did Finnegan pick her? Perhaps she's candy to keep the engineer happy.* He sat back, not seeing anything of the countryside or traffic on the motorway as they approached Heathrow airport. His thoughts were lingering on Tomas. *I'd forgotten how handsome you are. I miss you; not seeing you each day is torture.* He relived his deliberate, coquettish touches. They aroused such pleasure, stoking the fires of desire. Awkwardly he felt his penis engorge with blood. His hand went down to ease the uncomfortable swelling. *If only I was alone, I could masturbate.* The thought made him look down and a small moan came out, before quickly disguising it as a cough. *She's watching me, the foul, fish-smelling bitch.* He wiped a small trickle of saliva from his mouth using his handkerchief, before he carried on with his favourite daydream; Tomas naked, waiting for him in his bed.

'The traffic is slow. You might miss your flight.'

He ignored her. Irritated she'd interrupted his daydream again. *I've watched them back at LCC, those devious little sluts, each one trying to entice you into bed. Tomas admit it, you've never shown any interest in a woman. You belong to me!*

Tomas was like an addiction. He knew it clouded his judgement, making him take risks. Bucephalus was worthy of a Nobel Prize. He imagined them sharing the celebrations and accolades together. He hesitated. What if Tomas proved reluctant to share it with him? *You owe me your career!* He remembered the unfortunate Christmas party when Tomas had lashed out with the broken end of his beer bottle. Some fragments of glass became embedded in the man's ear canal; dangerously too near to the brain to avoid surgery. *They wanted to charge you. I couldn't run the risk you'd be sent to prison. Inside you'd have been passed around like a plaything. I had to save you, so I told Finnegan, "Dr Olofsson must have everything he needs to make his idea work."*

He didn't dwell on what Finnegan might do if Tomas failed. *Finnegan relies on me to keep LCC at the forefront of innovation.* Smugly Professor Li flipped his talisman only this time he stopped, examining it carefully. The jade thorn was piercingly sharp despite its great age; a cruel reminder of how closely linked were beauty and pain. It reminded him of Tomas.

I'll ring Zhou once I get back to my apartment.

CHAPTER 5
JOSIE ACTS

Jon Maguire made the ideal lab assistant for Tomas, neither being comfortable with idle chitchat. As a technician he seemed content to be given repetitive tasks that required no independent decisions. He was in his early forties going on sixty. He had no outstanding features. The type of face you'd find hard to describe to a police officer. He was nervous and quiet; someone you could easily imagine being bullied at school. Professor Li had sent over little information on him to Josie. However, she did discover he came from a small community called Growly Bear in Washington State. His sister ran a B&B there.

Mike must have overheard their conversation because after that, at every opportunity he took delight in stabbing Maguire's stomach, pretending to be looking for his growler. She said nothing, suspecting his taunts were partially explained by having to move out of the bedroom he'd commandeered as his office. She hoped in time Mike would lose interest in his little game. At least Tomas and Mike had called a truce to their enmity as they tried to resolve the challenges Bucephalus gave them; only now there was someone else living with them. The sense of a quest had disappeared. It felt like any other LCC project, with targets and deadlines. The final indignity came when Tomas banned her from entering the laboratory at all. In future Maguire would bring down parcels and their meals. She felt ostracized, annoyed and useless.

She tackled Tomas, 'Don't you think I deserve an explanation?'

He looked tired and exhausted, his skin blotchy – from lack of sleep, she assumed.

'I've found something,' he said. His answer was pretty much as she'd come to expect. It explained nothing.

'Why won't you tell me what you are working on?' hoping their former intimacy counted for something.

'Remember how much this means to Finnegan.' His face was serious. 'How few people know what we are doing?'

She wondered if Tomas was in some bizarre way acting chivalrously, trying to protect her from Finnegan's wrath. But it didn't help her itch.

♦

Josie didn't like the person she'd become or the situation she was in. She'd forgotten who she was and why Bucephalus mattered to her. It was time to act. She needed Finnegan to acknowledge the debt he owed her.

She thought about Finnegan's desire to keep Bucephalus hidden. To her knowledge six people knew: Finnegan, Professor Li, Tomas, Mike and now Maguire. She thought about Eliot and decided she knew the name of the project but nothing more. She doubted the LCC board knew about Bucephalus. She decided he was financing it from his own resources. Finnegan was as rich as Croesus but he'd not used that name for his project; instead he'd chosen Bucephalus, a horse. Suddenly she laughed out loud. What were LCC and Genco if not about horse power? She'd never thought Finnegan had a sense of humour. Somehow it didn't fit the man. There must be more to it.

He'd married the English aristocrat Lady Alice Leal. He'd used his wealth to save the Leal family from the death duties and taxes imposed by a post-war Labour government. Genco was on the Leal estate, as was Ham Farm; business and marriage intertwined. The location of Bucephalus reaffirmed her suspicion. This was private, family business. She knew he'd not divorced Lady Alice even when she failed to provide him with an heir. And from society magazines and press archives, it was clear the president's mother Martha Lintel Montgomery and Lady Alice were close friends. Finnegan no doubt used the friendship to further his own ambitions. Uncharitably, she decided Lady Alice was more valuable to him as a business asset than as a brood mare.

What was it about Alexander and Bucephalus that appealed to Finnegan? Josie jotted down what she knew about Alexander: a legendary warrior, conqueror, worshipped as a god, possibly poisoned by someone close to him, a homosexual and with a wife and sons; none of this fitted Finnegan. If only she could get inside his mind, she'd have a clearer understanding of the scale of his ambition. There'd be no altruism behind what he was doing. He'd take full advantage of any commercial gain. This felt more like the man she knew. She looked again at the name he'd chosen. It was deliberate, not a joke or a name appearing in Lady Alice's West Mountain stud book. Alexander, like Finnegan, was a man with an enormous amount of self-belief and ambition. Alexander had conquered his world. Finnegan was consciously alluding to a similar destiny.

Too many thoughts flooded in. She found an A1 sheet of paper and wrote down any idea or word that came to her. She let them wander over the paper like a disorientated drunk. Some led to another, others came to nothing. But the exercise freed her imagination, allowing her to capture all her random thoughts. If she saw a link, she highlighted it with a coloured marker pen. The drunk's progress now looked like a Jackson Pollock painting. Her marker hovered over the word Alexander and as if moved by a finger at a seance, it shot across to the word "childless", the connection made by her subconscious. That was it! It did matter. He wanted a legacy. Finnegan could accept he had no heir, as long as he wasn't forgotten. He wanted to be remembered like Alexander. All she now had to do was discover what would guarantee an automotive giant such a legacy.

She had a starting point. It involved fuel and an engine. Car manufacturers were all desperately seeking cost-effective alternatives to the petrol/diesel engine; aware petroleum would eventually run out. Engines also burned fossil fuels creating greenhouse gases, and these emissions were responsible for climate change. *Stupid, stupid, stupid.* She banged her forehead with the palm of her hand. Tomas and Mike must be working on a new formula and configuration that cut emissions, thereby extending the viability of petrol and diesel engines for decades. Emerging nations would be able to grow their economies using clean transport, and governments wanting to reduce their carbon emission would legislate, ensuring the worldwide adoption of LCC's Bucephalus range. No wonder Finnegan was paranoid about keeping it a secret. Why had it taken her so long to figure it out? She cringed. Until now she'd focussed on getting the job done, desperately wanting Finnegan's approval. Her neck reddened at her naivety.

She needed a break. Josie got her bike out. She selected the Gloria Gaynor anthem and set it on replay. She sang along enthusiastically before running out of breath going up the steep, long haul of the Trundle. At the summit as she recovered her breath, she thought surely it would be the name of the scientist who'd found the formula and the engineer who'd got it to work; their names would be remembered, not Finnegan's. So where did that leave Finnegan and his need for a legacy?

Josie decided to get her hair cut. Her long, discarded hair lay like strands of washed up wet seaweed on the floor. The asymmetrical bob suggested by the hairdresser was startlingly different. It suited her thick lustrous hair, framing her face and accentuating her eyebrows, grey eyes and black lashes. She felt surprisingly light headed as she walked back to the 4x4. In a shop window she caught sight of herself, barely recognising the woman looking back at her. She liked it. It expressed her sense of being a woman, not the nanny, servant, chauffeur – or any of the other roles the men in this project had given her.

Naturally it was Mike who commented, 'Hair today and gone tomorrow,' he said, amused as always by his quip.

'Nothing escapes you,' she said light-heartedly before striking a pose, while he pretended to be the photographer snapping away on their fashion shoot. It felt like their old camaraderie had returned.

'You look radiant, by the way,' he said.

'You look like shit.' He did too, his beard unkempt and thinner, puffy bags under his eyes; he seemed thinner too. Josie planted a kiss full on his mouth, 'I've got a secret too.'

CHAPTER 6

WASHINGTON MEETING

They were told to wait. The Chinese Ambassador would see them shortly. Finnegan remained stony-faced. He wasn't used to being kept waiting; uncharacteristically he paced, revealing how much this meeting meant to him. Finnegan glared down at the professor. 'I want to know what they are saying.'

Professor Li was nervous. This was an important meeting for all of them.

Ambassador Zhou arrived accompanied by a large entourage of men all dressed in identical dark suits. But before the meeting began, Professor Li stepped forward. He bowed with a show of deference and presented the Tang ceramic horse to the ambassador. It was from his private collection, 'A token of our future relationship.' He'd told Finnegan a gift would be expected.

Ambassador Zhou bowed slightly. 'The Tang period was one of great expansion,' his words translated by an aide.

The Chinese bowed and took their seats. The formalities over, Finnegan wasted no time. 'I need three factories built producing cars, 7.5 and 13 tonne trucks. And I want them up and running as soon as possible.'

The professor looked directly at Zhou as he translated, neither man acknowledging that they knew each other. The ambassador turned to his party and a series of rapid interchanges began.

Finnegan leaned in. 'What are they saying?'

'They are wondering why China should agree to your proposal.'

Finnegan interrupted their discussions, 'It's about making money.' Immediately the room fell silent with all eyes focussed on him. Finnegan spoke directly to the ambassador, 'Today's market is highly competitive and your labour costs are lower. I'll provide the tooling and you the raw materials. Together we will produce a range of vehicles, at a much lower unit cost.' Then he looked at each man in turn. 'We'll all make money out of my deal.'

There was a moment's silence before Ambassador Zhou spoke through his interpreter, 'How will your workers feel about us producing an iconic American brand?'

'Leave that to me,' Finnegan's voice was assured. 'They'll be badged as LCC vehicles, but produced under licence in China. It's not an uncommon practice.' Finnegan leaned to his right and in a low voice asked, 'Are they going for it?'

Before the professor could answer one of the anonymously dressed men asked, 'Do you trust us with your brand?'

Finnegan replied instantly, 'A word of advice, no one crosses me without there being consequences.' He deliberately glowered at the man who'd spoken. The message was clear, only a fool would try it. Finnegan's bulky presence implied it would be physical and painful too.

The professor wiped the perspiration from his forehead. He was worried Finnegan's bombastic approach would offend their hosts who were more accustomed to subtle negotiations. He flipped his talisman and looked directly at Zhou, before lowering his eyes.

'You'll pay me a licensing fee on each unit produced, and in return I'll make sure the president opens up the US market to your exports.' He paused. 'It's a one-time offer and a great deal.' Finnegan sat back in the chair, convinced this was the deal clincher.

The professor tried to relax but he knew Finnegan wouldn't countenance rejection. Professor Li was listening hard, trying to understand the shifts and nuances when Finnegan's voice again interrupted the conversations around the table, 'If I discover you've attempted to reverse engineer any of my component parts, I'll make sure the president slams the door shut in your faces, and imposes – eye-wateringly high tariffs on all your goods, am I clear?' It appeared he'd had enough of their prevarication. He'd reverted to his bully-boy tactics.

The atmosphere changed. The professor looked straight ahead his heart pounding; he concentrated on keeping his expression neutral as he translated. He was waiting for the Chinese delegation to stand up and walk out. But Ambassador Zhou remained seated.

'And where do you want these vehicles delivered to?' Zhou asked again through his interpreter.

'Durban, it will be my contribution to the president's aid programme.'

The ambassador rose bringing the meeting to a close. His officials filed out one by one. Finnegan stood up. 'Do we have a deal?'

Ambassador Zhou was half Finnegan's height, but with equal authority he said in perfect English, 'We see this as an opportunity that will greatly benefit China.' Zhou was on the point of leaving when he added, 'Does the president know about the licence fee arrangement?'

CHAPTER 7

BANG, BANG

Josie dropped the shopping bags, momentarily unsure what to do. Every kitchen door was open. Strewn across the floor were broken crockery, cutlery, the contents of glass jars and eggs mixed into an inedible concoction. Cautiously she navigated her way across. In the sitting room the cushions had been slashed freeing feathers from their dark incarceration; the sofa upturned like a beached whale. The television lay shattered.

Bang, bang – it sounded like an open window caught by the wind. Warily she crept up the stairs, her ears straining to hear if someone else was still in the house. Bang, bang – there it was again. She went into Tomas's room and then her own. The rooms trashed with the same wilful destruction; the contents of drawers and cupboards scattered and beds upturned. At least no one had peed, shit or covered the walls with obscenities.

She crossed the landing to Mike's room. His window was open, banging against the wooden frame. She peered down towards the barn fearing some terrible tragedy. She'd known senseless violence at home; bloody knife attacks and bodies left butchered by the roadside. The door to the barn was closed. The yard looked as it always did, abandoned and unused. She felt instant relief and closed the window.

Before calling the others, she checked each room carefully, seeing if anything was missing whilst trying to decide if it was opportunism or a deliberate attack. She knew industrial espionage was lucrative and they had a secret worth stealing. She couldn't discount the possibility. She started in Mike's room. No matter how many times she'd told him to keep his laptop locked up in the laboratory safe, he'd persisted in using it in his room in the evenings. She began searching for it, her frantic actions resembling those of the intruder as she threw his clothes in the air, looking for it buried under the mess.

'What the hell are you doing?' Mike stood in the doorway, his tone changing to one of amusement, 'I don't think much of your cleaning methods.'

'Mike, is your laptop down in the lab?' Her voice was desperate. This was no time for one of his jokes. Suddenly they were both at it.

'Who'd want my laptop?' Mike answered his own question, 'A druggie feeding his habit.'

'Possibly – anything small they could resell.' She doubted her own words. Nor did it fit the profile of a group of bored teenagers. The destruction was too theatrical, as if it had been staged. 'What's Finnegan going to say?' she said, worried.

'Don't panic. The server is in his office. He has all my work.'

Josie didn't know the server was in Finnegan's office. She'd assumed it was in LCC's laboratory. The information didn't surprise her though. Bucephalus was his private obsession.

Mike bundled her out of his room as he continued to search. 'Check the other rooms. See if anything else has gone.'

She clung on to the thought it was a mindless burglary. Her stomach churning, fully aware a skilled hacker would open his laptop like an ebook. She returned a moment later.

'Mike, did you use the word Bucephalus anywhere on your laptop?'

His silence answered her question.

'We need to get the others.'

♦

Mike and Maguire sat round the kitchen table; Tomas leaned on the sink, looking as if he might be sick. Josie paced up and down.

'Did it have the details of my formula?' Tomas demanded turning towards Mike.

Mike shook his head, though he avoided eye contact. 'It had details on the modifications to the engine and exhaust systems; details on the catalytic converter, the reconfigured baffle in the exhaust, the reordered honeycomb structure and the changes to the metal proportions in the washout.'

'The whole damn lot,' Tomas glowered at him.

Said quickly it didn't reflect the brilliance of his engineering work. However, from his slumped posture Mike was clearly mortified. For a moment Josie felt sorry for him.

'Will it look like a new design for a high performance car?' Josie said, searching for a way out of their dilemma, whilst trying to make Mike feel a little better.

Mike stood up. 'I might have referred to a new fuel.' He waited for Tomas's reaction. It seemed this time they might actually hit each other. 'But not the formula I swear it.'

She stood between them as she grabbed Tomas's arm. 'Sit down both of you!' Josie shouted. They sat. 'Was it a random burglary or have we been targeted?' No one answered her.

'Is there anything on the CCTV?' Maguire spoke for the first time.

'No, I checked. The kitchen door isn't covered. When I installed the system I was more concerned about the barn and the yard. They must have come over the fields.'

'They waited till they saw you leave.'

'That's bloody brilliant Sherlock.' There was no humour in Mike's voice.

'Why did they target Mike's laptop?' Maguire said looking around.

Mike threw his arms in the air, suggesting exaggerated frustration before leaning across the table and repeatedly stabbing his index finger inches away from the technician's face. It was deliberately provocative. He turned and stared at Tomas. 'Does Sherlock here know what Bucephalus is exactly?'

Together they looked at Maguire.

'No, no,' he protested weakly staring from one to the other, his forearms raised as if in the act of surrendering. 'Professor Li gave me explicit instructions. I was following his orders that's all … I'm telling the truth.' The colour drained from his already pallid face. He appeared uncomfortable, more nervous than normal. Suddenly he got up and rushed out. A few minutes later they heard the toilet flush.

'You realise we cannot involve the police.' Her heart was thumping, and after a long pause she added, 'What the hell am I going to tell Finnegan?' She leaned forward, her short hair covering her face. She turned, looked at Tomas and then at Mike. They both avoided her stare.

Maguire came back in and apologised, 'I've not been feeling too good lately.' No one was interested.

'Don't tell Finnegan,' Mike said. 'Scan the internet, see if anyone has picked up on something new being developed, if not,' he paused, 'we might have got away with it.'

'Should I tell Professor Li?' Maguire looked at Tomas.

He shook his head. 'If Mike referred to a new fuel, but not the formula – Bucephalus is still a secret,' Tomas added, 'and I can carry on working.'

There was a metaphorical sigh around the table. Josie wasn't so easily convinced. What was so important about Mike's work? Josie couldn't decide. She looked at Mike. After the initial panic in his room, he now seemed sanguine.

Yet she couldn't shake off the feeling something didn't fit. Was it one of them? Her head spun, she swallowed hard. It took several minutes before her nausea was under control. It couldn't be Tomas her lover, or Mike her friend. She wasn't so sure about Maguire. She saw less of him because of the long hours he spent down in the laboratory, and as a consequence she had discovered little about him. Why had the professor suddenly decided Tomas needed help? Did she believe him when he claimed he was only a technician? They must have spoken about the work and what Tomas was trying to achieve. He had access to all of Tomas's work but not necessarily Mike's. She tried to settle her nerves. But one thought wouldn't go away. The three men had been together during the burglary, so whoever had trashed Ham Farm it wasn't one of them. Was someone else involved?

♦

Alone she tackled Tomas. 'Does Bucephalus work without Mike's designs?'

'Yes and no.'

'Well thanks – that's really useful,' her intonation clearly underlining her irritation.

He held her gaze. There was a long pause. 'My fuel powers any vehicle, but it needs Mike's modifications to get the full benefits.'

She assumed that was as far as he was prepared to go. At first she'd found his strong silent nature appealing, now it was annoying. Would they target Tomas's work next? She'd have to review their security procedures. It was annoying especially as they were so close to the end. For it to fail now would be a disaster. She felt the sulphurous "or else" of Finnegan at her shoulder.

'He works for Genco.'

Tomas's words brought her out of her reverie. 'What are you saying?' she asked, bemused. She knew Tomas didn't like Mike. But to accuse him of betraying them, it was ludicrous. 'I don't think it's him,' she dismissed his suggestion. He might be intuitive when it came to chemistry, but she doubted he had the same understanding when it came to people. Yet it was interesting that he hadn't accused Maguire. Perhaps being scientists they'd become close working in the laboratory side by side.

CHAPTER 8
FIELD STUDY PLANS

Professor Li cleared his throat, 'Science as dramatic as this will be scrutinised by every laboratory in the world. We need to be absolutely sure it delivers and,' he paused, 'there are no unforeseen consequences.' He directed his remarks towards Finnegan.

Andy Lucky Malone noticed Finnegan's features harden. The professor obviously had qualities Finnegan valued. It explained his position in LCC and his presence at the meeting.

Professor Li persisted, 'TD50 tests on mice are not the same as human trials.'

'Are you sure we need human trials?' Finnegan challenged him.

Andy spoke out, 'If there's something wrong with Bucephalus, I need to know. It's the future of my company we're talking about.'

'We need to be certain.' Professor Li was resolute.

'I don't intend to be the patsy, if shit hits the fan.' Andy pushed his chair away from the table making his position perfectly clear.

'Don't worry Lucky.'

Finnegan walked over to the professor and standing behind him, he put both hands on the professor's shoulders. From anyone else this gesture might have conveyed a degree of good-natured intimacy, but with his full weight bearing down it looked like Finnegan was crushing him into the black leather conference chair.

'I'll give you your field study. And you'll give me the green light to launch our vehicles worldwide.' It was clearly an order. He returned to the head of the table. 'We're going to carry out the environmental trials in southern Africa.' Andy was about to ask why when Finnegan carried on. 'We'll be able to do it without anyone knowing what's going on. I think conjurors call it misdirection.' Unexpectedly his belly laugh filled the room.

Andy felt uneasy. 'As I see it, you've got two problems. Firstly AMOIL isn't a major player in southern Africa and secondly car ownership is low. A sudden influx of vehicles will stand out. You'll have the media crawling all over you.'

'I expect it will be on every TV channel in the world,' Finnegan continued to laugh. 'How big a sample do you suggest, would Botswana with a population of 1.8 million do?'

'Are you crazy? Even you wouldn't consider using a whole country as a laboratory just to prove Bucephalus works.' Andy was shocked.

'I don't need such a large sample.' The professor remembered Finnegan's reference to Durban.

Andy got up and helped himself to a drink, knocking it back in one.

'I'm going to persuade President Montgomery to announce a new humanitarian crusade in southern Africa.'

Andy was reminded of their first meeting, when Finnegan had hinted at supporting the president's re-election. He was beginning to understand the scale of Finnegan's plan.

'I'll even give him a name for it – Feed Africa. Its purpose will be to end hunger in Africa.'

Andy regretted taking that drink. He thought he knew Finnegan with his outspoken, racist opinions. But now he was espousing a good cause, directed at benefitting black people. It didn't fit. He looked at Finnegan's thickening waistline. His bloodshot eyes suggested lack of sleep. Yet despite his physical appearance, it was clear – he was very much in control.

'I'll be an enthusiastic supporter on the understanding I get the sole monopoly on all the vehicles they use,' he laughed, 'and there's your field study, Professor.'

Finnegan turned to Andy. 'I want you to buy out the competition, so that you hold a monopoly on all the gas stations. You've done it before – bribery, exclusive contracts, cut-throat pricing at the pumps, aggressive marketing; you know how it's done. Feed Africa will need fuel for its vehicles, specifically Bucephalus fuel.'

Andy now understood. 'You'll supply 'em and we'll fill 'em up,' both men enjoying their old camaraderie.

But Finnegan hadn't finished. 'I can see pharmaceutical and agrochemical companies being delighted to trial their new drugs and GM products in an unregulated market like Africa. If they can shorten the process, it'll save millions. And they won't have to worry about litigious groups campaigning about the side effects. People die all the time in Africa.'

Andy looked across at Finnegan's heightened colour and his shallow heavy breathing. *The man's getting off on this*, he thought.

'The president's mother funds a hospital at Matsane in southern Africa,' Finnegan said, looking directly at the professor, 'I'm sure it'll be useful to you in your field study.'

Son of a bitch, Andy thought, *he's even figured out a way to involve the president's mother!* Not for the first time he was relieved they were friends.

'Professor Li, I want you to start work immediately,' Finnegan said. 'Design an environmental monitoring programme that satisfies the EPA; prove we have a safe and credible emission-free vehicle. I don't care what it costs.' Finnegan got up and poured himself a drink.

Andy joined him. This would be his last big deal before he retired; reassured he'd be leaving AMOIL in an unassailable position.

♦

Professor Li had a lot to consider. The field study was thousands of miles from his laboratory, in a complex outdoor environment where any number of other factors had the potential to upset the results. Passive air sampling would be the easiest to organise using automated stations. The mass spectrometry system GLC/MS examined a wide range of air pollutants and when connected to a base station, E-MDMS transmitted the data via satellite in real time. He could monitor all the data coming out of Africa back in America. The reports sent directly to his PC. No one else at LCC would see them.

Nearly all the components of motor fuel are damaging. He focussed on the additives' ingredients and those produced by the complex chemical reactions inside the car's exhaust system. It was always a question of which combination offered the least harm. Over the decades the range of toxic emissions had grown longer: carbon monoxide, carbon, nitrogen and sulphur dioxide, lead, benzene, xylene, toluene and hydrocarbons or aromatics like methyl-tertiary-butyl-ether (MTBE); each advance brought with it its own problems. He remembered standing next to Tomas at Ham Farm and him pointing to the manure heap, saying that's what gave him the idea to use urea as his additive.

In his laboratory mice were eating, breathing and having Bucephalus fuel applied to their skin; technicians monitoring their behaviour, looking for increased signs of aggression or confusion. He hoped the mice would react quickly; then at least he'd have some early indications it was harmful. It was the one area that worried the professor. Because problems like these only emerged over time and Finnegan would never agree to lengthy environmental studies or social observation.

TD50 tests on mice did not go far enough; he needed to test changes in humans. The simplest and most obvious way was to use blood tests. Red blood cells last for up to 120 days, white cells are more fragile. The lymphocytes last only seven days. It was imperative therefore that the blood samples were delivered quickly to technicians for analysis at a dedicated blood clinic. But taking blood samples in Africa presented him with particular problems. He'd have to refrigerate them as soon as possible, as well as avoiding excessive agitation in their transportation. If these factors were not addressed the blood cells would degrade and be of little use.

Analysis of the constituent parts of blood would provide him with important clues. Red cells carried oxygen round the body and removed waste (carbon dioxide) through the lungs. White cells produced antibodies and fought off infection and attacked tumours. While platelets were the clotting agent, sealing up insect bites, wounds and internal cuts. His technicians would look for any changes in the number, shape, quantity and distribution of red and white cells and platelets. If people presented themselves at the hospital with symptoms like respiratory infections, muscle seizures, meningitis, kidney and heart failure, these could easily be the results of existing known viruses, bacteria, parasites or simply inherited genetic conditions. What would lead them to Bucephalus as the source? There'd be no reason to even consider car exhaust fumes, because who knew about Bucephalus.

In Africa wild and domesticated animals roamed freely, mostly unfenced; insects and birds acting as transmitters of diseases. He'd need a team of veterinarians to monitor the health of animals and the impact Bucephalus might have on them. He wondered about collecting data from other living samples. Organisms like plants and fish were useful indicators, as they tended to accumulate significant quantities of material from very low concentrations because they were constantly exposed to the physical, biological and chemical influences in the environment. Instead he chose a simpler route. Farmers collected winter rain for crops and livestock, storing it in tanks. In rural areas where water was scarce, people would use the same water for their own needs. Harmful pathogens were frequently transmitted via microbiological organisms such as bacteria and viruses in water. Regular sampling would flag up problems in both animal and human populations.

Acrylamide was one of the key ingredients in Tomas's emissions-free fuel. The literature on acrylamide was confusing. In animals it was a known carcinogenic, as well as having toxic effects on their nervous system. It was found in processed food products like crisps and tobacco. He contacted a laboratory in Sweden working on acrylamide research. They were surprised; he was the second scientist from LCC to contact them. The professor knew immediately who the other one was. The Swedish professor was happy to confirm their findings. Acrylamide should be re-designated as a substance of very high concern because it damaged male reproductive glands and if ingested affected fertility. At first Professor Li was shocked, before realising Finnegan would be delighted by his findings because here was another candidate to blame if people fell ill.

The professor accepted research was a balancing act, offsetting an incremental advance in one area, only for there to be an unforeseen change somewhere else. He wasted no time in worrying about such intangibles. He was certain. Science was always at the forefront of innovation. He had dedicated his working life to it. It was up to others to decide whether it was a step towards a greater good, or – and he dismissed the thought – a step towards an irreversible catastrophe.

He wasn't concerned about the morality of it. That was for others. There were always risks. Besides, in his mind he knew the greater goal was the reduction of atmospheric pollutants. The consequences of global warming would affect far more people than this study. Cities like Cairo and countries like Bangladesh would entirely disappear under the rising oceans. No country with a coastline would escape the consequences, as rising sea levels redrew the topography. The east coast of America would be under water, bringing it to the very front doors of financial institutions and ordinary Americans. Whole communities would be abandoned, the lives of millions changed as they demanded help. This threat would lead to mass migrations, social unrest and political instability on a scale never experienced before. It would trigger an economic crisis that could literally flood the world; a twenty-first century biblical disaster. Only those governments with autocratic powers would survive; democracy was riddled with self-interest, special pleading and the need to maintain popular support.

The effect of climate change on the biosphere would be equally catastrophic. Some species would not adapt quickly enough and become extinct, pushing human life to the brink too. Set against this agenda, Bucephalus was a lifesaver if it slowed or stopped climate change from progressing further.

CHAPTER 9

FEED AFRICA

President Joseph Montgomery welcomed his two guests before asking Jim Morgan, his chief of staff to leave, well aware their private discussions would be recorded on tape.

'And how is Lady Alice?'

'Fine, she has a three-year-old running at Churchill Downs. She thinks it has the potential to win the Triple Crown.' Finnegan's tone was amiable.

The president smiled, turning to his other guest. 'What do you think Andy?'

'It's how I've made my fortune, taking chances,' Malone replied.

The president chuckled, 'Whereas we politicians are risk averse.' He pointed to a framed cartoon on his desk. In it he was portrayed as Gary Cooper walking slowly down a dusty Western street; someone you could trust to do the right thing. He liked that image of his presidency; unfortunately comedians (and his opponents) took a different view. They'd come up with a different interpretation of the cartoon.

"Slow-Hand Joe" was his mother's little boy, dressed up in his cowboy suit.

'Can I congratulate you on your re-election?' Malone said.

The president indicated they should all sit. Finnegan squashed the Schiaparelli pink cushions under his bulk, glancing up at the Rothko. Each president redecorated the Oval Office to his taste. Amateur psychologists would interpret this as an insecure man still tied to his domineering mother.

'We consider our investment well spent.' Finnegan's words were offensive. They implied he owed them a personal debt and it left an aftertaste of something illegal.

The president changed his demeanour instantly. He'd wondered what they would ask for. Nothing in politics was straightforward or without its price.

His chief of staff had told him it wasn't good public relations to be seen in their company. They were major contributors to global warming; an issue which was at best divisive.

He'd replied that he couldn't ignore their handsome contribution and apart from a few private conversations, they'd kept a low profile – until now. He told Jim, 'They'll want a commitment from me not to agree to any proposals that will damage their industries. It'd be straightforward horse trading.' But Finnegan's last remark made him wonder just how big the favour was going to be.

'Mr President, we know how sensitive the administration's position is on energy exploration, especially when it brings you into conflict with the green lobbyists,' Malone said.

Here it comes, he thought.

Finnegan jumped in. 'I fully understand why America doesn't want to take the lead in dealing with global warming because it would upset too many industries and lead to an economic downturn, as manufacturing costs rise in an effort to meet the new standards. Inevitably the consequences would be fewer exports and rising living costs. Alongside this, images of dole queues and homeless people at soup kitchens. Not something you'll want to be remembered for.'

Montgomery believed little would be achieved. The ship of state moved imperceptibly forward; continually balancing the different self-interested factions represented by the senators and congressmen, businessmen and bankers. His administration was comfortable to sit on the fence, ahead of the next world conference on global warming. Besides everyone knew India and China were hardly likely to vote for stringent reductions in emissions, as these would damage their burgeoning industries.

Finnegan outlined the problems, 'But without tackling global warming, the costs associated with rebuilding the infrastructure damaged by natural disasters such as rising sea levels will run into trillions. The strain on the administration will be immense. Voters are never happy paying more taxes. It will be an uncomfortable time to be the president.'

Montgomery rather hoped it would take years to agree any changes. And if there were a genuine problem, he'd no longer be in charge and having to make those painful and unpopular decisions. He looked at his guests. He saw two men in their seventies, still wielding immense power. A small doubt crept in. Should he have achieved more? His mother thought so, as she so often reminded him, 'You're a Lintel, we matter', totally forgetting any contribution his father might have made to the family.

He knew his mother and Lady Alice Finnegan were friends. No doubt like all women they'd shared intimacies. He regretted now not talking to her before the meeting. He should have been better prepared. But he'd thought he could handle it. Now he was having his doubts.

'We're not going to be asking for any special consideration,' Malone said, taking him by surprise.

Finnegan stepped in quickly, 'Despite the failure of communism, capitalism is now perceived as some ungodly evil. Every day corporate America is on a TV station somewhere in the world, defending itself against a Jon Doe petition. Hell, even the beefburger is portrayed as a plot to destroy the culinary traditions of foreign cuisines.'

They all smiled. The mention of food or his guests (whichever it was) made the president's stomach ulcer gurgle. It reminded him too, he was having dinner with his mother. He wanted to take a pill, but didn't want to show any sign of frailty, not in front of these men. It was all about image.

'What Gene is saying is we've lost the respect we used to command in the world. No one believes in America or its values.'

'We are bankrupt. Fort Knox is metaphorically empty.' Finnegan managed to make it sound personal.

The president eased his collar away from his damp, reddening neck. 'And just how am I going to change that?' He was uncomfortable. The burning sensation in his guts wouldn't subside. He deeply regretted he was without the support of his advisers. 'Look, I'm not sure where you two are going with all of this.' He needed to get rid of them and as soon as possible.

'I'm suggesting you launch a programme. I've even given it a name – Feed Africa,' Finnegan said bluntly.

The president forced himself to stay seated and not get up and wander round the room like a lost five-year-old in a shopping mall. What the hell was Finnegan talking about? He felt exposed.

'It'll put America and, more importantly you, centre stage.' Malone's words sounded seductive.

'You'll go down in history as one of the great presidents.' Finnegan smiled at him, giving him time to try on the image. 'Mr President, Feed Africa will begin to redress the poverty and in particular hunger that prevents the Third World from developing its true potential. If hunger was eradicated there'd be nothing to stop them. Africa is rich in natural resources and land for agriculture. It has a youthful population eager to work.'

'It would be a magnificent humanitarian concept, led by you,' Malone chipped in.

'With your vision there'd be nothing to stop them achieving their potential as dynamic, economically successful countries. The political and economic benefits are incalculable, enough to steer the agenda away from global warming and on to a concept ordinary people will understand.'

The president's ulcer started to subside.

'And Feed Africa would promote the American values of self-determination and enterprise. It would support community action and education too. What politician would want to be seen vetoing such concepts?' Finnegan added.

Feeling more relaxed, he got up and walked over to the Oval Office window and looked out across the lawn. He turned to ask, 'That's all fine and dandy, but how will it work and who will pay for it? Because if it's so simple, why hasn't someone else come up with this idea before now?'

'It's easy. You announce the concept and invite the other nations to join in. You'd get it rolling by – let's say setting it up in a part of southern Africa where it is politically stable. Your mother through the Lintel Foundation has many useful connections out there.'

It felt like a double act because Malone then said, 'Other countries, with links to parts of Africa through their colonial past, could be persuaded to join your initiative by simply rebranding their existing foreign aid packages under the banner of Feed Africa.'

'I still don't see how we'll end hunger.' He was buying time.

Finnegan told him, 'By exporting wheat to Africa. It's time for you to redeem those promises you made to American farmers during your election campaign. Right now they're in a difficult position. Europe and the rest of the developed world are reluctant to buy GM foods, but in Africa with hungry bellies, there won't be the same objections.'

He needed more time. But he liked what he was hearing. 'How will we pay for this, because I'm assuming there will be other costs,' his politician's brain kicking in.

Malone said, 'If you guarantee AMOIL exclusivity on the fuel and LCC a contract to provide all the vehicles, we'll give you our wholehearted support.'

'As will other corporations. Just as we can, they'll see the benefits of supporting Feed Africa because it will open up new markets.' There was a pause. 'I'm sure between you and your mother you know all the major company presidents and CEOs in corporate America.'

'Just imagine the media coverage,' Finnegan said. 'Every American is going to know who Joe Montgomery is, and how he made America great.'

Montgomery wasn't sure he fully trusted the man. He didn't like the way Finnegan operated. He was too – he searched for the right word – domineering, just like his mother. His ulcer returned. It made him wince. He seriously needed to get rid of them.

'Thank you gentlemen,' he got up and offered his hand, signalling the meeting was over. 'It's an interesting concept; we'll take a look at it.' Inside he was beginning to think – perhaps he could run with it. It might be a way to define his presidency. At least he hadn't been pressed on climate change. It felt like a successful meeting.

His secretary Elizabeth showed the two men out. He opened his drawer and took two pills. Looking out across the lawn, he wondered; Vernon his speech writer would find the words to inspire the world and he'd be the man on the podium delivering them. His name would be linked to Feed Africa, ensuring him a place in history.

The word Bucephalus was never recorded.

♦

Sometimes opportunities presented themselves and it is a clever politician who sees how to use them to his advantage and in doing so broker other more sensitive deals. He thought about the upcoming conference and knew how irascible China's stance would be on agreeing reductions in global warming. Did this give him an edge, a bargaining tool? It was clear they'd invested heavily in Africa; building roads and infrastructure to get access to ore, minerals and the other commodities they needed. But this investment did little to grow local communities because China shipped in the people to work, run and manage these so-called development programmes. It stank of old-fashioned imperialism, wrapped up and agreed to by local politicians who grew immensely wealthy at the expense of their people.

At some point ordinary Africans would wake up to this corruption. Feed Africa had the potential to be this catalyst as individuals and communities prospered from the impact of America's intervention. It would restore America's position in the world and show the Chinese they weren't in charge of the continent.

The president also saw how well Feed Africa would play to the ordinary Christian voter in America too with their deeply conservative principles. They believed in everyone's right to prosper, based not on state handouts, but the endeavour lying within each person. With each thought he was warming to the possibilities.

Thinkers, campaigners and the press were regularly saying feeding the world's expanding population was going to be a defining challenge in the next millennium. Africa had the undeveloped land mass and potential to become the epicentre of food production. He accepted there would be fierce arguments: man versus animals, biodiversity versus GM. But those arguing against change were in a difficult position. It stank of "I'm all right Jack," whereas he was opening his arms to humanity; in time a whole continent.

Who could argue against everyone's rights to the most basic needs of food, shelter and a better future for their children?

For Slow-Hand Joe, Feed Africa was starting to feel like a dearly loved duster coat, one he'd worn all his life.

♦

'I understand you had a meeting with Gene Finnegan and Andy Malone today.' Martha Lintel Montgomery kept a close eye on his diary. She looked across at her son, a man in his fifties, whose face had grown thin – etched with the worries of his office. He represented her life's work. She'd got him into the White House despite him being single, using her fortune, influence and contacts. Her reward was she now acted as his consort and ignored the politicians who mocked a president still living at home with his "mom". They didn't have the ear of the president. She did.

'I can see why women find Andy Malone attractive.'

Martha didn't offer an opinion, a slight pink blush on her neck.

Joe raised his eyebrow. It was a Lintel characteristic beloved by political cartoonists. 'Mother, is that a no comment response?'

'So what did they want?' She ignored his fishing expedition.

'I expected to be squeezed, after all it's men like them who've got us into this position. But they surprised me. They've come up with an idea called Feed Africa.'

Martha was surprised too. Lady Alice hadn't said anything to her. But then she never discussed her husband's business affairs. Martha often wondered if it was snobbery on Lady

Alice's part, for despite being one of the wealthiest men in the world, selling cars was akin to trade. Not something aristocratic Lady Alice would have felt truly comfortable with.

'There's no reason to think they are any less entrepreneurial than the rest of the world.'

'It will take more than that,' her tone was dismissive.

'Of course it will, but America will be taking the lead.'

Her piercing eyes concentrated on her son's face, 'What about corruption, bribes, self-interest, tribal wars?'

'I expect you to fully support me on this. Use your contacts and the Lintel name,' he said.

She was irritated by his show of independence. She threw her linen napkin onto the table, signalling their meal was over. Rarely did he take the initiative when it came to policy ideas.

There was a knock on the door. 'Sorry to interrupt you Mr President, but I thought you'd want to know the Chinese Ambassador is on his way.'

He got up. 'How do you feel about a couple of pandas at the White House?' He laughed, giving his mother a perfunctory kiss on her powdery thin-skinned cheek, 'I don't want them vetoing my proposal because they feel their noses have been put out of joint. You know how sensitive they can be.'

♦

'Put me through to that smug bastard!' The president was incandescent. 'Finnegan, you set me up. I've just left a meeting with Ambassador Zhou, and guess what he had to tell me?'

Finnegan guessed it was about his car factories.

'You've done a deal! You've invested in a major car plant in China. They're going to be flooding the US market with cheap cars. Where will that leave Detroit? I'll have workers on the streets protesting, or lining up in dole queues – looking for handouts. That's not the sort of prime time TV coverage I want. Never mind what it'll do to the balance of payments.' He paused. 'Why the hell didn't you give me a heads up when we last met? It felt like I was caught with my trousers down. With them it's all about face. Well I've got shit on mine!'

'Mr President I can explain.'

'This better be damned good.'

Finnegan reacted. He had an overwhelming urge to crush the man at the other end of the line. He felt his heart squeeze tight. No one spoke to him like that, not even the President of the United States. 'Feed Africa will give you worldwide publicity. But this is politics. How long before economists and your Republican opponents start asking how this humanitarian programme is going to be paid for? Or the man in the street says why are you helping black Africans when you don't help us?'

'Too bloody right and what do you suggest I say?' He took a breath. 'And while we are at it, let's just ignore all the extra pollution your Chinese cars will cause.' He was in full swing now, 'Even my own scientists are telling me, New York will be ten feet underwater, and as I see it – you are to blame.' His voice was screaming down the line. 'But it's fine and dandy because LCC will be selling even more cars. What do you care if they are manufactured in China?' He gathered himself. 'You're no more than a car salesman.'

‘Exactly,’ Finnegan said.

‘What…?’ the president stuttered, deflated.

‘Mr President.’ Finnegan wasn’t concerned about being polite. ‘They pay me a licence fee on every vehicle they produce. They pay me and I pay you.’ He added, ‘It will be my contribution to your Feed Africa initiative. You don’t need to worry about it.’

‘And how do you imagine that’ll keep the doom mongers and green lobbyists off my back?’

‘Trust me, once they know, it will.’ Finnegan hung up before he began laughing. You can never have enough bargaining chips in your back pocket when putting a deal together. And he’d just added another.

CHAPTER 10
STATE DINNER

'I don't think you should wear that particular bow tie.' Martha Lintel Montgomery walked straight into the president's dressing room. She ignored his valet William and selected the one she preferred. She held it up for William to take. 'This polka dot one says you're confident, youthful, not some old fuddy-duddy.'

'Mother, will you please knock before coming into my room.' He changed his tie. He didn't want to upset his ulcer so early on in the evening.

She looked at him in the mirror. 'Your father for all his faults did have a full head of black hair.'

There it was, that barbed criticism he'd come to expect each time they met. Sometimes it didn't even matter what the words were, her cold stare and tone of voice were enough to convey the undercurrent of disappointment. She had perfected it over the years; an uncanny ability to irritate him. Occasionally he responded, 'Yes, but he wasn't President of the United States.'

Ignoring him she said, 'William, next time cover the grey streaks,' and without pausing for breath, 'and who got you to Pennsylvania Avenue?' Her question didn't require an answer. The inference being he owed her everything. He was merely a walk-on part in her production.

He waited for what usually came next, the importance of the Lintel name. There was a whole litany of phrases. He knew them off by heart. He'd come to realise no matter what he achieved – even a second-term presidency – it wasn't enough. He knew how her mind worked. She was already working on his next career move. After this, she planned to make him head of the Lintel Foundation. His father's name conveniently airbrushed out of the narrative. Her legacy would be the Pope's seal of approval; the Lintel name pre-eminent in the world of humanitarian giving. Privately he reminded himself, *I'm the one on the hustings and in front of the cameras. Feed Africa will be good for me.* He glanced at William, registering the colour of his skin. When the media focussed on another case of racial unrest, caused by a white police officer killing a black youth, he'd be able to remind them of Feed Africa and his proactive stance on improving the welfare of black Africans.

'By the way I've told Christina to change the seating plan. You need to sit next to the Chinese ambassador's wife. I'll sit next to the head of the United Nations.'

He raised his eyebrow.

'Don't give me that look! You know it will send a very positive signal. And the first dance—'

'This is not my prom.' POTUS walked out furious. He forgot his pills. He saw his chief of staff Jim, arguing with Christina Fairfield. Vernon his press officer stepped forward with his speech. 'Not now!' He slammed the door shut. At least in the Oval Office he could pace without interruption.

His PR team had worked hard over the years to reassure the American voter that Slow-Hand Joe was a safe pair of hands, despite not being married. It was a tightrope act he'd perfected. On the one hand he needed to show he understood the issues surrounding families. Middle America approved of him having his mom around, along with their public show of affection and the Lintel good causes he attended. It reinforced his persona as a caring man. While the younger, glamorous women he escorted to various functions encouraged just the right amount of speculation and gossip in the media. This man-about-town image did him no harm either. It played well to the male voter who secretly thought he was a lucky bastard, and to the female voter who waited for a Cinderella moment. So far no one on the outside was privy to what went on behind his bedroom door. A door jealously guarded by his mother.

He needed to calm down. The next few hours would be important for him. He would make his announcement about Feed Africa. Two hundred of the most powerful men in America had been invited. This was networking on a grand scale. He'd also invited the Secretary General of the United Nations, head of the World Health Organization and representatives from Save the Children Fund and UNICEF. The gathering included the presidents of four southern African nations and the Chinese. It was a protocol nightmare that his mother had just upset. He'd have to work the room, smoothing ruffled feathers. At the last minute the Chinese Premier had refused the invitation and sent their Ambassador in Washington. This *volte face* had perplexed everyone at the

White House. He hoped Finnegan wasn't the reason for it. He didn't like the man. He was too much like his mother.

The fanfare of the anthem announced his arrival. As he stepped forward smiling and waving, he remembered he'd forgotten to take his emergency pills from his desk drawer in the Oval Office. Hopefully he wouldn't need them tonight. He scanned the room as the pre-dinner drinks and canapés were circulated by staff dressed in black, wearing white gloves. It reminded him of the southern states and slavery. But Martha insisted. He'd long ago developed a sense of when to make a stand; the wearing of gloves at a State dinner wasn't one of them.

Excited by the evening he began to circulate, his personal secretary Elizabeth Findlay discreetly at his elbow in case he forgot someone's name. She spoke several languages including Mandarin, which was useful tonight. Across the room he caught sight of his mother and Lady Alice talking, their heads conspiratorially close together. Finnegan seemed to be accompanied by a Chinese man. He leaned in towards Elizabeth. She whispered, 'Professor Li, head of LCC's R&D.' It surprised him.

'Good evening Ambassador Zhou.' He needed to be careful and avoid any enquiries that would give offence, when really he wanted to know why China had snubbed his invitation. He was just about to thank him for coming when Finnegan butted in.

Ambassador Zhou bowed. Finnegan spoke directly to the ambassador, virtually ignoring the presence of the president, 'I have a small gift, I'm sure you'll appreciate.' Professor Li stepped forward and said something in Mandarin. Finnegan handed over a small marquetry box.

Elizabeth whispered, 'The key to a Genco car.'

He suspected Finnegan had a fleet of cars to give away tonight. He forced a thin smile, deeply offended by the bribe he'd been forced to witness. The man was treating the White House like a car showroom!

The president spoke to Ambassador Zhou, ignoring Finnegan's presence, 'I hope our new trade deal will lead to more opportunities.' He didn't refer to LCC's factories; instead he drew the ambassador's attention to the number of potential business partners in the room.

Through his interpreter the ambassador replied, 'China is always looking for new ways to succeed,' followed by another staccato outburst in Mandarin, his words translated by the interpreter as, 'Our future lies in the wellbeing of our neighbours.'

What was he saying? Montgomery looked blank for a moment. He wasn't sure who these neighbours were exactly. It felt like it was an important message, but what did it mean? He caught sight of Jim Morgan, his chief of staff, and Douglas Dennison the vice-president. He beckoned them over. They needed to be part of this conversation.

'Does that mean China has asked to join the ASEAN alliance?' Douglas Dennison spoke directly to the ambassador.

Ambassador Zhou spoke rapidly to his aide.

'Sorry I didn't catch it.' Elizabeth glanced at Dennison, 'He might have given offence. China doesn't ask.'

Montgomery let it pass; tonight they were here to discuss Africa. He beckoned President Abyoie over. 'I'm sure your country is delighted with the Truth and Reconciliation Commission's work. The world has been truly impressed by the maturity and humanity your country has shown.' He paused. 'We can all learn from it.'

'It was the wisdom shown by Madiba.' President Abyoie smiled, unaware he'd been used by POTUS to remind China of its poor record on human rights.

Ambassador Zhou addressed his next words to the black president, 'China is pleased to support the forthcoming meeting of the African Union.'

The president wondered if in attempting to remind China about its human rights record, he'd touched a nerve. Meetings with the Chinese were full of carefully orchestrated rituals where it was easy for misunderstandings to arise. Very little was said openly, messages hidden in subtext. It was not the American way. He whispered to Jim Morgan, 'Put China on the agenda for tomorrow's meeting.' He thought, *Is this their way of pointing out China has influence and friends in Africa, and they don't like what I'm about to propose?*

The president turned to President Abyoie. 'I see you have been given a gift too.' He wondered how Finnegan organised the hierarchy of horsepower within each box; his corrupting largesse tainting everyone it seemed. It was a petty reaction but he was anxious about this evening.

Ambassador Zhou took the box from his aide, as if weighing the contents up and comparing it to President Abyoie's; again this action conveying more than it seemed. Ambassador Zhou spoke in English, his words directed towards Finnegan, 'Beware of Americans bearing gifts,' he paused and turned to look at the surprised president, 'because Troy ended in flames.'

He had no idea what Zhou was alluding to. He knew his face looked flushed. He'd lost control of the swiftly moving currents of diplomacy. However, with the two of them together, it was an opportunity for the White House photographer to record the scene. His press office would add the appropriate words, none of which bore any resemblance to those just spoken.

He moved off towards firmer ground. 'Bob, good to see you, I hope you'll get on board with my initiative.' He gave him a gentle slap on the back and a vigorous firm handshake. Bob Bernau was the CEO of a major agrochemical company.

'We're all very excited by your proposal.'

Of course it had been leaked judiciously beforehand. No one came to an event like this unprepared. Bernau had been talking to the Congressman from Ohio who added, 'Time to make good on those promises.' The three men smiled at each other. He moved on, more relaxed. He understood what these people were saying. They were interested in profits and business expansion.

Just before they went in to dinner, he pulled Douglas Dennison to one side. 'I thought you were keeping a close eye on the Chinese.' He didn't trust his vice-president. He was an old friend of his mother's. 'It seems the Chinese are more interested in doing trade deals with their ASEAN partners than with the US. It's not what Finnegan promised me.'

'I'm not sure what you are referring to? What did Gene Finnegan promise you?' Dennison asked, clearly on a fishing expedition.

'He's promised to come on board with Feed Africa. It's what tonight is about, isn't it?' He quelled a sense of foreboding. 'You know I'm counting on your support.' The two men parted, apparently easing back into the ebb and flow; apparently on friendly terms.

'Elizabeth, I want you to chat up Finnegan's man. See what you can discover.'

This was his moment. He'd been reassured it would be well received; the White House machine working hard to build a consensus. Everyone agreed. It made great economic sense and as he surveyed the other businesses here tonight, his anxiety subsided. Feed Africa was a worthy cause. It would be his personal legacy.

'It's time for dinner.' Uncannily his mother appeared by his side. She clutched onto his arm smiling indulgently up at him and for the cameras.

The president's stomach grumbled.

Douglas Dennison materialised, 'You're looking magnificent as always Martha.' He gave her a perfunctory kiss on the cheek. The cameras flashed again capturing the White House scene.

As Martha passed Elizabeth she whispered, 'Tell William, he'll need his pills tonight.'

CHAPTER 11
GO HOME

Josie rang Finnegan's number. She didn't mention the burglary. 'It's finished.'

'I'm coming over.' His voice took her by surprise. He'd never visited nor spoken to her before. There was no hesitation either, as if he'd never doubted the outcome. 'I need to speak to Dr Olofsson.'

There were no words of congratulation for her. She felt her heart rate rise. What did he want with Tomas? Until now she'd been the conduit. All the men involved in Bucephalus knew the purpose and they'd excluded her. She barely held her temper. 'I told you I could keep a secret.' She cut the connection. She had done what he'd asked for. He owed her.

Two days later Finnegan arrived. She caught sight of the high-performance Genco. It came to a halt, sending the resident pigeons scattering into the air. Finnegan strode towards the barn, not looking to his left or right. He opened the door and walked in.

A few minutes later Maguire came out. He was still

wearing his hairnet, overshoes and laboratory coat. He stood bewildered, before coming up to the house where Josie was waiting for him.

'I've been told to go home,' he said, shaken.

'What, back to LCC?' Josie was taken aback, 'what else did Finnegan say?'

'He's closing us down. Told me to get out, he needed to talk to Dr Olofsson.'

A few minutes later Mike came out.

'What did Finnegan say to you?' Josie asked Mike as he arrived in the kitchen looking angry.

'Told me it was over, I was finished.' Mike rushed upstairs taking them two at a time. A few minutes later he reappeared with his helmet, dressed in his leathers. They both heard the roar of the Augusta, followed by the birds, before they settled back down in the trees.

Maguire shrugged his shoulders. 'I won't miss him.'

Josie wasn't surprised. She found Mike amusing but knew how he taunted the others. Why was Mike so upset? He'd been keen to leave a few weeks earlier. She turned to Maguire. 'Is there a problem with Bucephalus?' She was struggling to understand why the sudden rush to close Ham Farm down. *Did it have something to do with the burglary?* she wondered. She felt vulnerable.

He avoided her gaze. 'I'm only a technician.'

'You work alongside Tomas, you must discuss things.' She sensed he was hiding something. She concentrated her grey eyes on him.

'He wasn't ready to sign it off.' He was clearly uncomfortable, staring down at the floor, not at her. He looked dreadful, as if he were about to collapse.

'But Tomas told me it was finished.' Her voice was harsh. She was upset.

'Tomas wanted to do more testing. Finnegan's not a man you can easily say no to.'

'Surely Professor Li would support Tomas.'

'He's just a different kind of bully.' He went upstairs to pack.

Well that was interesting, she thought. She sat on the chair, drumming her fingers on the table. Had Tomas made a mistake and Finnegan was taking the project out of his hands? Typically Tomas hadn't said anything to her. She could have delayed telling Finnegan. She felt foolish. She waited thirty minutes, her feet and hands now tapping out a rhythm. Suddenly she heard the crows, a sure sign something was happening. She stood up quickly, only to see Finnegan drive off at speed, sending them and the skittish pigeons skyward. *He's gone!* She was enraged; holding her stomach she rushed upstairs; waves of nausea and anger making her retch into the toilet bowl.

♦

'Get out!'

'It's me Tomas,' she called out.

'It's my reputation.' He thumped his fist hard on the bench, sending a glass stirring rod rattling against the measuring flask. He picked up the glass flask and threw it against the wall. Josie ducked to avoid the missile. 'I told him it still needs testing.'

She noticed the laboratory appeared unchanged, liquids distilling with yet more samples ready for analysis. 'You said it was finished. That's what I told Finnegan,' her voice matching his actions.

'I said,' he turned angrily, 'I'd found the formula and the right distillation. This is only the beginning.' He stared at her. 'No one understands!' Tomas unexpectedly collapsed, putting his head in his hands, leaning on the bench.

She put her arms around his shoulders hoping he wouldn't pull away, rather open up as he had done once before. And suddenly it slipped out, 'Tomas, we're going to have a baby.' She regretted her words immediately, blaming it on the strain of the burglary, worries about the future but mainly, having to keep her pregnancy a secret from him. Tomas pulled away from her. She saw the expression on his face and was appalled. Neither of them moved. All she could hear was the steady whir of the air conditioning. She stared at him open mouthed. He looked ragged. His normally warm flesh tones looked grubby like used student bed linen. 'Are you all right?'

'Leave me. Stay out of here.' There was no hint of tenderness or love in his voice.

They both stood on the edge of an abyss. Then he grabbed her and kissed her hard, crushing her against his chest. She could feel his heart beating through his lab coat. He pushed her away, his eyes moist; then without saying another word, he dragged her tightly by her upper arm and out of the laboratory.

'You're hurting me!'

He pushed her out and rolled the door shut in her face. All she could do was run away, devastated by his reaction. Everything was spiralling out of control. She wanted her mother and the others at Tugela. She needed to feel safe and loved.

Josie ran crying into the field, her vision blurred by her tears, as a sudden gust of wind whipped the wild grasses into a maelstrom. Tomas had said nothing to her about their baby.

♦

After that Josie and Tomas avoided each other. Her daydreams for a happy-ever-after evaporated. His reluctance to say anything cut her deeply. She was too proud to forgive him or try to understand. How you could love someone and then reject them so totally? Didn't he want to be a father? Perhaps she had misjudged him. She thought she understood the reason behind his dislike of physical intimacy. She forgave him the dedication he lavished on his work. Now she wondered if he was unable to forge a real long-lasting relationship. She remembered his pain when he'd told her about his father and the phrase, "He abandoned me." Yet it seemed he was prepared to do exactly the same to their unborn child. How wrong had she been to let him into her heart! She should have become Mike's lover. It would have been far less complicated.

There was no camaraderie between any of them now. Consequently when Maguire left there was no party or even a meal together. Josie did her duty and drove him to the airport. Her last words were, 'Forget about Bucephalus', as if any of them could.

They were three again, no longer innocent characters having an adventure. Mike spent his time down at *Grey Goose*. She got on with packing up the house and Tomas stayed in the laboratory doing the same. After another bout of morning sickness Josie sat miserably on her bed. She left a message on Finnegan's phone telling him the date they'd be returning and that Mike planned to go sailing on *Grey Goose* before returning to Genco. She doubted Finnegan cared about Mike's holiday. But she was keen to be professional right to the end.

However, she felt increasingly uneasy about her own position and returning to LCC and facing Finnegan. She tried to imagine the scene in his office. She wasn't sure she could maintain the lie, pretending nothing untoward had happened. She knew he would find out about the burglary and then what? Equally she didn't want him to know she was pregnant; the instinct to protect her baby was paramount. Instead of feeling joyous about completing Bucephalus and her pregnancy, the nightmares returned.

She went down to the laboratory. She had to face him at some point. They needed to talk. He had a child to consider, however much he wanted to escape the responsibility, and with only a few days left before the contractors arrived to take everything away, time was running out.

Josie walked straight into the first portacabin. Tomas used it as his office. It appeared untouched; with a quickening stride she walked into the next and then the next. The laboratory was the same as it had always been: full of equipment, machines running, nothing had been packed up ready for the move to LCC. She found him sat hunched over, reading something.

'You know we leave in a few days' time,' she shouted at him. Josie waved her arms around. 'What the bloody hell is going on! You were meant to be packing this up.'

Then she saw his sunken eyes, as if he hadn't slept for days and his skin was blotchy, his face gaunt. He didn't get up.

'I'm sorry Josie, sorry for everything.'

Not again, she thought. She didn't want to always be the strong one in the relationship, navigating them through choppy waters. How much did she love him? The question balanced uncertainly between her heart and her head.

She clung on to hope. 'Tomas I love you, I want us to be a family.' If only they could put Bucephalus behind them, they'd be all right. She felt him momentarily pull back, as if the force of her embrace had winded him. She kissed him tenderly. Her stomach flipped over as she tasted and breathed him in. Her desire reignited. Josie held his hand on her stomach.

'It's a baby – your baby. He needs his father.'

He looked at her belly. 'It's a boy?'

She nodded. 'Say hello to your son.' She'd been too selfish, too focussed on her own needs over the past few weeks.

Tomas sat down on the stool, physically exhausted. He picked up a piece of paper and thrust it towards her. 'I warned Finnegan.'

She didn't read it. Instead she sat down beside him.

'Josie it's not safe.' He looked devastated.

Is this why he seems so ill? It's got nothing to do with me and the baby, Josie thought. 'Back at LCC you and Professor Li can resolve any problems.'

'You don't know him.' He buried his face in his hands. 'I'll be blamed, my career and reputation gone. It's all over.'

'I believe in you.' Josie touched his arm. 'Finnegan wouldn't risk it. He's got too much to lose,' she said, trying to be positive. 'We can still be a family.'

He pulled away. They were adrift again, heading for the rocks. She knew it would always be like this. Yet she still loved him.

He got up, tore up the paper and said, 'It doesn't matter now, it's too late anyway.' He took her hand and walking slowly towards the door he said, 'Let's go sailing.'

Surprised, Josie felt enormously relieved. 'I've never sailed,' she said, grinning up at him.

They laughed. He planted a light kiss on her lips. For the first time in months, Josie felt happy. They would work something out. As they reached the door Tomas said, 'You're still banned.' Slowly he closed the sliding door.

She walked back to the house; the constant commentary of the crows made her look up. 'You can have it back. We're going home.'

"Home", where was that?

CHAPTER 12

GREY GOOSE

It must have been the realisation they were at the end of the project. The mood lifted. An end of term madness gripped them. Tomas disappeared, as he had done on different occasions over the past weeks.

The yard was full of contractors' vehicles.

Dismantling the laboratory proved to be so much quicker than installing it. The dark despair of a few days ago was gone. Josie relaxed. They agreed today was the day. They'd spend it aboard *Grey Goose*, as a sort of farewell party. Tomas and Josie came down the stairs dishevelled.

'Young love – how charming.' Mike's sarcasm was obvious.

Josie flashed a diamond ring. 'He sneaked off and bought this.' She held it out in front of her, humming and twirling round Mike.

'So he's faced up to his responsibilities.' He grabbed her hand and pulled her close into him. 'A little bird told me a secret, you've never sailed!' He pushed her away and slapped her bottom with some force.

'Ouch!' She turned, looking at Mike. He wasn't smiling.

♦

They'd finished packing the few items needed for their day into the boot of the 4x4. Mike jumped into the driver's seat, calling out to Josie, 'Hurry up – we'll miss the tide.'

Josie came out and locked the front door, then immediately reopened it. 'Sorry boys, I need the toilet again.'

Mike got out of the car, calling out, 'I don't want you being sick on *Grey Goose*.' He rushed up the stairs to his bedroom where he opened his sports holdall, chucking out stuff till he found his yellow chamois gloves. He waggled them like puppets as he raced down the stairs past Josie.

'So I can hold on tight to you. It's going to be wet out there.'

She closed the window in the toilet and checked the others. Mike had a tendency to leave his open, saying he liked a cold bedroom. It was open. Amongst the discarded paraphernalia on his bed she saw a laptop. She was curious. He hadn't given her an invoice for a new one. She ignored the beep of the horn and flipped open the lid. The password command was blinking at her. He wouldn't be so stupid to use his old one, would he? She typed it in and the laptop sprung into life. She opened the file explorer. The most recent document was a job application.

Beep, beep, beep…

She wanted to open up the other files but realised Mike would know she'd sneaked a look. She shut it down and went downstairs slowly, each step like a walk to the gallows. She liked him. He was her good friend – the lovable bear. Slowly the thought came to her. He was also a really good actor too and she'd played along, delighted by his jokey, over-the-top performances. She'd even thought he fancied her. She felt foolish and hurt. She'd thought she knew who he was. He'd seemed like a good sport, straightforward and honest. Now it seemed he'd been playing a character all along, biding his time, ready to benefit from Bucephalus in whatever way he could. Her neck reddened with shame. She'd misjudged him completely. Men weren't to be trusted. It was a hard lesson to learn, but a part of her now understood her mother's fierce independence.

She climbed into the back of the 4x4 without speaking. On the thirty-minute drive to the estuary she had time to think. She replayed the day when they'd discovered the burglary. Mike had been genuinely shocked and searched as frantically as she had done. Then she remembered he'd ushered her out. Did he want to look for something on his own, a hidden laptop, one not connected to Finnegan's server? In the brief time she'd had to scan his laptop she'd seen a list of CAD drawings and assumed all the other technical specifications he needed to replicate his work for someone else would be there. She hadn't had time to see if he had Tomas's formula. He might have lied about that too. Why not? She could believe anything of him now. It appeared Mike did have secrets after all. She muttered out loud, 'Bastard.'

She caught Mike's eyes looking at her in the car's rear view mirror. She held his gaze. Then opened the window and stuck her head out, as if she was about to be sick. 'Do you mind if you two go sailing without me? I don't think my stomach is up to it.'

For a moment Tomas was concerned. Mike grinned across at Tomas. 'Now we'll see who the better sailor is.'

Generally midweek the harbour was empty. Today was a blustery wet one. It had discouraged retired day-trippers or if they were about, they were sheltering in the small cafés dotted around the picturesque village, one street back from the tidal roadway. Local people were in The Ancient Mariner keeping warm by the log fire. From here they could see the estuary with its bobbing boats. They talked about the latest piece of technology they'd bought and trips they planned to do when the better weather came.

Grey Goose was moored mid channel. Josie held back as Mike brought down the last items from the 4x4. They loaded up the dinghy, apparently still in good humour; Mike giving Tomas a playful shove, knocking him off balance.

'You're sure you don't want to come?' Mike shouted back up to her.

Josie waved back. 'No.'

Mike came running up the concrete slipway, 'Last chance?' He hugged her, growling in his usual manner, his face snuggled into her neck, only this time the hairs of his beard scratching her.

She pulled away. 'Mike, will you forget about Bucephalus?' She was giving him one last chance to redeem himself.

He looked quizzically at her.

'I mean, what will you do now?' Her eyebrow rose.

For a moment they stared at each other. 'Did you find it?' he asked.

She nodded.

'For God's sake Josie, I'm sitting on a gold mine. Just imagine the package I can negotiate. I'll buy a new boat, even a top-of-the-range Genco.' He grinned. 'Everyone will be trying to find out what LCC have done. And I know,' he laughed, pleased with himself.

'You imbecile, what have you done?'

'It was simple. I duplicated everything onto my own laptop.' He winked. 'You're not going to tell on me are you?' He flashed her one of his broadest smiles and planted an unwelcomed kiss on her lips. Suddenly his voice changed. 'You should have chosen me.' It had an edged to it.

Josie didn't react for a moment. The wind blew a sudden gust, partially covering her face. From behind her black veil she spoke in a calm unemotional voice, 'Finnegan will never let you get away with it.' She turned away.

'You and your obsession with Finnegan, the bogeyman,' He waggled his yellow fingers at her, 'Woo – or else.' He laughed, mocking her.

'You're a fool.' Her eyes were cold like the English sea.

Tomas came up to them. 'I thought you wanted to catch the tide.'

Mike slapped him hard on his back.

'Be careful, that's my fiancé,' Josie said. She tilted her head up so Tomas could kiss her.

'When you're quite finished,' Mike said tetchily.

She stood watching them go out to *Grey Goose* in the dinghy, securing it alongside before clambering on board. Josie retreated inside the 4x4. The rain on the windscreen obscured the boat's outline, only the ripple from the propeller and the disturbed gulls indicated the direction of their progress as *Grey Goose* moved towards the English Channel. She could see them preparing the mainsail and jib. The chugging engine stopped. And for a brief moment there was silence; before a deafening noise and a fireball lit up the horizon.

Josie screamed in horror. The boat disappeared in a yellow and white flash, the flames expanding over the whole boat. Suddenly people were appearing from everywhere, running towards the tidal breakwater. Others stood pointing, animated, not believing what they had just seen. A siren sounded, several men rushed towards a boat, the engine whining as they raced towards *Grey Goose*. Josie got out of the vehicle and slid down to the ground crying and screaming, her body shaking, shivering with cold. A stranger came towards her and pulled her up, holding onto her shoulders to stop her from falling to the ground again. The piercing sound coming from her mouth stopped. She felt numb. Had it been real? She looked into the person's eyes, as a coat went round her shoulders.

'Did you see it?' she asked, stupefied.

'Yes, it was horrible. It just suddenly exploded.'

Another voice close by said, 'They'll find it hard to identify anyone after that fireball.'

Josie began to sway, her words a deep moan of disbelief. 'No, no, no, no.' She broke free and ran to the water's edge, scouring the estuary for any signs of life. *Grey Goose* burned intensely, fed by the fuel on board. An oily iridescence kept the shattered pieces alight like floating torches. She wanted to jump in and swim out to Tomas, desperate to believe he was alive, knowing no one could have survived. She screamed 'Tomas' over and over again.

♦

The Harbour Master's office became the incident room, with people constantly moving in and out with purpose. Radios crackled with messages; she may even have heard a helicopter's blades. A man in uniform seemed to be giving the orders.

She watched as if disembodied, cocooned from the urgency and the activity around her. Her tears stopped. Her mouth was dry, the mug of tea cold in her hand. The blanket around her shoulders slipped to the ground. She didn't notice it falling nor did she pick it up despite still shivering with shock.

It wouldn't take them long to identify the owner of *Grey Goose* and that would lead them to Genco and Mike's next of kin. The police were interviewing people at the scene, trying to establish a reason for the explosion. Someone might have seen the three of them together. She was trying to get her mind to work but like her body it remained paralysed. What if someone heard her calling out Tomas's name?

She couldn't face going back to Ham Farm. Where could she go? She didn't know anyone locally – that had been the point, invisible and hidden away from other people. Suddenly and in spectacular fashion it wasn't a secret; everyone was talking about the incident. It would be on the news for days. Journalists were already gathering outside, TV cameras and microphones; they were bound to ask her what she'd seen. She looked out through the window at what seemed like divers going out in a rubber dinghy hoping to recover human remains. In her mind she knew Tomas would be unrecognisable. Who would claim his body? No one from LCC would come forward, leaving the local authority to bury him in an unmarked grave. Tears ran down Josie's face. She knew she'd never see him again. He'd become a ghost, alive only in her imagination. Her hand went instinctively to her womb.

How long before an appeal would go out asking for witnesses to come forward with information? Someone was bound to remember a pregnant, distressed woman at the scene calling out a name. It wouldn't take them long to check the local hospitals, checking on a woman coming in for her twenty-week scan. She'd be identified. Someone pointed in her direction.

♦

Josie drove back to Ham Farm, not remembering anything of the journey. Where else did she have to go? In Tomas's old room she found his suitcase with his clothes neatly packed. She opened the case and took out his blue shirt and held it to her face, breathing in his smell; she rocked backwards and forwards. She stuffed the shirt into her bag. Would she ever stop crying?

♦

Maybe it was panic or fear but she decided to abandon Mike's clothes in a charity shop's skip. His riding gear was too memorable to do the same. She looked online and found several charities seeking second-hand riding gear. She'd parcel it up and send it off anonymously. The bike was more of a problem. Eventually she decided she'd leave it in the barn. She heard herself say to the watching crows, 'The bastard', as she struggled to wheel it across the yard. The barn had been cleared and looked as derelict as that first day she'd arrived. She covered the bike in straw, turned off the lights and locked the door. Walking around like an automaton she set about cleaning the house. In each room she wiped away every possible fingerprint and vacuumed up as much bodily detritus as she could; removing anything that could give someone a clue as to who had lived here. She was erasing Bucephalus, just as Finnegan had done.

Mike was a brilliant engineer; he'd spent hours tinkering with *Grey Goose*, there was no possibility he would have missed a faulty connection, and besides it was such a devastating explosion. It must have been a bomb. For a brief moment she wondered if Finnegan planned for all three of them to die in the boat. The media and inquest would tell him the truth soon enough; two bodies, not three. Once Finnegan had the formula for the fuel and the engine designs, he had his legacy. No one's name associated with it; only his. Like a tyrannical despot his hand swept the chessboard clear, brushing away any evidence, keeping Bucephalus as his secret.

She now understood the magnitude of his threat. She'd never go back to LCC. There was only one thought in her head. She had to escape. Her life was in danger. She had to admire his planning. He'd chosen each one of them carefully. Who would miss them and raise the alarm? She had run away from home, cutting all ties. It was the same for Tomas. His father was dead and he hated his mother. He had abandoned her a long time ago. No one would believe her alcoholic ramblings about a missing son. Tomas wasn't close to anyone at LCC (apart from Professor Li) and no doubt he'd invent a story to explain his absence. Besides there was nothing to link Tomas to the man who'd died in a boating accident in England. That left Mike. Finnegan must have judged him correctly: too ambitious and greedy, someone that had to go once he'd served his purpose. Should she warn Jon Maguire?

She logged onto Mike's private laptop, praying no one at LCC knew about it. She booked a flight to Frankfurt, transferring the following day to Dubai, before flying on to Johannesburg; all on different airlines. She paid for the tickets using Mike's bankcard. Next she drove to the town and withdrew her money. Finally she parked her 4x4 on a back street, leaving the doors unlocked, hoping someone would steal it, or if not it'd be weeks before anyone reported the car as abandoned. She paid for her railway ticket with cash and caught the train to London. From there she bought another and arrived at Heathrow in time for her long flight home to Tugela, Mike's replacement laptop safely stowed in her luggage.

CHAPTER 13

GG42/OO

Professor Li had been right to insist Tomas have an assistant, someone who could carry out the mindless repetitive distillations, increasing the component parts milligram by milligram until he found the optimum concentration of the right chemicals. He needed someone who would do as he was told. He couldn't rely on Tomas. Bucephalus was too important for there to be any mistakes. His laboratory would be credited with a discovery that changed every industry relying on fuel; confident his name and reputation would soar, achieving everything he had striven for.

Maguire collapsed into the chair. He looked terrible. 'Finnegan ordered us home.'

'It was a business decision. Ham Farm had served its purpose. It will be finished here.'

'So it had nothing to do with the burglary?' Maguire asked, surprised.

'What burglary?' Professor Li leaned forward. 'Why didn't you tell me?'

'It was a collective decision not to.'

'When did I give you permission to act independently?' The professor was deep in thought. His concentration was broken by Maguire coughing and spluttering, his body shaking like a man with palsy. In disgust Professor Li got up and pulled off a handful of paper tissue from the dispenser.

'Was anything taken?' He handed the tissue over before wiping his hands with barrier cream.

'The engineer's laptop, that's all.'

'What else haven't you told me?' *Perhaps Maguire wasn't such a good choice*, he thought.

'There was a problem.' Maguire crumpled up, coughing in pain.

'I know all about the acrylamide,' the professor said, relieved it wasn't anything more serious.

'It wasn't that.'

Professor Li stopped, his glasses catching the light, turning them into spotlights focussed on the hacking, nervous technician.

'Tomas named it GG42/OO, after a boat his father owned.'

The professor sat shocked by the revelation. Each night he checked the results, searching for errors or mistakes in other people's work. He hadn't found anything. It was impossible!

'Why didn't you tell me?' He was disappointed that Tomas hadn't asked for his advice.

'He knew what I was doing.'

The professor's mouth twitched. 'You mean telling tales, spying on him.' He pulled his silk handkerchief out of his top pocket and dabbed the corners of his mouth. 'Remember who pays your salary.'

Let him sweat while I think what this means. He'd set up a complicated spider's web, hiding it amongst other projects so individuals and teams had no idea they were working on Bucephalus. At the same time he oversaw the environmental field study personally; every day new information came in that only he saw. No one at the lab knew about Bucephalus apart from the man in front of him. And he looked seriously ill.

'I thought you'd want to give him more time.' Maguire's body doubled over in another spasm.

'It looks like you'll need your LCC medical insurance.' He'd seen all the read outs, they showed nothing out of the ordinary, only traces of hydrogen, nitrogen, oxygen and carbon, as one would expect. He hadn't seen anything to worry him; no trace of a new compound. 'Where is the evidence for this GG42/OO?'

Maguire managed a smile. 'He said you'd miss it; hidden in the carbon signature printout. You'd think it was a slightly heavier line or a smudge.'

I had missed it!

'He said you and Finnegan would insist the project go ahead.'

He imagined his peers laughing at him, calling into question his thoroughness and ability. Slowly he took off his glasses to clean them. 'What did Dr Olofsson say to Finnegan?'

'I don't know.' Maguire looked directly back at him.

I don't like his streak of defiance. He knew Tomas wasn't interested in building a career at LCC. His work was all that mattered to him. Tomas would have been forthright. Whatever concerns Tomas expressed, it wasn't what Finnegan wanted to hear. Panic rose in the professor's mind. *I haven't waited all these years for it to go wrong now.*

'Can I have a glass of water?'

He saw Maguire's paper towel was spotted with blood.

'The air smelt peachy, it was the acrylamide. He told me he'd turned off the air extraction.'

The professor looked closely at the technician. The Swedish researchers had been right; it was a dangerous chemical. He reassured himself. In the confined space of Ham Farm the concentrations would be abnormally high. It would not be the same in Africa. Perhaps that explained why he hadn't spotted it. He'd have to review all the printouts.

Maguire continued. 'I asked him why he'd done it. He said it was his responsibility. GG42/OO was too dangerous to ignore. He's right isn't he?' The question contained both pride and doubt. 'He was testing it on himself too.'

He heard the technician's words. They sounded distant. Feeling a dreadful numbness grip his chest, his legs went from under him. He collapsed into the swivel chair, dropping the cup of water as his hands grabbed the arms, to stop himself from sliding to the floor. It took him a moment to recover. 'Leave and don't tell anyone.'

♦

What would Finnegan do if Tomas told him Bucephalus wasn't ready to be launched? He'd have to reassure Finnegan, tell him the young man's work didn't mean the end of the project; they still had a green vehicle. He'd reassure him, he'd personally oversee it. He'd never let Finnegan down before, and look at what he'd achieved. Finnegan didn't need to know about GG42/OO. He just needed a little more time, but he was confident he could find a way to mitigate the effects of this new chemical compound.

♦

'What's the meaning of this?' Finnegan picked up the report before tossing it aside.

'I strongly recommend we wait until the field study is complete before we announce our breakthrough. It may take longer than I'd first envisaged.' The professor tried to remain impassive, his hand itching to fiddle with his talisman. It always reminded him of his greater purpose.

There was a moment's silence before Finnegan raised himself up, arms akimbo, leaning forward on the desk, 'Do you mean delay it?' It may have sounded like an open question but it wasn't. They both knew it. 'I've given you everything you asked for.'

He felt hot and clammy.

'I thought your laboratory tests proved we have a green car.' Finnegan's gaze focussed on him.

'Yes, but…' He didn't finish the sentence.

'And the field study was merely you being paranoid. You've had long enough. I order you to finish the field study. Do it now before someone finds out what we are doing.'

He persisted. 'Dr Olofsson had concerns about the body's ability to produce healthy blood cells.' He was uncertain how much to say about the problem, still worried by what Tomas had said to Finnegan.

Finnegan reacted at the mention of Dr Olofsson's name, his eyes bulging. 'You want me to throw away millions of dollars, my investment in China and the support of the President of the United States because…' he took a deep breath, 'because your boyfriend is concerned about some fucking blood cells.' He stood upright and slammed his fist down on the desk.

Finnegan's action and words hit their mark. Professor Li felt them like a body blow. He knew Finnegan would not delay or abort Bucephalus. He always got what he wanted, whatever the human or monetary costs. He had seen and felt Finnegan's wrath before. Normally he absorbed it, consoling himself with the knowledge that despite Finnegan's far-reaching power and autocratic behaviour, he didn't know everything.

'Dr Olofsson tested it on himself.' He had to hold his nerve, gauging the extent of Finnegan's knowledge.

Finnegan picked up the report and threw it at him this time. 'You know what I need and it's not this. If there's a problem, fix it.'

The professor remained seated. 'Dr Olofsson hasn't returned to LCC.' He waited, hardly daring to breath.

'He died in a boating accident.'

The colour drained from the professor, his hand pulling his silk handkerchief out to smother his cry of anguish.

Finnegan looked at him, disgusted. 'I don't want to hear about more delays.'

Professor Li tried to stand up. 'I understand.' His emotions were in turmoil. *Tomas dead!* He could barely comprehend it. His world imploded, and Finnegan stood there unmoved, wanting – no, demanding that Bucephalus work.

The sound of Finnegan's buzzer ended the meeting.

As he slowly walked out a thought grew, tiny at first before it took hold. *He could claim it as his own.* With Tomas dead, the plaudits and the glory would all be his. He imagined the Nobel Prize tantalizingly within reach of his fingertips with each step.

Eliot was surprised to see a small smile on the professor's normally expressionless face.

PART TWO

HOME TO AFRICA

CHAPTER 14
HOMECOMING

Doctor Kate Ryland was late; opening the Land Cruiser's door a hot blast of dry air engulfed her. Immediately she regretted not parking it under the jacaranda tree, at least then she wouldn't feel like a chicken about to be roasted. She could barely hold the steering wheel. She flipped the aircon switch. The powerful engine dropped the temperature to a shivering coolness. Years in the sun had shrivelled the skin on her arms. They now looked like a dried-up river bed and her liver spots, tobacco stains.

The hospital was on the outskirts of Matsane. She'd chosen the site because of the river and the slight rise, the wafting early morning breeze welcomed by the TB patients. Kate drove at speed towards the airport; braking hard at the junction she rolled over the stop line and caught sight of the policeman in the car waiting ahead. She swore under her breath.

'*Dankie*,' she said sarcastically as she threw the ticket into the glove compartment, along with the others, knowing no one bothered to collect the fines.

As soon as she pulled up into a parking space and opened the door, Kate regretted using the aircon. The mid-afternoon heat felt oppressive. She made her way to the airport's terminal. It was built in the 1930s when rich Americans and the English aristocracy came to hunt big game; now all that remained of its Art Deco glory were the narrow bronze and glass entrance doors, and thin elongated lettering spelling out the airport's name, 'Matsane'. Two palm trees flanked the entrance. The only area of green was where the abandoned yellow hose pipe dripped; sparrows squabbling over the oasis. The building was white except where the copper-rich earth splattered up the walls, staining it the colour of congealed blood. Behind a high wire security fence were two hangars, offices and a maintenance building. The flying school's Cessna and Piper aeroplanes were lined up, ready like taxis to take rich tourists to private game lodges in the bush. An avgas truck was filling up a light aircraft with aviation fuel.

Inside the airport people milled around leaving footprints on the polished red concrete floor, overhead the fans turned the air slowly without having any impact on the temperature. Kate found a seat, only half listening to the announcements as she waited for Josie to arrive on the daily flight from Johannesburg, her foot tapping up and down.

'Hi Mom.' Josie dropped her bags. She looked exhausted. Her eyes were red and puffy.

'You look dreadful AND pregnant,' Kate said bluntly.

'Thanks for the welcome.' Josie's sarcasm didn't help the reunion. She rubbed her belly before bursting into tears like an overwrought child.

Kate felt awkward. 'When's the baby due?'

'Just over sixteen weeks.' Josie wiped away her tears.

Kate gave her daughter a long, appraising stare. The person in front of her looked so different. Gone was the daughter she remembered. Instead all she saw was another desperate mother needing her help. As they got into the vehicle Kate wound down the windows.

'Johannes asked me every day, "When is Josie coming home madam?"'

'And Balipi and Mary, I've missed them.'

'A postcard would have been nice.' Even Kate was surprised by her reaction. The hurt and worry of her daughter running away instantly returned, reigniting all those feelings she thought she had buried. She wasn't sure what she felt by her daughter's return. The Land Cruiser was new when she'd left; now the hospital's name on the doors had faded, the bodywork chipped, and the mileage indicator showed over 240,000 miles. The women sat side-by-side like strangers; each uncomfortably aware of the silence that had lasted for nearly a decade.

♦

Josie avoided making small talk. What could she say? Where to begin? Inside she was hurt by her mother's welcome but equally too worn out to explain why she had come home so suddenly. Instead she concentrated on the view as they drove down Main Street. It appeared familiar. The architecture belonged to Africa's colonial past: single storey buildings with green or red corrugated metal roofs and overhanging porches offering protection from the sun's glare. The peeling stucco and faded signboards recalled the hopes of long-ago proud shopkeepers; now irrelevant to the goods on display inside. Outside one shop she saw a table covered in a mishmash of different telephone handsets, their wires trailing up and over and into the dark interior. People stood on the street using them to do business or call home. Lone vendors found shade where they could. The unlucky ones sat in the dazzling light and heat, in front of them on patterned cloths a miscellany of goods. In single numbers to large piles, everything was for sale: pencils and boiled sweets, shoelaces, bottles of shampoo, clothes, kitchen utensils, oranges, and even live caged chickens. Young men hung about waiting for something to happen, calling out to friends. Women carried bags in each hand, balancing another on their heads. The air was dusty and dry. Trucks and cars navigated round pedestrians, cyclists and the occasional mongrel intent on crossing the street. It looked vibrant and chaotic.

At the end of Main Street the OK Bazaar had gone; in its place a new shopping centre. The car park at the front was busy. Checkers supermarket dominated the centre, its windows covered in garish posters advertising Omo washing powder and Castle lager at slash-down prices. The names stirred long-forgotten memories for Josie; the brands different to the ones she'd bought in England. She noticed a group of excited black children, each carrying a balloon, come rushing out of the Wimpey. They narrowly missed an African woman with a baby wrapped in a blanket tied on her back; traditional Africa and the new avoiding a collision.

When she'd left, apartheid was beginning to crumble, but even then a black person had to carry a Dompas explaining why they were in a white area. Now black and white people walked on the same pavement; politeness, not skin colour determining who stepped aside. Josie had watched Nelson Mandela walk free, without fully understanding how it would change the country. It seemed the rainbow nation shopped and ate together. It was a shocking and profound change. She felt like a visitor; conscious she might inadvertently say or do the wrong thing in this new country.

The Land Cruiser pulled up at the robot, the first of several along this new stretch of the road. The lights went from red to green. Kate pulled away. Beep, b-e-e-p, the driver behind kept his hand on the horn, annoyed at Kate's slow acceleration. Josie saw Kate glance up, and glare into her rear view mirror.

Kate glanced across at Josie. 'If it's late at night, don't stop for a red light and keep your doors locked at all times.'

Josie's expression was dismissive. Kate answered the look with irritation in her voice. 'Remember, that Dutchman behind will have a gun in his glove compartment and he'll use it without a second thought. Some things haven't changed.'

Josie turned her face away not wanting to confront her mother, afraid she'd break down. Her memories of the explosion were still raw and vivid. A flat bed Datsun Sunny truck passed them at speed overcrowded with men. Some were seated. Everyone else stood nonchalantly hanging on, seemingly accustomed to their precarious situation.

The road soon petered out with unfinished buildings, piles of rubble and shredded plastic littering the ground or pierced on barbed-wire fences. She spotted a group of men sat drinking amongst the rubble; a brown dog flopped down and fell asleep in the afternoon heat.

The municipal bus station was still on open wasteland. There was no new investment here. The orange-bodied buses with pale yellow roofs and green horizontal stripe were notorious for breaking down or crashing. Lines of passengers stood around while others sat patiently on their jumbo tartan polypropylene bags waiting. In a dust cloud two white minibus taxis arrived. Josie saw their doors slide open and people scramble out, moments later they were full. They sped off down the gravel road, leaving khaki-coloured vapour trails. The taxis were controlled by rival gangs who sorted out their routes using machetes. Two disinterested policemen sat in their patrol car.

The black township spread out to the east. Josie remembered the weekend sounds of crowds at the football match, drumming and the brass band playing Sunday music. To the west were the citrus farms. One of her earliest memories was of their intoxicating perfume in spring. Sprawled along this road were ramshackle houses; a town planner's nightmare. Along the straight road were giant advertising boards and roadside stalls selling fruit, while people walked on the edges beside the chaotic flow of traffic. Kate's car overtook a laden cyclist. He wobbled precariously into the gravel like a trapeze artist, before remounting and setting off again. This road eventually joined the highway. It took goods and people north across the border or south to the major cities of the Transvaal. In Kate's experience each truck carried the HIV virus; the drivers indifferent as they spread Aids across a continent to prostitutes and wives, girlfriends and children.

Kate turned off before they reached the junction and carried on out into the veldt. They passed isolated houses, the homesteads surrounded by abandoned blue cooking oil drums, orange twine holding makeshift fences together and washing hung out to dry. Solitary cars overtook them at speed, music blaring out. A small group of young children and their yapping dogs appeared from nowhere. They ran alongside the Land Cruiser, their hands out begging before giving up and waving goodbye. Some way off Josie caught sight of a boy swishing the long grass with his stick. He looked up, before carrying on watching the cattle.

Her eyes grew heavy and she drifted off to sleep. She awoke as the Land Cruiser came to a stop. Kate jumped out to open the gate. She pushed the three Nguni cattle out of the way, encouraging them to rejoin the others. With their distinctive horns and low humps they looked so different to English cows. Josie breathed in deeply. The air was alive with the sound of insects. The landscape shimmered in the heat. Mirages flickered ahead, disappearing as they drove closer. Josie's mouth was dry. She was nearly home.

Kate drove on, turning the steering wheel back and forth avoiding the boulder-strewn surface, reminding Josie of Ham Farm. Then Tugela appeared; the property named after the great river in southern Africa. Here it was a trickling stream for most of the year but it provided enough water for the cattle and wildlife in the dry season, changing character in spring when the late afternoon and early evening thunderstorms turned it into an eddying torrent.

Josie caught sight of the water pump, the afternoon air catching the blades; beyond it the tall elephant grass hiding the brick-built servants' quarters. Josie instantly remembered eating mealie pap and stew with the others, sat out here on the low branches of the fig tree; its shade in contrast to the stifling heat inside the dark interior.

The bungalow was exactly the same: a deep stoep at the front overlooking clumps of agapanthus, their heads the size of footballs, strelizia and vygies with their daisy-like flowers and glaucous fleshy leaves. She remembered the acacia tree, with the yellow weaver birds' nests, hanging down like melons suspended in string bags and the shocking pink and purple bougainvillea. As a little girl, she'd sit here looking through this kaleidoscope of colours at the pale indigo kopje in the distance, listening to the night sounds of crickets; the air still warm from the day's heat before suddenly the sun fell below the horizon. She never imagined she'd come back to it alone and pregnant.

Josie heard their voices before she saw them. Tooting the horn, Kate pulled up as Josie slid out of the vehicle before it had fully stopped.

'Welcome, welcome home.' Johannes' smile radiated genuine delight. He grasped her hands in his, before Josie threw her arms around him.

The previous owners of Tugela referred to him as their garden boy. No matter how many times Kate asked him to plant the flowers in a straight line he'd plant them in clumps. There was no malice behind his actions, only a different understanding of nature. In his world straight lines didn't exist. He spent most of his days now tending his Nguni cattle. Kate assumed he was responsible for a much larger family living somewhere else because from time to time he'd ask "madam" for money. There was never any explanation as to its purpose nor did she enquire.

'You're going grey,' Josie noticed the flecks, before giving him a kiss.

Mary was next. She wore her house girl's outfit, neatly ironed. It was pink with a lace frilled apron and triangular headscarf. Mary was looking at Josie's big belly. She started giggling and clapping her hands. Josie hugged Mary; her roundness fondly familiar and comforting. 'You've not changed at all.'

Like Johannes, Mary had worked for the previous owners. She did the washing on Monday mornings and insisted on using Maizena starch and Reckitts blue. Kate was surprised by how often she bought these items. If Kate bought a different brand, it languished unopened in the cupboard. Mary had her favourites too when it came to polish and window cleaning; tearing up old sheets to use as lappies. She also had firm ideas about where everything belonged. For example Kate's black high-heel shoes were in her eyes Sunday shoes, so they lived in a cardboard box in the bottom of the wardrobe, while takkies were everyday shoes and they stayed in the basket next to the washing machine. In the end Kate gave up and let Mary run the house and look after Josie. As a baby, Josie was carried round tied securely to Mary's body, with Mary constantly singing and talking to her. Mary put her to bed at the same time each night, whether Kate had come home or not.

Josie saw another woman, surrounded by faces peering out from behind her. Winnie, it turned out, was Mary's sister. She'd arrived one day with her four children: Isaac, Moses, Brown, and Precious. There was no mention of Winnie's husband, Kate assuming he'd died from Aids. Winnie became the cook, enabling Balipi to become the hospital's driver.

From time to time others would join them. Kate was never quite sure how many mouths she was feeding. Each fortnight she filled the Land Cruiser with sacks of mealie pap, sugar, crates of fruit and meat. There were also the dogs and chickens, none of which Kate ever consciously bought, but who now seemed to be part of Tugela, along with the wildlife that passed through or lived there. In the end it worked perfectly and suited Kate. It left her free to get on with her work while they took care of the house, garden and her daughter.

'Where's Balipi?' Josie asked over her shoulder.

'Working.' Kate opened the back of the Land Cruiser, 'Isaac, bring the bags.' Kate disappeared inside, the fly screen door rattling shut behind her.

Left alone outside, Josie and the others were soon clapping, swaying and singing in welcome; Josie joined in instantly remembering the familiar call and answer songs; the dogs barking too, not wanting to be left out.

For the first time in days Josie relaxed. *Let Finnegan try and find me out here in the middle of nowhere*, she thought. She was home and more importantly, safe.

CHAPTER 15

WAITING FOR BABY

The two women sat on the stoep in silence as the sun disappeared in its dramatic red, orange and gold flourish.

'Did you see them?' Kate asked, 'The newly dug graves, we're on our fourth cemetery at the hospital.'

Josie didn't know what to say.

'Eight hundred people a day die in this country.'

Josie wanted to say something about seeing Tomas and Mike die, but couldn't face her mother's interrogation. It also seemed too horrific and intimate to be shared with a stranger.

'That's 5.5 million in southern Africa living with HIV and Aids.' Kate got up. 'I'm tired.' She put her hand on Josie's upturned face. 'See you in the morning.'

Sadness overwhelmed Josie. She wanted her mother to reassure her she was safe. But Kate had not asked about the baby, who its father was, nor had she once said, "It's good to have you home." Josie felt she was still being punished for leaving. She didn't know how to rebuild their relationship, so much had happened. She listened to the crickets and the distant rumblings of a truck, the sounds carrying far in the vastness of an empty landscape. Exhausted, she dozed off in the chair before Mary woke her and helped her into bed. Mary lit the oil lamp and left it to burn; as she had done when she was a small child afraid of the dark. Josie watched the revolving scene; a band of native Indians were chasing a fleeing settler's wagon. The present had arrived when she was a baby. Kate never said who'd sent it.

♦

Josie and Kate found it easy to avoid each other. Kate carried on working as before and Josie pottered about in sleeveless loose dresses and flip flops, fitting in easily with the daily routines at Tugela. Each morning at seven Balipi tooted the horn. The sound brought the children running, squabbling with each other over whose turn it was to sit by the window. The dogs jumped in too, ignoring the children's squeals as their paws trampled over legs. They also wanted to stick their heads out of the windows. With his passengers on board, Balipi drove off. Some days he pretended the Hilux was a buffalo with an early morning cough. As it jerked forward in stuttering bursts he'd say, 'This buffalo needs its muti,' and everyone would join in coughing, trying to make the loudest sound, before shouting out the name of another animal. Their joyful cacophony set off the baboons down by the stream. Occasionally, egged on by the children and with the dogs barking as they stood like surfers on the children's legs, Balipi drove the Hilux at the potholes. Everyone screamed with delight as they sat, feet off the ground and arms folded, waiting to tumble into the foot well; the bumpy landings creating a hodgepodge of dogs and children. But Balipi mostly chose to ignore their pleas of, "Again, again," knowing it could break the axle and that would mean no rural clinic until the replacement part arrived.

'One day you'll shake the baby out,' Josie said, laughing along with the others whilst holding on to her belly.

'The baby will be very happy to see the sun.'

Josie was eager to have the baby now. Because she looked like she'd swallowed an extra large space hopper. Grace, the midwife at the hospital, told Josie the baby was in the breech position so she would have to come in when the time came. Despite what Grace said, Josie hoped the baby would be born at home at Tugela. She wanted the first faces her baby saw to be the faces of the people she loved. She wanted him to be and feel African. She already knew his name, Tomas Johannes – TJ for short; but for now she kept his name to herself. In Africa a baby's hold on life is slender: bacterium gives them tuberculosis, flies malaria and viruses measles. Measles is so prevalent many mothers don't name their baby until after they've survived the disease.

Walking back one morning, with the boys running ahead pushing their homemade metal cars along using sticks and Precious, the youngest of Winnie's children beside her, Precious told her, 'I'll help you with the baby – and make sure the python doesn't eat it.'

Josie was bemused. 'What python, Precious?'

'He's this big.' Precious stretched her arms out straining, making the snake frighteningly long. 'Isaac says he's seen him, and he could eat a baby – easily,' her head nodding earnestly. Before Josie could ask her more, Precious, bored by her impending grown-up responsibilities, let go of Josie's hand and ran off to play with the others.

Josie remembered Johannes teaching her as a little girl, never to poke sticks into the termite mound because that's where the black mamba liked to sleep in the afternoon. But she hadn't heard anyone talk about a python at Tugela. She must ask the others, in case it was true and not some story made up by her older brothers to frighten their baby sister. It brought back another memory for her, that of her best friend Pamela at boarding school. They used to walk around arm in arm, Josie retelling stories from Johannes' encyclopaedia of animals, while Pamela told her about the antics of Tootsies her dachshund. They were both very excited when Tootsies gave birth to seven puppies. Pamela got special dispensation to bring them in for everyone to see. Then one day Pamela came to school in tears. It appeared her mother had been hosting her regular bridge afternoon and Pamela was playing with the puppies in the garden, when a python had suddenly appeared and swallowed Tootsies whole. Josie wasn't sure if she believed Pamela. But for several weeks afterwards she found herself lying perfectly still in the dormitory, convinced the ridge of blankets running along her back was the python as it lay patiently still, waiting for her to fall asleep before devouring her.

Josie looked down to her feet to see if she wasn't about to step on a puff adder.

♦

Sitting on the stoep she remembered the games she used to play out here on her own. Her favourite was shopping. Each cane chair became a different shop. One sold animals from her Noah's Ark, another balls of wool, Johannes gave her flowers and if she asked nicely, Balipi gave her a couple of hard-boiled eggs to sell which she then ate for lunch. They were as varied as the items she'd seen in Matsane. She and Molly, her mother's cloth dolly, shopped together using her marbles as money. Molly, faded and worn, joined her on walks, dragged along the ground or used as a pillow when she lay under the tree looking up at the azure sky, imagining the occasional clouds to be the head of an elephant or mysterious faces. Some afternoons she lay on her stomach and watched the ants walking in a line, carrying leaf fragments on their heads like African women. On other days she persuaded Balipi to make her a banana milkshake, which she poured out into her tea set, inviting the others to join her. They preferred their Rooibos. As the hostess, she duly spooned in the six spoonfuls of sugar they each took in their tea.

Bored with Molly or her own company she'd run off to find Johannes. She loved Johannes, following him round like his shadow; wiping her wet thumb on her shorts before putting her hand in his. Johannes told her lots of stories about the animals that lived around them, each one filling her imagination. Her favourite story was of the little dung beetle because despite its size, it used all its strength and determination to roll balls of dung far larger than itself around. She'd sit on her haunches sucking her thumb, marvelling as the tiny insect struggled to manoeuvre the huge ball round stones and out of the hollows along its path. Johannes told her the Nguni cattle and the dung beetle were very good friends. They helped each other like friends should. The cattle gave them dung so they had somewhere to live and food to eat. Sometimes they buried the dung, turning it into a nest for their eggs; this Johannes explained sweetened the earth, making the grass grow tall, giving the Nguni plenty to eat. The dung beetles also cleared away the dung so the flies didn't worry his Nguni as much.

'Mary's like a dung beetle because she's small, is always cleaning the house and moving things around.' They laughed like children sharing a silly joke.

On another day Josie said, 'When I grow up, I'm going to be strong like the lioness.' She roared and told him to run away so she could chase him. He didn't run very fast. She easily caught up with him and jumped up into his arms, covering his mouth with kisses, pretending to smother him like the lioness did to its prey. He struggled for a few minutes, playing his part before she said, 'Johannes you are a very tasty impala.' They giggled. He put her down. Looking up at him she asked, 'Why do antelopes have black socks round their ankles?'

'They're scent glands to tell the others, the lioness is coming – so run, run away.' He'd give chase as she ran, jumping up and down like a springbok.

Later walking along amiably she told him, 'You are the cleverest person I know.'

And he told her, 'When you grow up, you'll be beautiful like my Nguni.'

Secretly Josie decided she'd prefer to be the lioness.

♦

Josie's recollection of her mother was of a more compassionate person. It was in sharp contrast to the hard, bitter, overworked person who came home each night too tired to eat the meal Winnie left out, but who'd down several glasses of white wine instead before Balipi came round to make sure the doors and windows were locked.

Josie wondered why the need for such security out here. They were too far from Matsane and the township to be a target. She asked Kate one night, 'Do you have a gun?'

Kate stood up and took Josie into her bedroom. She opened the drawer beside her bed. The hand gun was inside an embroidered nightie case. 'Mrs Clarkson left it here when I bought the house, all those years ago. I'm not sure if it even works.'

Josie took the gun. 'What would you do if we had an intruder?'

'I'd hope the dogs would bark.'

Josie thought about their other guardians, the monkeys and baboons down by the river, living in the big trees. Like an over-vigilant neighbourhood watch, they screeched warnings at anything that disturbed them. She hoped that included burglars.

'I've sewn up too many bodies to want to add my own to the list.' She put the gun back and shut the drawer.

♦

Lying on her bed having a siesta, Mary woke her with a cup of Rooibos. Josie noticed Mary had brought in a jar and teaspoon with her. As a child she remembered it. The unctuous malt extract. It was one of her daily treats. Evidently Mary decided she still needed it.

'Mary, what's in this?' Josie said screwing up her face. It tasted bitter, not at all as she remembered.

'The sangoma gave it to me. It will make the boy strong like a lion.'

'Oh Mary, not witch doctor's muti – really!' Josie said it half jokingly.

Mary looked deeply offended. 'Madam will tell you. It is very good muti.'

The female sangoma's hut was near the baobab tree grove. Now called a traditional healer, they threw bones, ground-up medicinal plants and used animal parts in their muti; calling on ancestral spirits for guidance. Most had no physical benefits except in the minds of their users, like washing boys with water soaked in the bark of a baobab, believing this would make them grow strong like the tree. However, in some instances it was effective. Young pregnant girls ate ground-up leaves and as Kate later discovered they were more fertile and their babies survived. The reason was simple. The leaves contained essential nutrients, missing from their normal diet. Kate accepted local beliefs had a place; especially when they worked.

Johannes told her about the sacred baobab tree, looking as if its roots were stuck up in the air. He told her the baobab fell in love with four young girls who lived in its shade. When they reached puberty, they sought husbands and made the tree jealous. One night during a storm, the tree opened its trunk up and imprisoned them.

Josie didn't believe him. He insisted, 'Next time the wind blows you'll hear them cry out.'

'It's only the leaves rustling, you're being silly.'

When she asked her mother who was telling the truth Kate said, 'I think it's time for you to go to boarding school.

You need more education than the tales Johannes fills your head with.'

'But Johannes knows more than you. He told me when the baobab dies it turns to dust just like a spirit tree and I've seen it do that, so it must be true, so there!'

Besides Josie didn't want to leave Tugela and go to school. When she told Johannes he said, 'I'll always be here waiting for you to come home.'

♦

Sat on the stoep, Josie saw the Hilux and Land Cruiser bouncing home together. Surprised by the sight, she struggled out of the chair. The usual welcoming party was waiting as the vehicles pulled up.

'You'll need this soon.' Balipi passed pieces of the dismantled cot to Isaac and Brown, to carry inside.

Kate opened the back of the Land Cruiser. It was piled with parcels wrapped up in brown paper and tied with string: sterilising jugs, bottles, cloth nappies and a miscellany of baby clothes. 'I'd forgotten how much stuff a baby needs.'

Josie looked at Balipi. 'I thought I'd be using my old one,' she said as the pieces of the disassembled cot disappeared inside. She felt embarrassed that she had not thought about it sooner.

'The termites ate it,' Balipi told her.

Josie decided Kate must have thrown it out. She looked across at her mother's shopping spree. 'Sorry, I left in a hurry.'

'Don't worry these are mostly hand-me-downs.'

'Great.' Josie burst out crying, her tears trickling down her now bronzed cheek.

Mary pulled Josie into the soft mounds of her breasts and held her tight. Kate looked annoyed. She stormed off into the house; the fly screen slamming shut, adding to the drama of the scene. Balipi watched silently, before carrying the last piece of the cot into the house.

Josie found Kate with a glass in her hand sat on the stoep; the new bottle already half empty.

'Mom, I'm really grateful.' There was a shaky timbre to her voice. 'Tomas and I should have been buying those things. We should have been getting excited together.' Josie pulled her mother up from the chair and hugged her. 'Thank you.'

Kate broke free, her eyes moist. She finished off her drink, put the glass down and took Josie into her arms. They held onto each other fiercely.

'Mom I've been so scared. I ran away afraid he wanted to kill me too.'

'Who?' Kate asked, pushing her away to get a better look at her daughter.

Josie told Kate about Bucephalus and what happened to *Grey Goose*. 'Finnegan must have done it. It wasn't an accident.'

Kate looked astonished. 'I don't believe you. It's too far-fetched.'

Josie was suddenly angry. 'You don't know him!' her voice rising as the pink blush rose up her neck. She wanted to turn her back on her mother and walk away; instead she stood her ground and in a low, deliberate voice said, 'I saw Tomas die on *Grey Goose*. It exploded.' She stopped. With less confidence she went on, 'They are both dead.' Her lower lip was trembling. She breathed in deeply, desperately trying to hold her emotions in check. 'Tomas was TJ's father.' She showed her mother the ring on her finger.

Kate took her hand. 'You haven't worn it before.'

'No I know, it didn't feel right, besides you never asked me anything about my life.' She was at a tipping point. 'TJ will never see his father.' Josie started to sob.

'Like you,' Kate added quietly. 'I'm so sorry Josie. I've been punishing you for running away. You don't know how much it hurt. I thought I'd lost you forever.' She held her at arm's length. 'I know I'm not a good mother, but I do love you, more than you can imagine.'

They stared into each other's eyes. 'Because of you the Lintel Foundation paid for Matsane hospital. But there were conditions.'

'Mom, it doesn't matter. I love you too. You are so strong and indomitable.'

'What, like the buffalo?' Kate said, softening.

Josie's tears stopped and she smiled. 'This sounds like it's the start of one of Johannes' stories.'

They both laughed.

'I was hoping to be like the graceful egret walking across the top of the hippo's back.' Kate mimicked the bird; but with the wine bottle in her hand she looked more like a drunk trying to walk the line. Both women bent double, laughing – tears on their cheeks.

There was a knock. Balipi appeared by the door. 'The baby's cot is ready.'

Josie put her mother's hand on her belly. She called over to Balipi, 'Come, he wants to say thank you.' She placed his hand on her bump.

Josie took her mother's hand. 'You managed without a husband and I managed without a father, I'm sure we'll be fine. This is all the family I and my baby need.'

CHAPTER 16
INVITATION

The early morning briefing was about to start. Jim Morgan, his chief of staff, Ralf Sneider, Director of National Intelligence and the CIA, and the vice-president Douglas Dennison came in.

The president asked, 'Did any of you see the breakfast TV news coverage of Feed Africa? I think you could say – it was a good day at the office.' Everyone laughed. As the men helped themselves to coffee he used the intercom. 'Elizabeth, can you come in for a moment.' He took her to one side and asked, 'How many people know about the invitation from President Abyoie?'

She looked uncomfortable, glancing round the room. 'We've not had time to circulate it.'

'Come and see me at the end of the meeting.' He walked over to sit at the head of the table. 'Gentlemen, let's begin.' He turned to Ralf Sneider. 'What's happening with the Chinese? I thought the CIA was keeping a close eye on them?'

'I've nothing to report that need worry you. They appear to be focussed on their own internal affairs. They continue to arrest dissidents and keep a tight grip on social media. The State is very much in control. I'd say it was business as usual. Although there is one thing that might concern you, we've seen a build up of troops near the Vietnam border. But we think it is linked to some joint military manoeuvres going on in the region.'

'What's your view, Vice-President?' He put Douglas Dennison on the spot.

'As you know I've just come back from Thailand. The ASEAN partnership is a great success, and now that China and Hong Kong have joined, I'd say the region is pretty stable.' He sounded smug. He looked across at Sneider. 'I understand Australia is joining next. It makes sense.' He seemed pleased with his insider knowledge.

Sneider concentrated on the papers in front of him. The president watched the interplay. He felt his role as a second-term president was about keeping the members of his administration pitted against one another, in order to avoid cabals joining together to undermine his decisions. No wonder he had an ulcer.

'But what about the military exercises?' he asked, keeping Dennison centre stage.

'They have a mutual agreement on defence and aid,' Dennison added a little too quickly, clearly not wanting to be drawn into a deeper analysis. He glanced up at Sneider looking for support, but the DNI/CIA man remained silent.

These changing alliances and feuds were all part of Oval Office politics; if Douglas Dennison wanted to become his successor he needed allies. *That little interchange hadn't helped him!*

The president stepped into the arena. 'I can see how the ASEAN pact protected them from China in the past, but now they've invited the fox into the henhouse and he's disguised as a chicken.' Everyone smiled. 'Ralf, keep an eye on the situation for me.' Satisfied, he moved on, 'What's behind their interest in this African Union proposal?'

Sneider didn't need to open his morning briefing note. 'It's business as usual Mr President, profits and PR. We know China is extracting raw materials on a vast scale to support their industrial growth, while feathering the nests of African leaders. The African Union will end up as another toothless talking shop, a PR exercise. It won't affect Feed Africa if that's what's worrying you.'

He relaxed.

♦

The meeting over, Elizabeth came in with her notepad.

'First of all accept the invitation from President Abyoie. Secondly my mother is not part of the official party.' He stressed the word "not". 'Type it up and bring me a copy.'

She glanced up at him briefly.

'I know she's seen the invitation, now I want her to see my reply.'

Douglas Dennison knocked on the door and came in as Elizabeth got up to leave. He closed the door behind her. 'Mr President, I wanted to have a private word with you.'

'What's on your mind, Douglas?' he asked.

'I don't know how to put this, but there's some unhappiness about how the hell we're going to pay for your Feed Africa programme.'

Montgomery didn't answer him immediately, noticing his use of the word "your".

'People are asking is this a long-term commitment? We just don't see the strategic value.'

Again he noticed the use of the pronoun "we", when it should have been "I". He sat considering his answer.

'Douglas, I didn't bring you in on this at the beginning because sometimes, as the president I have to make the call.' He laughed lightly, suggesting camaraderie; neither man feeling it for a moment. 'But you can see how well this has resonated with the American voter. Individuals get to feel good and at the same time offset their charitable donations against their IRS returns. Corporate America also seems pretty happy too. I'd say everyone wins. Believe me, it will cost this administration less than you think.'

The vice-president didn't move.

Montgomery was annoyed. 'I'm having lunch with Martha. I'll give her your good wishes. Being friends, I'm sure you regularly get together and gossip like old cronies.'

Dennison bristled.

'If Feed Africa puts the Chinese noses out of joint all well and good; we need to remind them and the world, the United States is still top dog.' His smile appeared friendly and with his hand on Dennison's back, he manoeuvred him out of the Oval Office. As he closed the door he thought, *Son of a bitch, you're not the president yet.*

♦

He and Martha were sat opposite each other. She had an avocado salad in front of her, untouched – clearly she had something to say.

Ignoring her, he concentrated on his chicken.

'Lady Alice and Gene are flying out to south Africa.' She picked up her fork and immediately put it down. Her forefinger thin like a broiler's feet scratched away at a speck of imaginary dirt on the white linen tablecloth. 'Really Joseph, have you lost your tongue? I'm speaking to you.'

He stabbed the piece of chicken.

She admonished him, 'I don't like your behaviour.'

Her words ignited his pit of resentment. 'And I damn well don't like yours!' His voice was suddenly loud. He watched her neck colour. Before she could say anything he thumped the table. 'How dare you intimidate my staff and go through my post?'

William looked up.

'And take those white gloves off.'

Martha responded waspishly. 'Mind your language.' She turned to William and nodded her head. 'I don't know what you mean.'

From his breast pocket he took out a piece of folded paper and threw it down in front of her. 'Read it.' He watched as his mother's expression changed.

Her eyes at first quickly scanned the letter, before looking up at him, and then rereading it more slowly. The red anger crept further up her neck making him think of a turkey. Her mouth opened then shut.

He looked at her thin lips, the line of scarlet lipstick like a bloody slash. He savoured the moment. 'Just so that we are absolutely clear, I have accepted President Abyoie's invitation. I'll be visiting a number of the Feed Africa projects. I expect it will be a major event covered by the world's media.' He paused, before emphasising each word deliberately as if he was a five-year-old learning to read. 'And you are not part of the official entourage.' He stared across at her. 'I don't want to see you out there. Do you understand me?' Then in a mocking voice he added, 'Mommy's not invited.' He stood up.

Her eyes became moist. She dabbed at them with the corner of the napkin.

'Oh please God, spare me the performance of the wronged, forsaken mother who gave up everything for her only son. I know it off by heart. It's like an old scratched record.' He leaned in towards her. 'Did it ever occur to you, if you'd let me marry – I might have had a son.' He stood upright and thumped the table with his fist, 'Someone to carry on your precious Lintel name.'

Martha's demeanour changed. She looked furious, about to challenge him.

'Save it Mother. Feed Africa is my idea. It has nothing to do with you or the Lintel Foundation.'

He left the room, closing the door with some force. For the first few strides he felt wonderful. Then as his heartbeat returned to normal, he thought, *Am I acting like a petulant child, trying to deliberately hurt my mother?* His confidence wobbled, before something in him responded; Feed Africa made him feel differently about himself. He refused to let go of the euphoria. His gait changed; there was a swagger. He felt invincible.

CHAPTER 17

TJ

TJ arrived with all the usual pain and joy of a successful birth. Kate held her grandson, instinctively swaying him in her arms. 'He's got your eyes.'

'And Tomas's hair.' Exhausted Josie beamed up at her mother. 'Did Grace tell you, at the last moment he flipped himself round and came out head first.'

'Clever little boy.' Kate appeared reluctant to give him back.

'I could have given birth at home.'

Kate's look suggested otherwise. 'Sorry I wasn't here but I had an emergency.'

'Mom we're fine. When can we go home?'

'Let's make sure you can breastfeed first.'

Kate passed TJ back to Josie. In the crook of her arm he wriggled energetically despite being swaddled. 'Look, how strong he is.' She couldn't take her eyes off him. 'Mary will say it's the sangoma's muti.'

'She's probably right, but don't tell her.' They both chuckled.

♦

Seated in the Hilux, Balipi carefully passed the bundled baby into her arms. 'Isn't he gorgeous?' Josie looked at Balipi. His body blocked the sun, and for the briefest of seconds it felt like Tomas was standing in front of her. Her heart soared with excitement. She reached out to touch Tomas, but Balipi moved and Tomas disappeared. Her heart crashed.

'He's a fine boy,' Balipi said proudly.

She desperately wanted to believe it had been Tomas; her head and heart see-sawed between the two realities. She knew she was being irrational; looking at TJ in her arms she said, 'I expect everyone at Tugela wants to see him.'

'I can hear them singing from here.' Balipi shuffled his way round to the driver's seat dancing like an African.

As they drove along Josie noticed several billboards showing a seated African mother dressed in a brightly coloured African print dress and headscarf, holding a chubby baby in her arms, another child peering out shyly from behind her, with a third happily playing on the ground. The message was obvious – fecundity and prosperity, all thanks to Feed Africa. It was ubiquitous; her part of southern Africa chosen as the start for the Feed Africa programme of support and investment in Africa by the United States.

They pulled into the petrol station, no longer owned by SASOL. The attendants were now dressed in red overalls or black pants and red T-shirts. They all wore AMOIL baseball caps. Balipi got out and started chatting to one of the older men. Three others came over to wash the windscreen and windows and fill the Hilux with fuel; everyone moving to the township music blaring out on the forecourt. Josie recognised a Brenda Fassie song from her youth but none of the others. There were eleven official languages in the new South Africa.

Balipi said something, his head nodding towards her, suddenly everyone began clapping and dancing on the spot before one by one in a line, they waddled over to the window to see the new-born baby. Josie slid down from the seat to show them. The impromptu celebration ended when a vehicle pulled in. She looked across. It had tourist plates, making it an easy target for traffic cops issuing false speeding tickets; only when they got home would it appear as an extra charge on the hire car agreement. Balipi went inside the shop to pay. Two laden trucks pulled in one behind the other. They both had the Feed Africa logo emblazoned on the cab door. It was a simple pictograph, a blue rectangle with a yellow circle in one corner and a single green shoot. The words Feed Africa along the bottom were for those people who could read; everyone else looked at the symbols and understood the message.

'The garage is giving them away.' Balipi pulled a black T-shirt out of the canvas tote bag, the Feed Africa logo on the front.

'Isaac will love it. Perhaps you can get some more for the others when you fill up next.'

They passed the airport. It had grown bigger with more warehouses and offices. A cargo plane was being unloaded. Electric tugs whizzed around purposefully, pulling trailers laden with pallets covered in netting. Other vehicles were stacked high with cardboard boxes, held together by plastic wrapping; each item clearly stamped with the Feed Africa logo.

'Many aircraft come every day.'

She glanced across at Balipi. It was hard to tell from his expression how he felt about it. Everywhere there were signboards announcing this was the next place to be developed. It had the feel of a gold rush town with the same air of urgency and greed. Josie doubted anything worked properly. The electric supply would be intermittent, new junction boxes not connected to the grid, wiring stripped out along with the fitments despite the work being signed off. It would be the same with the toilets; few connected to a septic tank or the main sewerage. Not that Matsane's sewerage system was robust enough to cope with the current demand; effluent poured out, dogs scavenged through it and gangs of children played in it. In the expanding township more shebeens opened up. Run by women they sold mageu, a cloudy unfiltered mealie pap beer and alcohol. Men had wages to spend and that attracted the prostitutes, helping HIV and Aids to spread. There were the inevitable knife fights, the bloodiest bodies ending up at the hospital to be stitched up. No wonder her mother had missed TJ's birth and looked even more exhausted.

Two, then a third flatbed overtook them at speed, full of young men.

'Where've they all come from?' she asked.

'All over,' this time it was clearer, Balipi didn't approve. 'They are bad men.'

The sound of a blaring horn made Josie look up quickly. A whish and the dark outline of a passing lorry forced Balipi to swerve into the dirt by the side of the road. She cried out. Her voice and sudden movement startled TJ. He began to scream. Instinctively she rocked him, at the same time singing in a low voice, trying to calm him. As the cloud of dust cleared, she looked around. It had been some time since she'd been here. There were more trucks like the one that had just passed, parked up. Oversized concrete rings lay haphazardly abandoned along with other precast shapes. A line of looped wires ended at a portacabin in the distance. Fascinated, she watched as a large digger operated by one man shuddered as it tore voraciously into the earth before swinging round and spewing it out; the mini diggers darting in and out reminding her of hyenas scrapping over a carcass. Solitary men stood around while others were working in gangs. Josie noticed a lone woman talking into a walkie-talkie, holding the stop and go sign. She wore an orange overall and floppy hat, at her feet a plastic bottle of water. Feed Africa was changing the landscape in front of her eyes.

'How will the elephants cross this?' Josie asked, bemused because it was not uncommon to see a bull elephant wander across the road in Matsane; even truck drivers let it cross without impatiently using their horns.

'Perhaps this is not the way to the waterhole,' Balipi said half seriously.

'I don't expect anyone asked them.' She smiled back at him. Nothing was going to ruin her happiness. TJ whimpered. 'He's getting hungry.'

'Babies are hungry all the time.'

Josie realised she'd never asked Balipi if he had a wife or children. After all these years, she'd never asked him about his life. They had been her world, and she'd assumed Tugela was theirs. Each year he had taken two weeks leave, but she'd never wondered about the home he went back to, a place with parents, uncles and aunties, cousins – a whole family waiting eagerly to greet him.

'Do you have children at home?' she asked.

'Yes, I have two boys and a little girl.'

It should have been easy to ask him about them, but she was acutely aware of how awkward this new intimacy felt. In the uncomfortable silence Josie tried to think of words that wouldn't remind them both that even after the whites no longer ruled the country, black people were still not equal; their relationships still redolent of the old master-servant one. Her delight in being home and her happy childhood memories were tarnished. Josie felt her innocence drain away.

♦

The Feed Africa shipments fanned out taking American GM seed to all the farmers. New tractors ploughed up land for these fields of wheat; the companies insisting the new strain of seed was drought resistant and required less fertiliser. Farmers were given cattle feed as part of a scheme to improve the health of the indigenous breeds. Healthier cattle would fetch higher prices encouraging farmers to expand their herds, creating a dependency between them and the agro chemical companies. Even people with small plots were given water tanks. American businesses were making the most of the opportunities.

Josie saw the Feed Africa logo proudly painted on the doors of the lucky recipients. 'I wonder when we'll get ours,' she asked as they reached the gate to the property. Balipi didn't answer her. She wondered if there'd been some sort of disagreement, without knowing what it was about.

As expected, the reception party was waiting for them. Mary immediately took TJ from Josie's arms and proudly held him. TJ became the centre of attention, despite his crying. 'He's hungry,' Mary said as she proudly carried him off into the house.

As Josie watched her baby disappear, she touched Balipi's forearm. 'Thank you.'

♦

Josie tackled Kate, 'Mom, why haven't we seen Feed Africa out here? Isaac could help Johannes plant it.'

Kate gave her a withering look.

'What was that for?'

'Isaac should be going to school.'

Josie remembered learning from Johannes through his stories and puzzles, whereas at boarding school it had been problem solving and analysis using written words and books. She understood how important it was to get an education, but part of her wondered how quickly Africans would lose their cultural heritage and folklore if Western-style education became the only way to learn. Young people attracted to city life would mock the old ways without realising what they had lost; a richness and understanding of their world, created over thousands of years of experience and observation.

'Johannes isn't going to be happy,' Josie persisted. She'd seen him resting for longer periods under the tree, happy to leave Isaac following the Nguni. 'With a bigger boma and cattle feed, they won't have to graze so far away.'

Kate's expression hardened. She put down the glass with some force. 'Suddenly you know everything; coming back here, telling us how to live.' She paused. 'Why don't you just *voetsek*!'

Josie's neck reddened. 'You started it by saying Isaac had to go to school.' Josie stood up and stomped out.

'Josie – come back.'

Frustrated, Josie wondered if they'd ever be friends. Kate and Tomas shared the same single-minded, driven personalities. Neither accepted anyone else's interference or advice. She turned round and came back to face her mother. 'What was that all about?'

Kate didn't look at her, instead she peered out across the garden's dark shapes, now lit by the moon, the air still pleasantly warm. 'It's all over the news. The US President is coming out here. No doubt followed by the media, claiming his Feed Africa is the answer to Africa's problems.'

Suddenly alert, Josie's grey eyes focussed on her mother's face.

'He's a cowardly bastard with an overbearing and opinionated mother.' She sounded bitter and it felt personal.

Josie forced herself to say nothing, only her eyebrow rising.

Kate saw the expression on her daughter's face. 'Don't give me that look!' She paused. 'There's going to be a reception at Shindwalla and I've been invited.' She got up. 'There are too many ghosts in this house.'

At first Josie wondered who she meant, before she decided the ghost troubling her mother wasn't the same as hers. Josie rarely spoke about Tomas to the others and especially not to her mother. She wasn't ready to share him with them. Only now did she understand why she had fallen in love so quickly. Tomas embodied aspects of the people she'd loved at Tugela; Balipi's quiet, tall, handsome manliness and Johannes' musky smell. When she met Tomas, he filled a void, reminding her of home. But Tomas belonged to a different place and time; a place still too full of images and questions, the narrative far from logical or obvious, even at this distance. She often thought about it. She still hadn't forgiven Mike for his treachery, assuming it was his actions that forced Finnegan to act as he did. In her mind Mike's betrayal had caused Tomas's death. But where did that leave her? Was she unfinished business in Finnegan's mind, a weak link and therefore still a target? The idea lurked in her subconscious. Why the burglary, the sudden arrival of Finnegan and the bomb? It had the ingredients of a mystery but without any of the answers.

Standing in the doorway was Kate. 'These Feed Africa advertisements on people's houses, do they remind you of Moses and the plagues in Egypt?'

'Where the hell did that come from?' Josie struggled to see a link. 'No one's threatening to kill our first-born babies.' Suddenly her head throbbed as if too much blood had flooded it for a brief moment. The reaction caused by the idea of someone threatening TJ. She immediately thought of Finnegan; surprised her fear was still as potent as ever. Kate was right, between them they had too many secrets, but they weren't going to sort them out tonight. She was too tired. Even with Mary's help, she felt exhausted.

'Does TJ keep you awake at night?' she asked, wondering if this explained her mother's increased irritability.

'No, the wine and sleeping pills work just fine.'

'Really – is that such a good idea?' Josie regretted the words the moment she'd said them. She knew Kate would react. With other people it was so much easier, but with her mother, they simply rubbed each other up the wrong way; both women vying to be the alpha lioness at Tugela.

'I don't want Feed Africa here, are we clear!' Kate picked up the bottle and provocatively swung it under Josie's nose with a flourish and left.

Josie went into TJ's room. He looked so peaceful and perfect. His long body in a vest and nappy, the blanket scrunched up by his feet. She picked him up. He stirred and began to whimper. She really needed to think about what she was going to do.

CHAPTER 18
SHINDWALLA

Shindwalla was an exclusive five-star game reserve lodge. The complex was spread over the hillside with the private suites hidden amongst the huge granite boulders. From this vantage point looking out across the magnificent panorama, it was possible to see giraffe grazing the tops of thorny acacia trees. The camp's white rhino and leopard were more elusive.

The reception area and bar dominated the hill's summit. It was thatched, reminiscent of a giant's rondaval with its high ceiling supported on huge, roughly hewn tree trunks. Open on all sides it captured the early morning and evening breezes. Inside, the highly polished floor and fans kept it cool. The dark sombre interior was in sharp contrast to the lemon white shimmering sunlight beyond. Few people ventured out in the white heat of the midday sun. They preferred to sit inside on comfortable chairs and sofas being served long ice-cold drinks; telling fellow guests about the animals they spotted on their early morning or evening game drives.

The panorama was stunning, especially at sundown; the magnificence stirring feelings of infinity and insignificance simultaneously. In the rainy season cauldrons of clouds bubbled up reaching 9,000 metres, before a darkening sky crackled with repeated strikes of fork lightning as the booming thunder grew closer and closer, ending in lashing, drenching rain; the whole performance over in a couple of hours.

At night guests ate under the stars beside sunken fire pits. The tables lit by flickering candles and the Milky Way. Flares marked the perimeter of the dining area and beyond, a manmade waterhole attracted animals; their nightly arrival far more captivating than a cabaret. They appeared in slowly moving lines of ones and twos, until half a dozen gathered round the waterhole, their tails constantly twitching; before drifting off, disappearing again into the indigo black night. Occasionally guests were disappointed and no animals appeared. Only later, a guest would claim to have seen the leopard hidden in the shadows.

At the end of the meal, a game ranger carrying a rifle accompanied guests back to their suites. Newly arrived couples were amused by this ritual, assuming Shindwalla laid it on as part of the African experience. On their second night it was different. They walked quickly, conscious of the proximity of the deep, panting roar of the lion's pride nearby.

♦

With POTUS's arrival at Shindwalla there were even more guests with guns as the president's secret service checked the staff, visitors and the perimeter. The media circus stayed at the hastily built hotels and smaller private game parks nearby.

After all the rhetoric and meetings, Feed Africa was on the ground and delivering. Elizabeth Findlay handed POTUS the itinerary. The motor cavalcade would leave Shindwalla at 10.00. His first official function was at 10.40 for a walkabout with President Abyoie, which was followed by the unveiling of a commemorative plaque. They would then have a private lunch together. The afternoon was free. At 17.00 a game drive had been laid on lasting ninety minutes. At 20.00 the President of the United States would hold a reception for his host along with various other government ministers and VIPs. The following day Air Force One would take POTUS to Cape Town for a reciprocal reception hosted by the African president, then home to Washington. It was a short but significant visit. Not quite a vacation, but with the promise of more visits in the future and with time to relax and enjoy the country. His Feed Africa was as he hoped, making a difference – showering him with plaudits and positive media coverage.

'What do you think?' His press secretary handed over the latest approval ratings for him to scan.

'Pretty damn good.' He just knew it! Feed Africa was going to define his presidency.

'It's interesting to see what a positive change it's had on the young and black urban voters. Normally they are a segment we find hard to reach. Feed Africa appears to resonate particularly well with them,' Jim Morgan, his chief of staff added.

William proffered Montgomery his pillbox discreetly. He shook his head. 'And do you know what, I've never felt better.'

He couldn't remember the last time he'd felt like this. That wasn't quite true. He did know. It was when he'd banned his mother from coming with him. He'd been surprised that she hadn't broached the subject again. In fact Christina Fairfield told him she had gone to visit friends and handed over a handwritten note. It was brief. *I will concern myself with the Lintel Trust from now on.* He'd read it with satisfaction but a twinge of panic. She'd acquiesced too quickly.

He eased his collar. It was certainly hot, especially after the wintry weather they'd left behind in Washington. 'I'm ready.'

The fleet of black limousines sped along, outriders front and rear, holding vehicles at junctions until it swept past. They were followed by the usual entourage of journalists, photographers and TV crews from around the world, all travelling in LCC minibuses and cars. All along the route he saw posters of himself smiling and looking much younger. It reminded him to thank William. He'd done a good job on his hair colouring.

'Will the walkabout be covered by TV?' he asked.

'Yes, it'll make the East Coast breakfast bulletins.'

He smiled. Inside he did feel a little apprehensive. In America he rarely undertook these informal walkabouts. American politics seemed to attract individuals with a gun and a grievance. It was not the Kennedy headline he wanted.

Ahead he could see a crowd of excited children all bobbing up in front of TV cameras. There was the usual crush of correspondents, fiddling with their earpieces, waiting to go live to studios around the world. The crowd surged forward as the car came to a halt; lines of African policemen holding them back, their *sjambok* batons ready to strike out should anyone get too close. Montgomery stepped out into a haze of sun and flashlights. He tried to focus on the cheering children madly waving their flags and the women singing beyond the dark shapes of his bulky secret service guards. In the background he could hear the township's vuvuzela and a brass band playing an unfamiliar version of the Star Spangled Banner. Why had he been so nervous? Everyone wanted to grab his hand. POTUS smiled and waved back. In his gut he could almost feel his ratings shoot up another few percentage points.

President Abyoie and his wife stepped forward to greet him. They shook hands and all three stood together as the cameras flashed again, recording the historic scene. A group of uniformed school children began to sing the American anthem, their rendition making it sound like a gospel choir outing and not the more formal occasions he was used to. The South African anthem followed, before the official party moved off on the planned walkabout.

POTUS took one side, his secret service agents within feet, shielding his body. Montgomery waved to the crowds from behind this cordon. He remembered the sycophantic madness of his two successful election nights. This felt different. It was more genuine; a natural outpouring of affection that came from his promise of a new Africa.

On the other side, President Abyoie and his wife were stopping every few feet to shake the eager crowd's outstretched hands. A small blond-haired boy stepped forward, something in his hand. He held it up for the black president.

President Abyoie bent down to take the wooden toy. 'Thank you, did you make it?' The little boy nodded. 'I'll put it in my museum in Pretoria.'

The boy turned to look up at his mother.

President Abyoie reassured him, 'You can come and see it anytime.'

He walked on still holding the gift. His progress was slow, dictated by the warmth of the people both black and white. President Montgomery in contrast was walking quite briskly. He didn't stop as often or engage in conversation. He felt the perspiration begin to gather on his forehead, the glare of the bright sun forcing him to squint.

He whispered to Elizabeth, 'Where are my sunglasses?'

'Sunglasses make you look untrustworthy.'

It was time to leave. He crossed to join the others for the last few steps before everyone aware of the TV cameras paused to wave, smiling.

His next appointment was the unveiling of a commemorative plaque on a building site; the facility was a joint venture between an American multinational pharmaceutical company and a smaller African one. The local company had previously struggled to produce enough animal vaccines for animal disease like Snotsieke and Rinderpest. The new venture promised increased investment, greater capacity and higher production standards. The company's mission statement was simple: to halt the cocktail of pathogens that killed millions of animals, left others sick, reduced their lactation and growth or ability to work. It promised to concentrate on the particular challenges facing African farmers. There were no references in their glossy brochure to experimental drug trials, programmes to pump growth hormones into young animals or genetically modified DNA breeding programmes. Instead their advertisements depicted images of healthy cattle tended by young African herdsmen. It resonated with consumers at home concerned about GM and compassion in farming; but mainly with their shareholders.

He was about to leave when one reporter asked him, 'How are you enjoying your first trip to Africa, sir?'

Without thinking Montgomery said, 'I visited Cape Town as a young man, I've fond memories of it.' The moment the words were out he had a flashback. The image of his mother arriving unexpectedly and ordering him home immediately. He had done as he was told saying nothing to his girlfriend, not even a phone call. He'd just left on the family's Lear jet. Even after all this time, his acquiescent and cowardly act felt painfully shaming. His stomach tightened.

Another voice asked, 'Are you pleased with how quickly American companies have responded to your call for support?'

He paused, this time to collect his thoughts, grateful that no one was asking for more information about his first time out here. 'You need to see how busy Durban and Beira are these days. They look like the Washington Belt, gridlocked on the eve of Thanksgiving,' he joked.

In his briefing papers he'd read how Durban with its fifty-seven berths could turn around 4,000 vessels a year and the car terminal was used to handling 60,000 vehicles a month. He was sure Finnegan was using it as his point of entry for his fleets of trucks and cars. Even in the short time he'd been here, he was surprised by the number of LCC vehicles carrying the Feed Africa logo. He recalled the meeting he'd had with Finnegan and Malone. AMOIL would be using Beira in Mozambique with its facilities for unloading petroleum into harbourside storage tanks, ready for transhipment by road. He'd seen more than one red and black fuel tanker en route to the unveiling.

The day's official events were nearly over. All that was left was this evening's reception. He was wearing a cream Tom Ford linen suit, tailored to feel comfortable for a man in his fifties but with a crispness that had taken William hours to achieve. The colour perfectly enhanced the glow today's sun had given his face. With one final glance in the full-length mirror, he winked at himself and said out loud, 'Go get 'em cowboy.' He felt light on his feet, less stressed, genuinely looking forward to tonight.

The large open space was the perfect informal setting for the reception. African servers walked around discreetly offering drinks and canapés. Groups ebbed and flowed naturally and the occasional sound of laughter showed that people were enjoying themselves. Montgomery smiled at everyone and flirted with other men's wives. He caught sight of two men shaking hands. The confirmation he surmised of a deal struck; the African minister planning to grow his private wealth and an American CEO seeking to increase his share options. The Dow Jones was buoyant with the opportunities offered by an unregulated new market. Montgomery even suggested tonight Elizabeth could mingle, he didn't need her close by. Tonight he was amongst friends.

Someone slapped him hard on his back. He spun round about to good-naturedly chastise his assailant when he saw it was Gene Finnegan and Lady Alice.

'You look surprised Mr President,' Finnegan smiled, 'it's going well, isn't it?'

Finnegan was definitely smirking at him. Lady Alice offered her cheek for him to kiss. It was soft and powdery, like his mother's.

'I just love Africa, don't you?' she said, and without waiting for him to respond, 'When I was a girl we used to come out here often.'

'She's a far better shot than I am,' Finnegan said, looking fondly down at his wife.

'Pish darling, don't forget I was brought up in England where everyone hunted, fished and shot anything that moved.' She paused. 'Well, not the beaters that would be considered terribly bad form.'

Montgomery looked disconcerted.

'Darling, I'm only joking.'

Finnegan chipped in, 'I remember you shot and wore several of your trophies.'

'Darling, no one admits to wearing fur these days.' They sounded like any old married couple enjoying the familiarity of private banter.

'I'm sure Joseph has never done anything he's ashamed of.' Her china blue eyes piercing him, as she leaned in closer to whisper, 'No family secrets in your wardrobe.'

He laughed nervously, hoping to find a way to escape. Inside he was thinking what the hell was she alluding to? He immediately wondered what exactly his mother had said to her old friend.

Lady Alice lightly touched his arm, her grip becoming surprisingly strong as she held on to him. He glanced down. She had the same bony hands as his mother, with an oversize diamond ring on one finger and an equally impressive emerald on the other. Tonight it matched her necklace and earrings.

'Gene and I have some wonderful news. He's set up a charitable trust.' She glanced up at her husband. 'Our first project is a fully staffed laboratory for Matsane hospital.'

'And don't forget your wildlife conservation programme,' Finnegan added, smiling down at his wife.

'Darling, I thought it best not to mention that, after you told him about my prowess with a gun,' she laughed lightly.

'That's wonderful news.' Montgomery managed a smile as Finnegan grabbed his hand; the passing photographer capturing the moment. He felt an overwhelming desire to wipe away Finnegan's sweaty handshake.

'Your mother's work has inspired us to do more out here in Africa.'

He stepped back, his pulse racing, his stomach about to react. Was he never going to be free of his mother's interference? He thought he'd made it plain Feed Africa was his baby, not hers. She was more tenacious than a stalker and far more devious. Only he understood what was going on between them. It was a simple threat. She was telling him, "I know all the wealthy important people and you'd better not exclude me in the future because I have the power to influence them." She was a frightening matriarch worthy of a Shakespearean play. He caught himself glancing down at his hands, fully expecting to see blood on them. His stomach complained. The pain was unbearable and sharp. He doubled over, groaning.

'Martha, Joseph's not well,' Lady Alice called out.

He straightened up to see his mother dressed in a long, dark-purple silk taffeta evening gown advancing towards him. At that moment the thin wisps of her hair reminded him of vipers. His colour drained. If he'd had a gun strapped to his leg, Slow-Hand Joe would have used it.

'Did Christina not tell you, I'm out here as the guest of the Finnegan's?' She leaned forward allowing him to give her his usual perfunctory kiss. Half turning he heard her whisper, 'How dare you ban me, I'm your mother!' She kissed him as the cameras clicked. The President of the United States grabbed his mother's upper arm and strode out of the room – ignoring her protests. They were followed by the surprised look of President Abyoie and the other guests.

CHAPTER 19
HELLO DADDY

She sat, while he paced up and down, snarling, 'You couldn't stay away, could you? I knew you were up to something. But this is unbelievable, cooking up something like this. You know what I think of Finnegan. And all just to get your own back and prove a point! Did you think no one would have told me you were out here?' He'd have words with Elizabeth later.

He was angry with his mother, with Finnegan and with himself. He'd let his guard down and imagined the warmth of his reception was aimed at him, not his role as POTUS. His inner insecurities rose up. He knew he wasn't charismatic or a natural leader. He was, however, a man with integrity, someone you could trust in a world more used to back stabbing. He'd been happy to be portrayed as a safe pair of hands. He'd never imagined he could inspire those around him. He'd got used to his mother's constant insistence; his success was due to her and those around him who were more adept at state craft than he was. In his mind, state craft meant manipulation and self-interested dealing. It described Finnegan.

He'd let her have her way, he'd acquiesced, taken the line of least resistance because it had suited him, until Feed Africa. For the first time he'd felt like a man and a leader. He'd enjoyed the speeches – inspiring ordinary people, seeing business leaders and other politicians greet him with warmth; even if they were using it to further their own ambitions. He wasn't naïve. Yet he felt personally responsible for the positive zeitgeist Feed Africa had created around the world. He'd grown to be a statesman in his eyes. It was his achievement, not hers. So why did he feel his confidence slipping off his shoulders, like a bath towel leaving him wet and naked in front of her? It was years of being bullied.

'What have I done?' she asked innocently, standing up to touch his face. It could have been a tender gesture, instead he pulled away, repelled.

'What have I done,' his voice mimicking hers. 'Where do I begin?' He looked at her with hatred. 'You know what I'm talking about. Was it your idea or Finnegan's?' It didn't really matter either way. They had become an unholy alliance in his mind, determined to undermine him. Deep down, hidden in the recesses of his mind, he knew Feed Africa wasn't his idea but Finnegan's.

The truth dawned. He was being used by Finnegan to sell more of his cars. He'd seen them everywhere; sure, they were all badged with the Feed Africa logo, but southern Africa looked to him more like a LCC showroom. He felt used, stupid and diminished. His newly-found confidence withering before it had really taken root. But there was a bigger issue. Lady Alice had mentioned the Finnegan Trust.

He knew the man. It had nothing to do with philanthropy. Painfully he recalled Finnegan's words, "They pay me and I pay you." He had no doubt, Finnegan was laundering the Chinese money through his newly-founded trust. It meant if anyone discovered it, he'd be impeached. He wondered how many projects Finnegan was siphoning money into; his largesse corrupting others, ensuring he had a hold over their actions too. And there was no way he could start an investigation to find out because his position as President of the United States would be compromised. Finnegan had stitched him up, forcing him to keep their deal a secret.

He turned on his mother. 'What exactly did Lady Alice mean when she said there's nothing hiding in my closet?' His right eyebrow underlined the question.

Martha's exposed neck reddened. 'I made you. You owe me everything. What wife would have done as much as I've had to do?'

'What do you mean?' He wasn't going to let it drop, not this time. Anyway what was she referring to? Suddenly he saw all her projects in a new light. How many were covering up dirty little secrets, far from the philanthropy she claimed? It didn't take much for him to imagine. She'd paid off unsuitable women or worse, paid for abortions. He hadn't wondered until now, why there had been no paternity suits. He knew she wanted the Pope's blessing on her beneficence. He wondered if her soul was already damned, by the guilt of her actions. He felt a sharp pain in his stomach.

He'd never really given much thought to all the beautiful women in his life. There had been so many. Privately he saw himself as a Casanova, a sensitive man skilled in lovemaking. Suddenly he doubted his prowess; perhaps power was the aphrodisiac, not his manhood? Had they been procured by his mother to keep him in line and the gossip magazines and media happy? It was an uncomfortable thought; pimping out her son for her own ambitions. He was reminded of the few times he'd grown fond of a woman. She'd inevitably arrive and remind him of his greater destiny; insisting only a mother would be prepared to sacrifice herself in the ways she did.

He paced the room with a growing sense of unease. It reminded him again of his last visit, and Cape Town. What was her name? He'd come back from a private game farm – someone his mother knew, and was surfing at Camps Bay when the wave had dumped him at the feet of a beautiful girl with wild hair. What was her name? He couldn't remember, but she'd been a medical student doing a year's placement at Groote Schuur hospital. It lasted about a month before his mother flew in and ordered him home.

'Mr President, your guests are wondering where you are.' Elizabeth stood in the doorway, flanked by the Finnegans.

He turned to his mother. 'I think you should all leave now.'

President Abyoie came over, 'I hope nothing is wrong?'

He waved away his concern, 'Responsibilities of the office.' It sounded better than saying "I've just had a spat with my mother." He smiled thinly, still churning inside.

'In that case I'd like you to meet Dr Kate Ryland. She's the medical director at the hospital in Matsane. She does great work.'

They stood facing each other. It was one of those cliché moments when time stood still. He was just about to say something when she turned to her right and stopped, as an attractive dark-haired young woman, ashen-faced, fled the room.

'I'm sorry I have to go.' She ran after her.

He watched her leave; with the itch of a forgotten memory uppermost in his mind. Was that her? He looked towards his mother. She too was watching the fleeing couple, only her mouth was open in horror. Out of the corner of his eye he noticed Finnegan. He tried to read his expression. He might be – amused.

'Elizabeth…' He didn't know what to say.

'I know it felt like a Cinderella moment,' she laughed, 'do you know who they are?'

His eyes were firmly fixed on his mother. 'Give me a moment.' He turned to Elizabeth. 'Find them.' He didn't say why.

The incident brought the evening to an abrupt and awkward close, everyone sensing a scandal, but without knowing what it might be. Back in his suite he waited while his entourage searched for the two mysterious women. He took off his tie, opened his shirt and threw his jacket over the sofa. He sat down on one of the green dyed zebra-skin chairs.

'I think you have something to tell me?'

Martha looked directly at him, 'There's nothing to tell you.' She paused before adding truculently, 'The Finnegan's wanted a project and I know how much a new laboratory would help the hospital. I didn't think you'd get so upset.'

'A laboratory.' He threw his arms in the air, before deciding to go along with her charade. 'Was it your suggestion or his?' He was watching her closely.

'Really, does it matter?' She wasn't enjoying this, he could tell. She'd sat down. She got up. 'I'm feeling tired, can we talk about this tomorrow? The Finnegans will be wondering where I am.'

'Sit down.'

Rarely did Martha Lintel Montgomery do as her son asked, but on this occasion she did. At that moment the missing couple walked in, escorted by Elizabeth.

'Hello Joe, it's been a long time, just over thirty years,' Kate said without much emotion.

Suddenly Martha stood up. Her face was hostile. She turned towards her son, 'Look at her,' her breathing growing more rapid, 'she'd never have fitted in on Capitol Hill. She's just like all the others!'

It was an astonishing reaction. He was looking at the woman stood in front of him. She was thinner, her skin dry like an elephant's hide, dark circles under her eyes and her hair not as he remembered it; her glorious golden tousled mane gone, replaced by a short cut and dull streaks. Yet there was an echo, an echo of Kate – there, he'd remembered her name.

'This is a surprise.'

His mother grabbed Kate's arm, pulling her away. She was shouting at her, 'I've supported you all these years and in return we agreed – you'd never contact my son.' She was staring at Kate. The veins in her turkey crop were throbbing.

Kate shook herself free from Martha's grasp. The two adversaries faced each other; Martha stepped closer towards Kate. 'Be very careful what you say next.' The threat was unmistakable. 'You could lose everything.'

Kate stood her ground.

He turned to the young woman watching the scene.

She was tall with black hair and grey striking eyes. She was staring at him intently.

'I'm Josie.'

♦

After all these years of wanting to meet you, here I am and that's the best I can do! Josie thought.

'I'm Kate's daughter.'

She looked at him intensely, seeing him in the flesh for the first time. *We're the same height. His black hair appears dyed; the vanity of a man needing to look younger and vigorous, I suppose. We both have the same grey eyes.* She watched as his eyebrow rose. *It's the same gesture! Something else I've inherited, apart from his DNA. What should I do, shake his hand or hug him? Well it's now or never.*

'I'm your daughter.'

There, I've said it – hi Dad! This isn't how I'd imagined it'd be.

'Joseph it's not true!' Martha grabbed him, pulling him away. 'She's lying.' She stood staring at me, holding on to him. Her red lips were tightly drawn, as though at any moment she might snarl, exposing her teeth like a lioness defending her cub. 'This is what I've had to protect you from all your life; scheming women and their illegitimate children.'

I didn't feel comfortable calling him "Daddy", after that. Anyway he looked dumbstruck, maybe even horrified; obviously he's struggling to understand what's happening. I'll give him the benefit of the doubt – for now.

Mom stepped forward. 'I found out I was pregnant after you went home.'

'She told me she was going to keep the baby.' Martha turned on Kate, 'we had an agreement.'

Kate answered her, 'I never broke it, Josie figured it out.' She looked at me, both of us remembering why I'd left home.

'Then how did Lady Alice know about her?' he asked his mother.

'I never, never…' shaking her head in denial, looking like a confused old woman.

'Don't lie to me – you two must share all sorts of secrets.'

Mom turned towards him. 'I've never regretted keeping Josie.'

I felt so proud of her.

'I'd hoped for a boy,' Martha said looking at me, disappointment on her face.

'Why did you run away earlier?' he asked, looking at both of us.

I hesitated. I couldn't tell him who I'd seen or why he scared me. I didn't feel comfortable, revealing my inner fears to a stranger. My flight instinct was uppermost, even now. I hoped Kate wouldn't say anything about TJ.

Kate ignored his question. She faced Martha, her voice loud enough for us, or anyone listening in, 'Do you know how many babies you've killed?'

Martha took a step back. Her expression horrified.

'Don't pretend you don't know what I'm talking about. You know what you did.' She turned and faced the president. 'You're not entirely innocent either.' She had their attention.

I sensed this was something she'd wanted to say for some time. This wasn't going to be diplomatic or polite.

Kate launched her attack. 'The moment the Pope decreed using a condom was a sin, he condemned millions to poverty and worse. Your cadre of powerful Catholic bishops lobbied congress successfully.' She turned her focus onto the president. It was his turn. 'The politicians went further, ignoring your own Surgeon General's advice you refused aid for family planning clinics. It went to organisations that promoted abstinence and fidelity.' Kate glared at Martha. 'The Lintel Foundation could have taken a different stance. But instead you ignored my pleas for help.' Kate paused. 'Each day I watch mothers giving birth to HIV/Aids babies. Their innocent blood is on your hands.'

Martha stood upright, as if she'd been slapped. 'You're fired!'

'I don't think so.' Kate walked out.

My heart soared with pride. I followed her out.

♦

Back at home and after several glasses of wine Kate asked, 'Why did you run away?'

'I saw Finnegan.'

'Does he scare you that much?'

'Yes.'

'Well the truth is out there, your father is the President of the United States, and surely that means Finnegan cannot touch you. You have a powerful ally.'

'Really, do you think so? I'm not so sure he'll be on my side. He didn't seem that delighted to know he has a daughter.'

I knew Finnegan had access to the president through his wife. That's why I secured a job at LCC, hoping something would come up. Then Bucephalus came along and it seemed like the perfect opportunity. If I'd done a good job, I could have asked him to introduce me. It made me wonder. Did Finnegan know who my father was? Probably, he knew everything – why not that secret too? I'd always felt like a chess piece in his game. Now I knew. I was playing for my life, because I and one other person knew about Bucephalus.

'He knows I am alive and where I am.'

Kate looked at me quizzically.

'It's no use saying I'm being hysterical. I know what he did. Mom, can Mary look after TJ, there's someone I need to find and quickly.'

CHAPTER 20
JON MAGUIRE

Josie made an international call to LCC, 'I'd like to speak to one of your employees, Mr Jon Maguire.'

After a few minutes the switchboard operator replied, 'I'm sorry we don't have anyone working for us with that name. Are you sure he works for the Lexington Car Corporation?'

'Yes, he was one of the laboratory technicians under Professor Li.'

'Please hold.' The music started playing. The next voice identified themselves as a member of the Human Resources team. 'Who is it you're trying to contact?'

Josie explained. Again the woman at the other end of the line said she couldn't help. Josie persisted, 'I am a trustee of an estate and he is a benefactor. If you could check to see if you have an address, I'd be grateful.'

'But we don't…' she didn't finish the sentence.

'You will have his address or that of his next of kin. Please check with payroll. I know he worked for LCC. I'll hold.'

She heard a whole season of Vivaldi play before someone came back to her. 'Who did you say you were?'

Josie hesitated as if annoyed, her voice having just the right amount of irritated frustration and power behind it. 'I cannot close my client's estate without distributing the funds. It is quite a significant amount.'

There was a moment's pause; she heard a muffled conversation. 'We have an address for his next of kin: Annie Devereux, 1140 Mountain Drive, Growly Bear, Washington State, 98304. Can I have your name and details?'

Josie put down the phone, suddenly remembering the name Growly Bear and how Mike had made fun of him; stabbing his chest before laughing at him. She wondered how much force he'd used. He was a bully. She wished she'd been more assertive and not let him play the alpha male quite so often. Her excuse had been she was too preoccupied with the pregnancy to worry about his tomfoolery. Besides, by then they were making progress on Bucephalus. She didn't want to upset the team. But she should have made more of an effort to get to know Jon. His arrival had disturbed the dynamics, upset their routines, Tomas preferring his help to hers by banning her from the laboratory. She'd been hurt and angry.

It was a bit like Balipi and the others. She'd not seen those around her as individuals with their own lives, with stories to tell and dreams to share. Her world revolved around her. She felt ashamed. She had been obsessed for nearly ten years with one notion; that of meeting her father. And on reflection the meeting had been nothing like the fantasy she'd created in her mind. She remembered the evening. She tried to see it objectively, like a member of the audience watching a swiftly moving drama. But it was hard to see him as an ordinary man. His position as President of the United States and the occasion got in the way. She'd looked into his eyes, hoping for some sort of welcoming recognition, but instead – he'd seemed uncertain; not the strong father she had created in her head and longed for in her heart.

The scene had rapidly become volatile and explosive, disintegrating into a shouting match as her mother told Martha Lintel Montgomery exactly what she thought of her stance on contraception. The irony of the situation was not lost on Josie. She was illegitimate, the bastard daughter. Not someone the President of the United States would willingly want to claim as his own. She wasn't sure if she'd ever see him again. It depended on the reaction to her next phone call.

She didn't have much trouble in finding a phone number for Annie Devereux. It seemed Growly Bear was a small community outside the Mount Rainier National Park and she ran a bed and breakfast. With some trepidation, Josie rang the number she'd been given.

A woman answered.

'Annie, you won't know me but I'd very much like to talk to your brother Jon. It's very important.' She hoped his sister wouldn't be defensive or too curious. 'My name's Josie Ryland.'

She heard an intake of breath. 'I know who you are.' She sounded defensive.

'Is he all right?' She hoped he was still alive.

'No, he's not,' her voice rising angrily.

Josie remembered how ill he and Tomas had looked. She again chastised herself. Why hadn't she been more concerned? With her heart pounding she said, 'I'm sorry, but I need to talk to him about the project we were working on.'

There was silence.

'I could fly over and see him.' It was a statement and a request.

'What do you want with him now? Didn't you hear what I just said?' There was a long pause. 'Jon has cancer.' Her words were both hostile and defeatist, as if she now feared the inevitable outcome.

'I'm sorry, but that makes it even more important that I speak to him.' She was conscious of her heart's thud and her hand gripping the phone. It was worse than she'd imagined. At least she couldn't blame Finnegan for his death.

'He was fired from LCC, the moment he got home. They made him sign a confidentiality agreement. It was clear. If anyone approached him or tried to speak to him, LCC would stop paying for his medical treatment.' She took a breath. 'So you see he's not going to speak to you, or see you for that matter. Go away and leave us alone.'

Josie had to know. 'Did Finnegan fire him?'

'Professor Li did, and after all he'd done for him.'

Josie wondered exactly what Jon had done? It implied a lot more than merely helping Tomas around the laboratory. Now wasn't the time to ask. 'I can imagine how scared you feel, but let me reassure you, I don't work for LCC. I won't tell anyone we've spoken.' She paused, adding gravitas to her next words. 'He killed Tomas and Mike. I saw it happen.' She hoped that would be enough to persuade Annie to let her speak to her brother. 'Please believe me when I say, I might be next. So you see I really do need his help.' Again there was that slight delay. 'I have to stop Finnegan.' She gave Annie her number. 'Tell Jon, I'm sorry.'

It wasn't long before Annie rang back. 'You'd better come over and make it soon.'

Josie was exhausted by the three flights. She didn't dare risk breaking the journey by spending the night at one of Tacoma's airport hotels, instead she picked up a hire car and drove on. She still had some way to go. But she was afraid any delay might mean she'd miss her chance to talk to Jon.

The beauty of the snow-tipped mountains and the pine-scented air barely registered, as she struggled to keep her eyes open; afraid that a moment's lapse and she'd have driven off the twisting road or into one of the logging trucks that passed her, its horn blaring out a warning just in time for her to swerve.

Growly Bear B&B was a picture postcard two-storey log cabin with a stone boulder chimney. At the front were steps leading up to a porch and on it a double swing seat in white wood. A large American flag hung from a pole set at forty-five degrees so it was clearly visible even without a breeze to ruffle it. Josie saw the large satellite dish set up on the grass, making Growly Bear look like it was ready to receive travellers from outer space; not just cable TV. She could hear the sound of rushing water nearby. It was idyllically peaceful.

The front door opened. Annie Devereux stood looking at her from her vantage point, her arms crossed in front of her. She didn't move towards her visitor. Josie assumed normally her welcome was much friendlier. Josie lifted out her bag and Mike's laptop.

'How's Jon?' she asked as she reached the porch.

‘You look almost as tired as he does.’ There was a glimmer of warmth in her words, as she stepped aside to let Josie come in.

After sleeping for four hours, Josie roused herself and asked if she could see Jon. The room was downstairs, with a door that opened onto the porch; the stairs proving to be an insurmountable obstacle to him. The whole house had a honey, mountain herb smell to it. It was delightful. The perfume she assumed came from the exposed wood of the log cabin’s interior and the scented candles dotted around.

A hospital bed dominated the centre of the room, the bed hoist pushed against the wall, next to it the oxygen tank and commode; neither discreetly hidden but close by for when they were needed. The tallboy chest was devoid of themed knickknacks that would have made the room charming; instead it was covered with blister-pack pills, a damp facecloth and towel to wipe Jon’s face and ease his dry lips and a couple of plastic drinking cups with straws popping out. In the corner was an antique pale blue nursing chair, the cashmere throw tossed casually over its arm. Josie surmised Annie slept here with her brother rather than go to bed upstairs, leaving him alone.

She couldn’t help a small intake of breath. He looked corpse-like. His eyes were sunken; his flesh bruised, stretched over his thin bony hands. He’d lost his hair too. Jon had never been lively or animated. He now looked days away from a mortuary slab.

‘Hi, Jons’ she wanted to greet him like an old friend, someone with whom she’d shared an intense experience. He may not have added greatly to the camaraderie, nonetheless he had been part of Ham Farm, working on an important scientific discovery; the secrecy and jeopardy creating a bond between them. Also he had spent hours with Tomas. She was jealous of this intimacy and at the same time eager to reminisce. Who else was there she could talk to about Tomas? She looked at the man dying in bed. It reminded her – this wasn't a social visit; her thoughts and feelings were all jumbled up.

How many times at Tugela had she lain awake, going over the snippets of conversations and incidents, trying to remember exactly what had been said, hoping that hidden amongst those idle remarks were the clues to explain the final shocking days. She'd fossick, trying to find the gold nugget that would explain everything. If she and Jon talked, perhaps they might find it. Besides he'd have a different perspective. And although she couldn't change the past at least she'd feel she understood it. Not like a pawn to be tossed aside by Finnegan – her job done.

She was eager to ask Jon something she knew was too insensitive to be vocalised. But that didn't stop it from playing repeatedly in her head. If Tomas had lived, would he be lying in a bed somewhere dying too? In her mind she knew the answer, but was too frightened by what it meant. She felt sick in her stomach. She'd known something was wrong with Tomas. He'd looked ill. She remembered catching sight of his bruised chest. He'd told her he'd fallen over and caught it on the edge of the workbench. She chose to believe him, still angry at him for abandoning her and their baby. How self-centred had she been! She'd failed to care enough to help her lover/fiancé. She had abandoned him, just as his father had. She hadn't fought for him like the lioness she naively imagined herself to be. She wouldn't fail TJ.

'Annie said you saw Tomas and Mike die?' His voice sounded scratchy.

'They were on *Grey Goose* when a bomb went off.' She retold the incident without once breaking down. That was at least something. 'I think once Tomas told Finnegan Bucephalus wasn't ready—'

Annie interrupted her, 'Jon told me Tomas wouldn't sign it off.'

Josie looked at her but carried on without comment. 'Finnegan decided to act. He had what he wanted. We were in his mind a weak link.' Privately she grudgingly acknowledged, he'd been right about Mike. She looked at Jon. 'We'd done a great job in keeping it a secret.' She caught something in his face. 'I'm sorry, I should have warned you, told you sooner about the bomb.'

'No wonder they wanted to shut you up.' Annie took her brother's hand.

Josie persisted. 'At the time, he must have assumed I was on board too.' The memory of her fear and rising panic came back. 'I ran away, home to South Africa where I felt safe.'

'Jon you've got to tell her everything. There's nothing you can do now, but she can. They need to know how dangerous it is. Look at you.'

Josie noticed all the equipment and wondered about how many times a private ambulance had taken them to Seattle for his radiography or chemotherapy sessions. 'Do you think my baby's at risk?' Josie asked, afraid of his answer.

'He banned you from the lab to protect you.'

At least that explained one mystery! A bubble of love burst in her heart. Tomas did love her! She smiled broadly at Jon.

'He was a great chemist.' This time his words left him coughing.

She waited, watching Annie bring him a drink. 'I kept Mike's laptop. It has all the drawings for the engine and the formula.' She hadn't decided what to do with the information. 'I presume if I gave it to another lab, they'd be able to see where the problem was.' She wanted to rescue Tomas's reputation for TJ's sake.

'How – it was stolen?' He tried to sit up. Annie adjusted the bed, helping him.

'Yes, but he had his own personal computer, hidden away.' She looked out of the room. She remembered Mike's panic and then later his insistence on keeping it quiet, not telling Finnegan. 'He'd duplicated everything onto it, I assume so that he could sell it to the highest bidder.'

'Then who burgled the house?'

There it was again, the mystery of the burglary. Just like an old itch, Josie was transported back to Ham Farm and the feeling it had been staged. She shook her head and shrugged. 'I don't know.'

They sat in silence.

'Did Finnegan, or was it Professor Li who sent you over to spy on us?' It was crude but they were beyond pleasantries. She had to know and Jon had the answers.

Jon looked pained. Annie gave him a beaker and straw, encouraging him to take a sip. 'Professor Li was obsessed by Bucephalus and Tomas,' he said.

Why did the professor need Jon to report back to him on what they were doing at Ham Farm? Slowly it dawned on her perhaps he and Finnegan didn't trust each other. That old feeling of being a chess piece in someone else's game re-emerged.

‘Did he know about Finnegan closing us down?’

‘Professor Li was pleased.’ Jon looked at her. ‘Everyone knew he wanted to screw Tomas.’

Josie burst out laughing. That was one memory she was confident about. Tomas was heterosexual. ‘I met the professor once.’ She smiled at Jon. ‘I didn’t realise he was the competition. I thought my rival was his chemical formula!’

Her comment raised a smile on his face too. She regretted not getting to know him better.

Annie intervened. ‘I think that’s enough for now. You could probably do with some more sleep and Jon has to rest.’

Jon sank back into his pillow. Josie smiled and touched his arm.

Later Annie found her sat on the porch. ‘I’m sorry if I was less than welcoming but you can see how ill he is. When he came home, he wouldn’t say anything. He wants me to get his pension.’

‘But he told you about Bucephalus?’

‘I’m not sure how much to believe. He spoke about Tomas with awe, saying how brilliantly simple his idea was. He said his breakthrough came, walking past the manure heap each day. He tried urea. He and Mike Evans came up with something remarkable, only like all new ideas, it needed more development time.’ She looked away. ‘You should be proud of Tomas.’

Josie took Annie’s hand. They sat in companionable silence. Home seemed far away. Josie missed TJ, but she couldn’t leave. She had to know more.

‘I don’t think Jon blames Tomas for what happened. He was a scientist too. He understood. Tomas had to find out if it was safe, before Finnegan launched it.' She took Josie's hand and held it tightly. 'You know Tomas tested it on himself.'

Josie's tears ran down her face. 'I never asked. But I should have seen the signs. Now it's too late.'

Annie squeezed Josie's hand. 'I'm sorry.' She got up and left Josie to her private grief.

The following morning, Josie asked Jon if he was strong enough to go through the laptop so she could fully understand what it all meant. Annie looked askance. But Josie persisted, 'I know I'm asking a lot.'

'What made you seek Jon out now, after all this time?' Annie asked, still not happy.

'I thought I was safe but I saw Finnegan recently. He knows I'm alive and where I live.'

Jon reached out for Josie's hand. 'To get EPA approval he needs to test it in the real world.' He breathed in shallow, rattling gasps. 'Tomas turned off the extractor fans. It was in the air.' He gripped her hand. 'It'll be in the water, soil, food – everywhere,' his eyes concentrating on hers, 'GG42/OO, that's the problem Tomas found.' He sank back exhausted.

Josie realised there was no way Jon was going to have the strength to go through the laptop. Her best bet might be Annie. She might know more than she had said. It was clear he needed to rest. Josie closed the laptop.

The two women sat with their coffees, Jon asleep. Josie asked Annie how much she knew.

'I'm not a scientist. There'd have been no point in talking to me about it.'

Josie didn't believe her. She decided to tell her what she knew, hoping it would encourage her to talk. 'Obviously it's a new fuel, a step change, so important Finnegan risked everything to keep it secret.' Josie was remembering what Tomas had said. 'It needed Mike's input to work fully.' She hesitated. 'His drawings were as important. I've got everything.'

Annie looked at her. 'If you took the laptop to another car manufacturer, they'd only steal the idea, if it's as important as you say. They'd risk it, like Finnegan is prepared to. It always comes down to money.'

Josie shook her head. 'Finnegan wouldn't be so foolish. He's got too much to lose.' She remembered Bucephalus was all about his hunger for a meaningful legacy.

'Oh don't be so naïve Josie! Professor Li will do what Finnegan wants. There's too much at stake.' She looked at Josie. 'Besides, you already think he's capable of murder. He doesn't care about ordinary people. With you and Jon out of the way, who is going to look for GG42 or whatever it's called? It would take years. And even then, Finnegan will blame the scientists, saying they lied to him.' She paused, drinking her coffee. 'Who will believe you, even if you produce the laptop? He'll accuse you of industrial espionage and gag you.'

They sat in silence, each in their own world.

Annie spoke first, 'If I was Professor Li, I'd be very worried too. I might be next. Finnegan obviously doesn't want anyone who knows about it, or can contradict him, to survive.'

Josie added, 'And maybe that means you too. I'm so sorry for involving you.' Josie tried to think rationally; fear wasn't going to help them now.

'We need to know where he's testing it, Jon was right. There is still time.'

Josie felt her heart tighten. It explained why Finnegan was in Africa. 'I've got to ask Jon something.' She had to hear it from him. 'Jon, what's so special about Bucephalus?' Her eyebrow rose, demanding an answer.

He remained silent.

'Jonnie love,' Annie was beside him, 'tell her, please.'

'It's a green fuel; no carbon dioxide and nitrogen exhaust gases.' His eyes remained tight shut, as if he'd not seen anyone, and therefore not broken the confidentiality agreement. 'It's pure genius.' He paused, 'Pity about the cancer.'

She was surprised by his wry humour.

This final coherence brought on his last breath, as the rattle rose up from deep inside his lungs, struggling to leave, some would say releasing his spirit. As an epitaph his words lacked poetry but they had their impact. Josie ran from the room and vomited over the porch.

Annie came out.

'LCC cars and trucks are everywhere. I thought it was just part of Feed Africa, but he's using it to gather data for the field study. He's even set up a laboratory supporting my mother's hospital.' Her expression changed to one of defiance. 'Bucephalus is going to destroy the people and place I love.' She thought of TJ and the others. He was a small baby. At that moment all she wanted to do was to ring home and hear him giggling, burping; desperate to hold him and breathe in his lovely baby smell.

Josie rocked backwards and forwards, a primordial fear squeezing the breath out of her; Finnegan's "or else" mocking her.

'What are you going to do?'

Annie's question brought her back. 'I don't know.' She didn't say anything about meeting her father. She didn't know how he was involved. She doubted he would be on her side if she challenged Finnegan. 'I think President Montgomery is involved.'

'Jeez, that's quite an accusation. Can you build a case?'

'I'll need evidence.' Josie looked at Annie. 'At least I know where to find it. It's right on my doorstep.'

Josie stayed on for the funeral. She wanted to. The two women had become fond of each other. She'd rung home several times. TJ was fine. Mary was looking after him, along with everyone else. He was safe, growing bigger each day.

Together they cleared Jon's room and went through his paperwork. Everything had been meticulously saved and filed; as if anticipating one day someone would ask the right questions. Their last job was to send his death certificate off to payroll at LCC.

With Annie beside her, Josie rang Professor Li. 'Jon Maguire has passed away.'

'I hope our agreement was honoured.' He'd not offered any condolences.

'He didn't confide in anyone about what went on at Ham Farm or Bucephalus because I know and I'm still alive.'

'Who is this?'

'Josie Ryland, Tomas's fiancée.' She hung up feeling triumphant; at least that would pierce one of the professor's dreams.

'You're sure that was the right thing to do?' Annie asked, concerned but laughing at the same time.

'Well, it will force someone's hand. And now I know they are coming.'

PART THREE

GATHERING EVIDENCE

CHAPTER 21

WELCOME HOME

Balipi and Mary were waiting for Josie at Matsane airport, Mary holding TJ. Josie spotted them and ran over dropping her bags; she lifted TJ into her arms, squeezing him hard; his arms and legs thrashing around like a toddler in a paddling pool.

'He's grown so big,' she said delighted, 'he must love his malt extract!' Mary giggled, looking down at the floor. Balipi picked up her bags. 'Where's Mom?' she asked, not greatly surprised by her absence.

Balipi and Mary glanced at each other.

Walking along chatting to TJ she asked casually, 'Is everything all right?'

Balipi answered her, 'Johannes is not well.'

'Is he at Tugela?'

'Yes,' Balipi said.

She was reassured; it couldn't be too serious. They reached the Hilux. 'Can I sit in the back with TJ?' Balipi placed her two bags in the rear before getting in and locking all the doors. She was touched by his concern. After the quietness of Growly Bear, Matsane seemed frenetic with all the new buildings and construction still going on and with more people and vehicles filling the roads. All LCC, she noticed. She now knew why. She wound up the window, looking down at TJ.

Balipi turned on the air conditioning.

'No, leave it off.' She watched as the wind wafted the air into mini tornadoes. She felt sick in her stomach. There was no way of knowing if Bucephalus was out there – an airborne invisible killer.

♦

Josie hurried in, her eyes trying to adjust to the dark interior. Johannes lay on his bed, his forehead covered with beads of sweat. She went to turn on the single light bulb but Winnie's hand stopped her.

'No madam.' She shook her head, looking towards Johannes.

He moaned as Kate tried to sit him up. She flashed her torch across his eyes. They hardly flickered. It wasn't malaria because everyone at Tugela slept under mosquito nets. Josie felt like her five-year-old self, bewildered by the adult world and unsure what to do. The child in her hoped he'd suddenly sit up, pretending it was one of their silly games. When he didn't she sat down on her knees beside him like a supplicant. She took his hand in hers and squeezed it hoping he'd respond. There was nothing. She willed him to keep breathing, terrified of his death rattle; a sound she never wanted to hear again.

She leaned in and whispered, 'Johannes it's me, I've come home.' He murmured something. Relief overwhelmed her. She looked up hopefully at her mother.

'How long has he been like this?' Kate asked.

No one answered her.

'You should have told me sooner!'

'Madam is always busy,' Balipi's words were said without blame.

Kate looked at Balipi. Josie felt something pass between them. Kate strode purposefully out, towards the cattle boma followed by Balipi, Isaac and the other children. Kate got in amongst the cattle, pushing each one aside as she ran her hand along their backs, feeling for "staring coat". It's when the hairs on an animal's hide stand up rather than lying flat. There were other telltale signs; skin tightly drawn over their pelvis and exposed ribs from weight loss. Those with staring coat had a general lethargy about them, unlike the others who moved away agitated by her presence, bellowing loudly in protest. 'We need to get the vet out here to test them.'

'Mom, what is it?' Josie asked, confused by her mother's actions.

'It's sleeping sickness, Africans call it *nagana*. We haven't had an outbreak in decades.'

Josie still didn't understand.

'The last one was before you were born.' She turned to Balipi, 'I need to take a blood sample from everyone.'

'What's wrong with Johannes?'

'There's nothing I can do. It's too late.' It was the doctor, not her mother, who answered her.

Josie cried out, 'You've got to help him, it's what you do – you help people,' her voice now pleading.

'I'm fighting HIV and Aids without any medicines, and now this!' Balipi handed her the medical bag. 'Of course they won't come to me at the onset of their symptoms, when I can treat them, no – they'll go to the sangoma,' her frustration self-evident.

It was Balipi who answered her, 'You cannot change us, or Africa.'

Kate grabbed Josie's upper arm pushing her towards the house. 'Ring the vet.'

Josie pulled away, screaming hysterically at Kate, 'I don't know why you won't help him. It's Johannes!'

Kate's features hardened. She raised her arm, as if about to smack Josie when Balipi grabbed it.

'She's afraid – just like you,' he said, looking at Kate. They stared at each other in silence.

'Welcome home.' Kate stormed off back to the others, taking her medical bag with her.

After her phone call to Coetzer the vet, Josie went back to sit beside Johannes. She talked to him as if he were a child about to fall asleep before her voice faltered. She began to cry quietly, her head resting on his chest. She could hear his shallow breathing, smell his sweat, and felt the moisture of her tears on his warm skin.

She whispered, 'Don't leave me.'

CHAPTER 22
SLEEPING SICKNESS

The Nguni's thick hide normally offered protection from biting insects, as well as building up a natural resistance over generations; but if the indigenous cattle were ill, then what hope did the non-native breeds have? Bundled up under the auspices of Feed Africa, sending cows to Africa had captured people's imaginations. Overnight an influx of lactating animals from Europe arrived. They were welcomed by the women; giving them much needed milk and with the possibility of selling off the surplus. There would be money for school.

However, men thought differently about women owning cattle. It undermined their position and upset their traditional view that it was a man's job to tend cattle. They blamed the women for *nagana.* It was accepted women polluted cattle because of their menstruation, pregnancy, abortions or widowhood, and that is why they became ill or died.

Whereas sleeping sickness is transmitted by the tsetse fly. Each time the fly bites it builds up the reservoir and re-arms itself. Eleven to twenty-one days later with fevers coming and going, the infected animal becomes weaker. Eventually the animal's antibodies destroy the parasite; only for this to trigger the release of the trypanosome protein into the bloodstream causing the animal's death. In humans the first signs are fevers, headaches, joint pains, insomnia at night and swollen lymph nodes. It then progresses into a second fatal stage, when the spinal fluid enters the brain and central nervous system. The only way to diagnose sleeping sickness is through blood samples; technicians looking for the larvae.

♦

The sound of the doors opening and slamming shut brought Josie down from the stoep. She noticed Coetzer, the district's vet, was driving a new LCC 4x4. She mistrusted him immediately, fearing Finnegan's influence on his judgement and impartiality. Coetzer was a stocky Afrikaner who wore khaki shorts, a short-sleeved safari style jacket, thick long woollen socks and sturdy brown boots. His clothes made a statement about who he was. He had the swagger of a man used to issuing orders.

He didn't waste time with the normal pleasantries. 'Lady, you've got *Trypanosomiasis brucei rhodesiense*. It's the most virulent form of all of the strains.'

She was stunned.

'It's a notifiable disease.' He didn't explain he'd have to cull every animal for miles around, including the large stockholders' specially bred animals; destroying livelihoods and costing them millions of rand in lost exports.

'Why don't you vaccinate?' Josie asked.

'Don't tell me how to do my job.' He looked and sounded belligerent.

Another two vehicles arrived and a dozen black staff clambered out. Coetzer shouted over to the men, 'What are you waiting for?'

Josie didn't move. She folded her arms, challenging him in a way she suspected he wasn't used to.

'Look lady, every animal in the district needs to be shot. The air will smell of burning flesh for weeks; it's the only way to stop this,' he snorted, 'but only if the government acts in time.'

Josie's defiance evaporated. 'Mom's worried about how many people will die of sleeping sickness.'

'She's right to be worried.' Coetzer had been civil for long enough. He strode off.

Just then she saw Isaac running back. He appeared breathless and sweaty. 'What have you been up to?' she asked. He stopped in front of her, his eyes downcast, concentrating on the ground. He didn't speak. Josie heard the first gunshot. They both shuddered at the sound. It was followed by others, and the bellowing of distraught cattle. She put her arms around Isaac's shoulders, drawing him in towards her. 'Balipi told me you will be going to school now,' she said, trying to take his mind off what was happening. Isaac looked up at her, tears running down his face. She wiped them away and then her own; trying to smile and reassure him as she held onto him tightly.

The following morning, dressed in his white shirt and khaki shorts, she saw Isaac hand over his swishing stick to Moses. It had all the formality of a ceremonial occasion and the recognition of their changing lives. He then rode off on his bike; turning at the last minute, he waved at Josie. She waved back.

Moses called out to Brown who was playing under the tree. He got up and ran after his brother. She called out to them, 'Put your takkies on.' They wandered off into the veldt, Moses swishing at the long grass. A maternal bubble popped. She felt responsible for their wellbeing. At least out at Tugela, she thought, there were fewer vehicles passing close by. She hoped it might be enough to keep Bucephalus at bay.

♦

Josie chose the burial spot.

It was beside the marula tree, the place where she and Johannes often came. It was here he'd tell her his stories and she listen, enthralled. She was sure; this was where his spirit would be. She imagined him sat here watching over his now ghostly beloved Nguni.

The hairs on her neck rose. She spun round, certain he was behind her. There was nothing. The sense of loss overwhelmed her. She collapsed to the ground, sobbing. He had felt so real, within touching distance; as if nothing separated them but a dimension she couldn't cross because she lacked faith. Her heart broke. She couldn't be sure if she was grieving for Johannes, Tomas or herself. But out here she didn't have to pretend to be strong and coping. She let her fear and foreboding overwhelm her. Eventually her crying turned to gulping sobs as her tears dried up. Eventually she sat upright, her back resting against the smooth bark. Her heart and mind stilled. Then something strange happened. It was as if the tree, known for its healing properties, filled her with a sense of purpose. Finnegan wasn't going to destroy her. She had to carry on. She had TJ to protect and fight for, along with everyone else she loved.

A funeral is an important occasion, families often borrowing money beyond their means. Kate made sure everyone would say, "This was a good funeral." Everyone dressed in their best clothes. Mary put out Kate's black heeled shoes and insisted on wearing her ANC red beret. Winnie's children were neatly dressed, no one running around in bare feet, not today. Isaac walked with Balipi and the other men wearing a suit, several sizes too large. He looked serious but as he passed by, he briefly caught her eye and smiled broadly. She saw two images simultaneously; the child who played excitedly along with the others in the back of the Hilux and the emerging adult. She gave him her nod of approval. Josie was surprised by the number of people who came. There must have been a hundred or more unfamiliar faces. The procession carried his body to the marula tree, the women singing as they walked and the children for once subdued. At the open grave a black minister spoke. Josie threw Molly, her rag doll, onto the coffin. She looked down at her childhood companion and saw it disappear under the shovelled earth; each thud reminded her not of Johannes but Tomas. Had anyone stood by his grave and watched him buried? She made a silent promise. When this was all over, she and TJ would go and find him and mark his grave with a stone memorial.

♦

The following day Kate got up early to go to the hospital. Outside there were still groups of people sat around the dying embers, others walking slowly back to Matsane. Her face looked more drawn than usual. Ahead, the Feed Africa poster of the fecund woman mocked her. How the hell was she going to cope with an outbreak of sleeping sickness?

'What do you expect me to do?' she shouted out at the poster, unconcerned if anyone heard her through the open window. No one replied. Her impotence festered like an open wound and exhaustion drained her will to carry on. She hoped no one else at Tugela had contracted sleeping sickness. Inside she knew people died whether you loved them or not.

Her nostrils smelt the burning flesh of cattle pyres on other properties. It was shockingly different to the sweet blossom of orange trees. Coetzer had wasted no time. It was small comfort, but at least he had to tell people bad news. She wasn't the only one. The thought reminded her she needed to speak to him soon.

Kate worried about who would take over her role if she was sacked, following her spectacular outburst at Shindwalla, or even if Martha Lintel Montgomery would continue to support the hospital. She laughed out loud at the memory. It had felt good to have finally confronted her and tell her what she felt about her stance on birth control, as she struggled with HIV and Aids. It had been satisfying, if foolhardy. She didn't care. She remembered with pleasure, the horror in Martha's eyes when she saw Josie; and the same grey eyes and arched eyebrow being echoed in her son's astonishment. This was her granddaughter. Josie was her flesh and blood; she was a Lintel, an heir to the name and fortune. Kate immediately closed her mind to the future and what might happen, fearful of losing her family to that dreadful woman. She had no desire to rekindle the relationship with Joe either. It had been the briefest of affairs. She had no regrets.

Later on in her office, she and her team discussed the sleeping sickness outbreak. They had no space in the hospital for more patients and no specialist medicines to treat it.

'I'm not asking Martha Lintel Montgomery for help.' She caught Dr Wedderburn's surprised reaction. 'There has to be another way.'

There was a knock on her door.

Balipi entered. 'I have bad news. The men have said the women cannot come to the clinic.'

Kate was shocked. The rural immunisation clinic was a great success; it saved mothers and babies the long trek into Matsane.

'Do you know why?' she asked. He avoided her gaze. She still felt awkward, aware the rift between them hadn't mended. She took a guess. 'Has it something to do with the cattle being slaughtered?'

'Yes.'

'I knew it.'

'It'll be some half cocked, jumbled up mumbo jumbo, fuelled by rumours,' Dr Wedderburn said dismissively.

Kate and Balipi exchanged looks. She was lucky to have Dr Wedderburn. He was a good surgeon but his fondness for alcohol and other people's wives resulted in him being fired from the Netcare private hospital in Johannesburg. He'd narrowly avoided being struck off. She had offered him a position. He'd accepted but resented having to treat black Africans and not the wealthy woman of Rosebank, Sandton and Hyde Park.

Balipi ignored him. 'They say the animal doctor tells them their cattle are sick because a fly injects them with bad muti. They say, "You inject our babies."'

Dr Wedderburn laughed loudly. 'I suppose you can see their logic.'

Balipi remained dignified but clearly upset.

Kate didn't have time to begin an education programme explaining what they were doing or why. She needed Coetzer's support, but how likely was he to help her?

An education programme was no easy task, as she knew. Many Africans had a poor understanding about how diseases were spread, ignoring the role of insects, diet or living conditions. It would mean visiting all the outlying villages and returning several times to make sure the information had been understood, because confusion over words led to misunderstandings and misdiagnosis. Besides, she had no one who could do the work. Pamphlets were a poor substitute with so many official languages; not helped by vernacular words that were hard to translate and low literacy in adults. She knew too how strong a hold the supernatural had on people's ideas; its malevolence explaining a host of illnesses. Diseases were seen as part of a natural cycle. They came in their own season, making prevention appear foolhardy. She had long ago accepted each community prided itself on its own remedies as an affirmation of its identity and heritage. She respected the sangoma's pharmacopeia, except when it included the more imaginative solutions to diseases using such modern commodities as motor oil, paraffin, tar or Coca Cola. The battle to improve people's lives had once seemed an exciting challenge, now it defeated her.

CHAPTER 23
COETZER

'How can you help?' Kate's tone was dismissive.

Josie ignored her. She could see the strain around her mother's eyes and felt the continuing tension between her and Balipi. It was not for the first time Josie wondered if they had been lovers and her being in the house had upset their relationship. She didn't ask.

'This concerns me too. I'm coming to the meeting.' Josie wasn't thinking about the sleeping sickness outbreak, but what she'd learned at Growly Bear. Typically her mother hadn't asked her about the visit. She was too wrapped up in her own concerns. Josie understood Kate's life revolved around her hospital and this small part of Africa. However, Josie knew they were going to become the epicentre of a global crisis if she didn't act. And worse still, her father might be part of it. As Annie had said – she needed proof.

The introductions over, Coetzer spoke first, 'I've been told my priority is to organise a dipping programme for all the big cattle stockholders and erect blue nets around their water holes.' He looked round the table. 'It's the decision of the Minister of Agriculture. He's keen to avoid images appearing on foreign TV of burning carcasses.' His sarcasm was evident. He took a breath then surprised everyone by slamming his fist on the table. 'They need to be slaughtered. It's the only way.'

'Why dipping?' Josie raised her eyebrow, hoping she'd judged him correctly and that he'd want to put her straight.

'Oxpeckers predate the tsetse flies but they cannot reach down to the front legs, so we dip them.' He looked at her. 'Females reproduce every twenty to thirty days, fifty generations in one life time.' He paused. 'Now do you understand, lady?' His hostility towards her was obvious.

'What about all the lactating cows sent out through Feed Africa?' Josie asked provocatively.

He glowered. 'They are European cattle, not used to our climate and with no resilience either; bloody stupid idea,' his answer directed to everyone in the room.

Josie persisted, 'Then how come the Nguni are infected? They're native cattle?'

Everyone's attention turned to Coetzer. He looked bellicose but said nothing. Instead he pushed his chair back as if he were about to leave.

He doesn't have an answer! Josie thought, delighted. Perhaps he'd renew his efforts to find an answer, if only to silence her. She'd counted on him resenting her, especially as she was a young woman. What was it he had said to her the first time they'd met? "Don't tell me how to do my job." She smiled at him deliberately, hoping her expression would annoy him further.

But he wasn't done. 'And there's another thing,' his fist hitting the table again. 'Feed Africa is shipping out American

GM cereals to us.' He stared at Josie as if she was somehow responsible – the interfering outsider.

She was enjoying the contest.

'Cows develop severe health problems with it: liver abscesses and bloat. It kills them. They need grass to offset the build up of gases. Feed Africa,' he looked around the table seeking support for his argument, 'has come in here and expects everything to change overnight, without understanding the African's mind or their ways.'

She smiled up at Coetzer. 'Feed Africa must be doing something right,' her intonation mocking him. 'Tell me who's paid for all your extra staff, vehicles, and who knows what else?' Her insinuation was clear. She didn't stop. She saw the look on his face and his stance. 'I wonder how much you've been paid to turn a blind eye.'

'Josie, shut up!' Kate's outburst silenced her daughter. 'What the hell's got into you?'

Everyone sat there feeling awkward.

It's now or never, Josie thought. She looked directly at her mother. 'I hear Finnegan has set up a blood testing clinic and fully resourced it with technicians. How convenient, but why now?' She turned to face Coetzer. 'What's Finnegan asked you to do?'

Kate snapped back at her, 'I've had enough of your paranoia about Finnegan. It seems to me he's been exceptionally generous.'

'Yes, all those shiny new LCC vehicles. They're everywhere, aren't they?' She paused, letting her observation register with Coetzer, knowing he had a fleet of them. She slowly looked at each person in the room. 'He's doing it for a reason and it isn't philanthropy.'

'His blood clinic might well just save lives.' Kate looked grim.

'I thought Balipi said the natives are accusing you of killing their babies?'

Kate looked at the other medics in the room. Josie saw it and took a leap into the unknown. 'So the Africans are right, more babies are dying?' It was a high stakes game of poker. Josie played her hand. Her demeanour changed. She looked ashamed. She apologised to everyone in the room. 'Sorry, that must have been embarrassing for you, watching us fight.' She got up. 'I'll leave you to your discussions.'

By the door, she turned. 'Shall I check the hospital's records? It'd be useful to know exactly what's going on, and if it's true – more babies are dying.' She closed the door, a broad smile on her face. There was no way her mother could leave the meeting and stop her.

♦

One of the advantages of being funded by a charitable trust was they demanded good record keeping to justify their investment. The Lintel Foundation was no different. Grant applications or continued funding applications always demanded evidence-based information. Mrs Nkosi oversaw patient records and the hospital's accounts; the auditor never finding false documentation or sums of money redirected to support her family, or more tenuous dependencies. One salary often had to stretch a long way, but not with Mrs Nkosi.

Mrs Nkosi brought Josie the records.

Josie sat down. This was going to take some time. At first she noticed an improvement in infant mortality and assumed it was down to better inoculation and hygiene, as well as the positive impact Feed Africa was having by installing long drop toilets, water pumps and closed tanks that were checked regularly. However, if Kate failed to find a way to persuade people to attend her clinics this improvement would quickly go into reverse. Next she looked at mortality rates, discounting the shockingly high number relating to Aids. Professor Li wasn't interested in HIV/Aids and no one could have predicted the sleeping sickness outbreak. His interest was in Bucephalus. He'd be looking, as she knew now, for the impact of GG42/OO.

Jon Maguire had died from an aggressive form of myeloma. A good indicator for this was an unusually high white cell count. She looked for references to bruising; anaemia and bleeding. She found an increase in the number of people being treated for stomach ulcers and a spike in the number of amputations due to gangrene. Wounds were not healing. To anyone else looking at the information they would have dismissed it as evidence of the universal battle to defeat hospital infections. Josie thought otherwise. Next she concentrated on the antenatal and neonatal records. TJ was healthy but had the airborne toxin affected other babies? She found something: an increase in miscarriages beyond the first trimester. The African women were right to be fearful. There was another unusual feature, nose bleeds in babies and toddlers; a surprisingly high number. Josie wasn't a doctor, however she'd found enough to show her mother.

'What was that performance all about?' Kate stood in front of Josie.

'I wanted to make a point.' Josie crossed her arms with a flourish and accidentally knocked the stacked files onto the floor, creating a jumbled mess. Mrs Nkosi wouldn't be happy with her; she'd have to find a way to apologise.

'Finnegan…'

Kate broke in, 'Oh please don't go there again. Tomas died and you've no proof it was Finnegan. Leave it.'

'I do have proof.' Irritated, Josie stood up. She saw the look of surprise on her mother's face. 'Tomas created a chemical cocktail using an aromatic additive. It increased the aldehydes and in this case acrylamide. One of the side effects is impotency. He also tested his formula on himself by turning off the air purification system in the laboratory. He went further, though I didn't know it at the time. He was eating and covering his skin with it, in a desperate attempt to show how damaging it was. He knew Finnegan wouldn't listen to his concerns unless he did something drastic to prove how dangerous it was.'

'You're worried about impotency,' Kate's voice mocking her.

Josie was now really annoyed. 'The real problem is it destroys blood cells. It results in aggressive cancers.' She stopped. 'I've found in your records a higher incidence of blood-related problems.'

Kate reacted. Her mouth opened but nothing came out.

'I have Mike's laptop and Jon Maguire left meticulous notes,' Josie said, desperate to convince her mother, 'everyone is dead apart from me.' She looked at Kate. 'Finnegan saw me at Shindwalla. That's why I ran away.' Josie bent down and lifted the Feed Africa tote bag onto the desk. She took out Mrs Clarkson's gun and put it on the desk. 'Balipi and baboons aren't enough anymore.'

Kate swayed.

'Bucephalus is out here. I'm sure it's being tested on us.' She turned to the window, waving her arms. 'It is all around us, the air we breathe, on our food and in the water.' She paused. 'I have to get proof,' she stopped, 'and I think it is responsible for the Nguni dying, which means the animals are affected too.'

Kate's legs buckled under her as she fainted.

♦

At home in bed, Kate took Josie's hand. 'I'm sorry.'

'You've done nothing wrong.'

'I ignored you and now this.'

'Don't say that.' Josie saw the deep purple hollows under her eyes. 'You're exhausted. They'll have to find a replacement. You need a long rest.'

Her mother turned her face away, coughing. 'Josie, I'm not well.'

'Try to sleep; I'll make sure TJ doesn't worry you.' Josie didn't want to hear about her mother's fears. She had enough of her own.

Josie sat on the porch. She tried to think; the merry-go-round of unanswered questions and possibilities spun round. She made a list: how long before the launch, blood clinic reports, Coetzer's position and "Joe", friend or foe. She underlined his name repeatedly. Why would the President of the United States listen to her? She was one voice. Besides, he'd be more likely to take Finnegan's side. Lost in her thoughts, she didn't notice the approaching vehicles.

Coetzer came bounding up the stoep steps. 'I've come to take a blood sample.'

'What do you mean?'

'My native boy told me, you hid one of the Nguni because she was about to have a calf. Where is it?'

'I've no idea what you are talking about.'

'Look I don't care, but if it is alive. I need to test it.' He was agitated. 'The Nguni shouldn't be infected, not to the extent they are. I think it's more than sleeping sickness.'

Josie wanted to kiss him.

He looked at her, his stance still defiant. 'No one tells me what to do.'

'Not even Finnegan?' she asked, wondering what his answer might be.

'I don't know who you are talking about. I had dealings with some Chinaman smelling of perfume.'

She laughed out loud. It was the confirmation she needed. Professor Li had been out to Africa, setting up the field study. Then she remembered the ceremony she'd witnessed between Isaac and Moses. 'I know what he did.' Josie went to find Moses and Brown.

CHAPTER 24

LESEDI

Sat on the stoep, a rug on her lap, Kate apologised for not getting up. Dr Mokaba looked concerned. 'Thank you both for coming out here. We need to discuss how the hospital's going to manage in my absence. I don't think I'll be back for a while.'

'I'll be more than happy to step in. Until that is, you are ready to pick up the reins,' Dr Wedderburn said.

'I want Dr Mokaba to run the hospital, the staff respect and trust him.' Kate's decision was clearly not open for further discussion.

Josie watched Dr Wedderburn's reaction. He looked annoyed at being passed over in favour of a black doctor. 'What Kate hasn't said is – she has a different, more important task for you.'

Kate looked at Dr Wedderburn. 'To put it bluntly, Martha Lintel Montgomery and I had a blazing row. She threatened to sack me.'

The two men reacted differently to her words. Dr Mokaba looked genuinely shocked while Dr Wedderburn had a small smirk on his lips.

'She may go further and withdraw the funding completely,' Kate added, 'so you see Dr Wedderburn, I need you to go to America on a charm offensive. Persuade her – make her see how important Matsane is and how now more than ever, we need the Lintel Foundation's support.'

'I'm your messenger boy,' he said, still affronted.

'You could see it that way,' Josie laughed lightly, 'I'd say it's playing to your strengths. Older, wealthy women respond positively towards you. They like you and you know how to make them feel special.' She wasn't sure if it had come across as a compliment. It sounded… unsavoury. She kicked herself. 'Why don't I get you a drink? Let's leave these two to chat about swabs and syringes.' She stood up. 'I know how eager Mom is to hear about the hospital.'

Dr Mokaba pulled his chair closer to Kate's. He immediately began talking, with Kate repeatedly interrupting him asking for more details, and Dr Mokaba gladly filling her in.

At the drinks tray Josie took Dr Wedderburn into her confidence, 'I don't want Mom to hear this, but if I were you, I'd see it as an opportunity. Kate and Dr Mokaba are the same. They are only interested in bush health care. Whereas I'd say – Matsane for you is a dead end. Do you really want to spend the rest of your career treating black people out here?' She paused. 'When you could be running a private clinic somewhere more appealing?' She filled the highball with vodka.

He added a splash of orange juice.

'Martha Lintel Montgomery is a very wealthy, well-connected woman; she could open doors for you.'

He downed the drink in one, glancing across at the other two as he did so.

Dr Mokaba was telling Kate about something and moments later Kate laughed. Dr Mokaba slapped his thighs, rocking backwards and forwards laughing along with her. Josie kept her eyes firmly on Dr Wedderburn. *Did she really need to sell it to him?* 'With Mom eased out I suspect Martha Lintel Montgomery will be very grateful to you.' She raised her eyebrow and leaned in conspiratorially. 'A little bit of advice. Don't mention me.'

He looked quizzically at her.

'I don't know why – but she really, really doesn't like me,' Josie laughed, maintaining the intimacy. She whispered, 'I think it's because she's a good Catholic and I'm illegitimate. It offends her.'

Dr Mokaba turned towards Josie. 'Mrs Nkosi's daughter, Lesedi is expecting.'

'Is it her first?' Josie asked.

Dr Mokaba nodded. He turned back to Kate. 'She's a cleaner at the blood clinic, but the sangoma told Mrs Nkosi it's a bad place. She now insists her daughter leave. Do you think we can employ her at the hospital?'

'It's your decision, now.'

♦

With Dr Mokaba's help, everyone at Tugela gave another blood sample. Josie took the phials with her and walked into the new blood clinic. She asked to see Dr Holloway. When the receptionist asked why, Josie explained, 'Dr Ryland wants to know if anyone else in her household has been infected with *Trypanosomiasis brucei rhodesiense*.'

Dr Holloway came through wearing a white lab coat. She thought he was somewhere in his early thirties. She noticed he had an American accent. 'I'm sorry to hear that.' He invited her into his office.

Josie had taken particular care with how she dressed; short shorts and a tight T-shirt. From time to time she fiddled with her hair, her eyes wide open looking at him. 'Mom's sick, I'm terrified she's got it,' her voice sounding anxious. She began searching the bottom of her capacious leather handbag with one hand, while continuing to gush, 'Mom said what a fantastic facility you've got here, and how she'd never have coped without it.' She found a phial and put it on the desk with a flourish and a broad smile, before, head down, she began resuming her search; all the time giving the impression she was a ditzy, good-looking girl with big tits. 'I mean with all the good Feed Africa is doing, and then for this to come along.' She glanced up admiring his office for a moment. 'I saw the plaque in reception. Did you meet Lady Finnegan when she opened it?'

She waited for his answer.

He shook his head mesmerized.

She wanted to ask him about Professor Li but knew it would arouse his suspicions and not fit the part she was playing. Instead she continued her search before finally holding up the last of the phials triumphantly.

'Would you like to see what we do here?' He gathered the phials. 'I'll get one of the technicians to take a look at these.' He opened the door so she could walk out in front of him.

Outside his office she lifted her handbag onto her shoulder, leaving it there just long enough for him to see she wasn't wearing a wedding ring. She waited while he opened the security door and saw him glance at her naked hand. It reminded her of one of Johannes' stories, the ground-nesting bird feigning a broken wing to draw the predator's attention away from the bird's eggs.

The tour over, Dr Holloway said, 'Why don't you come back later today, collect the results and I could take you for a drink?'

'What time do you close?'

'The laboratory closes at five-thirty.'

She looked a little awkward. 'Can you leave them with the receptionist?' Her normal voice returning, 'I need to get home. My little boy will be waiting.'

He excused himself and disappeared back into the laboratory.

♦

That evening Josie drove the Land Cruiser back to collect the results. She took the gun with her. The blood clinic was a single-storey building. It looked prefabricated, as if it had gone up in a hurry. It had no architectural merit, unlike many of the other buildings put up by corporations responding to the president's Feed Africa call; many of them seeing it as an opportunity for long-term investment. The perimeter razor wire fence had floodlights to keep it secure. Two army guards sat in their vehicle outside. Josie parked. She caught a glimpse through the glass front door of someone pulling a metal bucket and mop. Josie tooted her horn and waved.

Lesedi saw her and came out. Josie walked over to the guards and explained why she was here. They were disinterested, waving her away with their AK 47s.

'Hello Lesedi.'

The young African girl unlocked the metal compound gates using one of the keys from the bunch that hung round her neck.

'I have some things for you and the baby?'

Lesedi looked down sheepishly, her hand on her belly.

'I know babies need so much. I've got a little boy. These clothes are too small for him now. Would you like them?'

Lesedi didn't hesitate, her face lit up.

'I've also brought some clothes for you to try on. They are all in the back of the Land Cruiser.'

Their arms overflowing, they carried the piles of clothing into the front reception. Josie laughed, 'It looks like you'll need some plastic bags to carry it all home. Where do you keep them?'

'My cupboard is in there.' Lesedi nodded towards the laboratory.

'Here, give me your keys, and I'll get the bags, while you try the clothes on.' Josie pointed to the toilets. 'Go on. I'll lock the doors so no one can come in.'

Josie wasted no time; having been shown round the laboratory earlier, she had a good idea of the layout and the function of the different work stations. She knew what to look for. She searched the trays on top of the filing cabinets. As in all offices, filing was the last job anyone tackled. She found some printouts. Next she hurriedly flicked through various report summaries. She didn't have time to read them now. She turned on the photocopier, hoping the noise of it starting up wouldn't reach Lesedi. It took only a few minutes. Next she ran down the lab to Lesedi's cupboard, found the bags and slammed the door shut. Moments later she was back in the reception area, waiting for Lesedi to change into her work clothes having tried on her old clothes.

'I was supposed to pick up some results. Can I have a quick look in the mail room?'

Lesedi opened the door, leaving Josie alone. Josie noticed a large manila envelope. It was addressed to a post box in America. She popped it into her bag, along with the one addressed to her.

'How will you get all these bags home?' Josie asked Lesedi.

'I can carry them on my head,' Lesedi said proudly. She shook Josie's hand, 'Thank you madam.'

Josie walked back to the Land Cruiser; as she passed the two men she waved the manila envelope calling out, '*Dankie.*' The soldiers looked back, bored.

CHAPTER 25
DU TOIT

Josie drove Mary into Matsane for their fortnightly shopping. The novelty of being allowed to sit up front with a white person still enthralled her. She wore her red beret. Josie noticed it. 'What was it like in South Africa then?' she said, nodding at the beret.

'The army and police were on the streets, shooting and killing people; even here. It was very bad. But once they released Madiba, we were so happy.' Mary began singing 'Nkosi Sikelel' iAfrica'.

'Didn't black Africans want land, like the Zimbabweans?'

'No madam, the Truth and Reconciliation Committee helped wash away our anger.'

Josie was deeply impressed by Mary's words. She noticed Mary had not called her Josie. She'd become madam, like her mother. Ahead, the traffic had come to a standstill. Josie wondered if it was another highway being created; the juggernaut of Feed Africa seemed unstoppable. They sat waiting. Suddenly there was a deafening explosion, followed by a billowing column of black smoke. The car in front reversed. Its red tailgate lights narrowly missed hitting their car, before it spun round and drove off.

'What the hell is going on?' Other cars were turning round and disappearing hidden in the dust clouds they'd created. In front Josie saw the burning AMOIL fuel tanker and around it, a group of young boys dancing, their arms above their heads in celebration. Unconsciously she registered – they were all dressed alike, black T-shirts, new trainers, some waving mobile phones. She turned the steering wheel hard and put her foot down on the accelerator, driving into the ditch. Mary screamed as the car's springs bounced down hard and up as they bounced out. Josie accelerated away. The gang jeered as she passed, before turning back to carry on enjoying the mayhem they'd caused. In her rear-view mirror she caught sight of the red and black outfit of the AMOIL driver. He was dancing too.

♦

'I don't want the children wandering too far from Tugela. It's too dangerous. Tell Isaac I want to see him when he gets home.' For the first time Josie was worried about their isolation. There were no near neighbours to call on for help if an army of youths came to the house looking to cause trouble. She'd buy a more reliable gun than Mrs Clarkson's old one and ask Balipi if he wanted one too.

♦

'You'd better come and see this.' Coetzer sounded agitated and elated

'This better be worth it,' she said, annoyed at being forced to drive back into town.

'I sent the samples from your cow and calf off to the Ministry in Pretoria,' Coetzer said, showing her into his office, 'I didn't want you accusing me of not doing my job,' a small smile emerged, 'they didn't find anything.'

'Do you mean the cow and her calf are clear of the disease? That's wonderful, the boys will be delighted.'

'No, the cow has nagana.'

Josie was confused. 'But you said nothing showed up in the sample you sent them.'

'Now do you see the idiots I have to deal with?'

'It doesn't make sense.'

Coetzer was actually smiling at her now. 'You'd have to call it stupid, incompetent, even corrupt.' He waited for her to figure it out.

Slowly she realised what he was hinting at and laughed out loud. 'I expect the Minister's driving a Genco.' The words were out before she could stop them. Quickly she glanced at Coetzer, aware he was driving around in a new 4x4 courtesy of Finnegan. She hoped he hadn't taken offence. She needed him. 'It explains why they've found nothing.'

He laughed, 'The official line is we are dipping cattle as a preventative measure, and though there have been some cases of sleeping sickness, it is not an epidemic.' Coetzer waved a letter from the Ministry in front of her.

'So what now?' she asked.

He sat there, saying nothing, waiting for her.

It didn't take long. 'You had it tested by one of Dr

Holloway's technicians.' Her admiration for him suddenly rose.

'I thought you wanted to prove Finnegan's up to something.'

'And what came back this time?'

'He confirmed the sleeping sickness. Now – and this is what is really interesting – he found traces of a new compound. Dr Holloway assumed it comes from one of the pharmaceutical companies' trialling a new drug.'

Josie was flummoxed. 'Impossible, Feed Africa hasn't been out to Tugela. We've been given nothing and besides the calf's been hidden. It's had no supplements.' She sat thinking for a moment before exclaiming, 'It's a smoke screen! Finnegan's setting them up, hoping they'll take the blame if anything goes wrong.' She looked at Coetzer.

'You're right; I would have come to the same conclusion as Dr Holloway, and accused them of illegal drug testing.'

'Whose side are you on?' Josie asked, hoping here was the ally she so badly needed.

'I've dedicated my life to animal welfare. I love this country. If some rich American thinks he can ride roughshod over it, he'd better watch out. I don't like strangers telling me what to do, whatever you might think.'

'Sorry, but I had to get you to act.' She told him all that she knew.

'Before you go, I've got more bad news. The game farms and private concessions are reporting dead antelope. It's not sleeping sickness.'

'Is this Bucephalus do you think?' she asked him, afraid of his answer.

'If it is – we need to find out and quickly.'

As an afterthought she asked, 'What will happen to our calf?'

'I let the boys keep it. I gave them antibiotics to strengthen its resistance and some dipping solution. You know the African's solution? They use sump oil.'

Coetzer's phone rang. He listened in silence, his face getting darker, 'You better come with me.'

'Why, what's happened?'

'My native boy is in police custody. It's this sporadic violence, the police are pulling in everyone. Du Toit isn't the brightest of police chiefs. When we get there let me do the talking.'

Coetzer pressed the intercom. Josie looked about. The compound resembled a fortress with ten-foot-high razor wire and lights on even higher posts protected by wire cages. Under a canopy were several police armoured vehicles with metal mesh protecting the windows and an armoured van.

'Is this normal?' she asked, nodding in the direction of the vehicles.

'It goes back to the riots. We had a lot of trouble here.'

'I remember reading about Steve Biko falling out of a fifth storey window while in police custody.'

Coetzer's expression darkened. His former good humour evaporated, 'You weren't out here. You don't have the right to judge us.' The Afrikaner gave her a hard stare.

'Sorry,' She looked apologetic.

'Tell them you work at Matsane Hospital.'

They waited in silence, before being shown into a small, windowless room. It was stiflingly hot. The air smelt of stale sweat and urine. A blue-uniformed officer stepped in.

Coetzer spoke first, 'Du Toit, I'd like my native boy back. Where is he?'

Inspector Du Toit pulled out a chair and sat down. He looked Josie up and down slowly. She felt herself colouring up, a light sweat developing under her armpits and around the back of her neck. She felt like a piece of meat being examined. Du Toit smirked, enjoying her discomfort, before turning to Coetzer. 'We've got trouble with the blacks, taken it into their heads to attack fuel tankers. What are you hearing?'

Coetzer took a moment. 'We are destroying people's cattle. They are bound to be unhappy.'

'I'm not talking about a few blacks with a couple of Nguni,' Du Toit said sharply.

'You've got my native. Have you questioned him?' Coetzer maintained his gaze. 'What's he told you?'

Du Toit quickly pulled his *sjambok* from his belt and slammed it down on the table. Josie jumped. He laughed, 'Nervous lady,' his remark hinting at some form of crude foreplay.

'Has my boy said anything?' Coetzer asked firmly.

Du Toit ignored him. Looking at Josie he said, 'Do you want to see him?' He got up, opened the door and barked out an order. The three of them sat waiting in silence. Mpho was hauled in. Handcuffed, his right eye closed and swollen, his nose bloodied and lips cut. She looked down at his hands. His knuckles bore the marks of Du Toit's stick being slammed down on them repeatedly. She wanted to vomit. The colour drained from her face.

'We're civilised, not like the natives. We don't chop off their arms or use burning tyres as necklaces.' He smirked at Mpho.

Scraping the chair along the floor, Coetzer stood up and was about to hit the man opposite him when Josie grabbed his arm as she leapt up too. 'This is outrageous. Take off his handcuffs. He needs a doctor.' Her grey eyes were staring unblinking at Du Toit. She took a step towards him, reducing the space between them. 'Now,' her face inches from his.

For a moment Du Toit looked surprised, then he said, 'You can have him,' pushing the youth towards them.

Coetzer grabbed Mpho. They walked him to the door. Josie turned to look at Du Toit. 'It's not the local boys causing the trouble. Someone is paying outsiders. But you're too stupid or too lazy to find out what's really going on.'

Sat in the vehicle Coetzer said, 'You've more balls than most men I know.'

'I'm not afraid of bullies like him.' Inwardly her heart was beating rapidly. She thought of Finnegan. For the first time his "or else" seemed like a puff of smoke in her eyes. 'Actually I felt like a tethered goat.' She laughed nervously, the adrenalin still pumping.

'If I'd gone in by myself, Mpho would have been dead by the time I got him out.'

'How can he get away with it?' she asked.

'People like Du Toit don't change. They don't want to.'

♦

Josie rang Annie Devereux at Growly Bear. The phone rang for some time before she heard a click and Annie answered.

'Hi, is everything all right? No repercussions, no one's come to see you, anybody odd hanging around or threatening you?' Her questions tumbled out in a torrent of concern.

Annie a little surprised said, 'I'm fine.'

'Sorry. I wanted to check you were all right before contacting Professor Li.'

'Why, what have you found out?'

'Well I have proof it's affecting domestic animals and the wildlife,' Josie said, without using the word Bucephalus. Even after all this time, she was paranoid someone might be listening in. 'I've got someone out here helping me.' She deliberately didn't use his name either.

'Great, well I mean – that's bad, really bad.'

'I know. I'm still trying to find out how it's affecting people.'

'Right – and Professor Li will tell you! Don't be so naïve, Josie. He'll tell Finnegan where you are and then you know what he'll do.'

'That's just it Annie. Finnegan saw me. I think he's always known where I was.' She paused. She didn't say anything about meeting her father. 'I don't think Finnegan was behind the bomb.'

'You've been convinced all along it was him,' Annie's voice rose in disbelief.

'I know, but I now think Professor Li was behind the burglary. He needed Mike's drawings. He didn't have them because they were on Finnegan's server, Mike told me that. What if Professor Li wanted it all?' She thought of Mike, 'Perhaps he planned to sell the idea to the highest bidder, just like Mike.'

'Why?' Annie asked.

'Love, money, revenge, who knows; I know he'd never hurt Tomas, but someone else might.'

There was a long silence on the line. 'So who do you think was responsible for the bomb?'

'Someone who wanted to cover their tracks, keep it a secret until they were ready...' Josie's words trailed off.

'Who has deeper pockets than Finnegan?'

'That's the problem, I don't know.'

The line went quiet. 'You won't want to hear this Josie, but what if Professor Li is genuinely worried about the results?'

'Then he could contact the media, come clean and save his reputation.' She took a big breath. 'Have you forgotten who we are talking about? He threatened and bullied you and Jon, he spied on Tomas; who knows what else he's prepared to do.'

'Calm down I get it, he's the bad guy!' Annie laughed, 'And all this time I thought it was Finnegan.'

'Finnegan's still to blame. First I need to meet Professor Li face to face. Thanks Annie for listening, and be careful.' She added as afterthought, 'Your back roads are very dangerous.'

'Look who's talking, I've seen the TV pictures on the news – yours don't look any safer. Good luck and take care.'

Josie wrote her letter.

CHAPTER 26
FINAL REPORT

Professor Li had been right to insist on a field study. But the results were worse than expected. It turned the glorious reality of an emissions-free car into an environmental catastrophe. It placed him in an impossible situation. Papers and files covered every surface of his once ordered apartment, muttering to himself whilst frantically searching, pushing piles of papers to the floor. They spread like a contagion. He watched them, seeing it as a metaphor for what was happening in Matsane. He closed his eyes for a moment. They were itchy and red with lack of sleep. On the sofa he drifted off, exhausted.

When he woke he felt no better. One last effort and it would be done. He began by reviewing the field study data. He hadn't anticipated the rapid increase in people in Matsane. The local water supply couldn't meet the demand so bottled water was shipped in. However, there were enough Africans drinking contaminated water from their tanks in the rural areas. He reasoned it would take years before low birth rates registered as a matter of concern and some researcher made the link to male infertility. And even more time before the link was made to acrylamide in the new fuel, if at all, because if they found acrylamide, there'd be no incentive to look further and discover GG42/OO. This gave him his opportunity. *I can still make this work for me,* he thought.

The most shocking data came from the blood samples; Dr Holloway's and more surprisingly from the veterinary technician's LCC had paid for. It appeared Coetzer needed to see him urgently. Something was amiss. Professor Li looked at the data and was surprised by the number of autopsies and range of species: antelope, zebra and buffalo as well as their predators and scavengers. Numbers were tumbling on the concession. No wonder Coetzer was worried about the wildlife within the private game park. He must be afraid the owner would pull out and sell it. Professor Li would offer him more money. He'd call it "restocking" the concession. But they'd both know it was actually a bribe, to keep his mouth shut. He'd seen Finnegan use a similar tactic. Coetzer had accepted the original handout without question, why not again? Everyone had their price.

Dr Holloway's latest report had not arrived, but he didn't need to see it. It would be the same as the others; a cocktail of pathogens highlighting a miscellany of illnesses. The results coming from a hospital where people had HIV/Aids, TB, malaria, sleeping sickness, diabetes, mineral deficiencies and blood disorders. He decided it was time to replace Dr Holloway before he began to notice a pattern: low concentrations of white cells. He could do it at the same time as seeing Coetzer.

Finally he considered the air quality results. They showed an increase in fuel particles, explained by the increase in traffic as a result of Feed Africa, but without the damaging climate change gases. It was the data the EPA needed. He looked for GG42/OO. It was there. He imagined countries with four- and six-lane highways and congested, smog-filled metropolises. He looked outside at the city, lit up by snaking lines of red taillights and white headlights. It reminded him of a dancing Chinese dragon and home. It would be overwhelming. In cities already struggling to create clean air zones, he expected to see the numbers of cancer patients rising rapidly, leading public health officials to demand extra funding and new laws to ban polluting vehicles. They would call on governments to outlaw the old petrol engine and demand the adoption of LCC's new green-fuelled vehicles. Sales would increase exponentially just as Finnegan had predicted.

In the confined space of Ham Farm's laboratory GG42/OO had acted swiftly; diluted in the vast landscape of Africa, he hoped it would barely register. But he found it. What made it dangerous was not the concentration, but the all pervading and cumulative effect. In the air it was deposited onto food, water and skin. As a consequence it was eaten, drunk and breathed in indiscriminately. No one escaped. How quickly it would degrade he had no way of knowing, and no time to find out.

He remembered Finnegan leaning on him, saying, "Give me the outcome I want." If he went ahead and ignored GG42/OO and it later came out, there would always be doubt about his work; no one would ever believe anything he published. If he refused, Finnegan's wrath would destroy him, his reputation and what would happen to the lifestyle he'd come to enjoy? *I'll lose everything I value.*

He wrestled with his conscience. By recording only the carbon/nitrogen results, he could be accused of manipulating the evidence; the word "falsifying" left a lingering, unacceptable taste. Still he wondered how many other reputable scientists had manipulated statistics in order to support the view of a sponsor or industry. *I'm no different,* he thought, easing his conscience.

It happened because decisions were never clear-cut; often a matter of interpretation. There were always outside pressures, checks and balances. The world was made up of shades of grey, not black and white. Reassured, he considered his dilemma further.

What if his cover-up was discovered? He'd be exposed, a pariah in the scientific world. It would mean professional ignominy. Colleagues would say he'd been sloppy and worse still, not rigorous. To be accused of devising a poorly conceived field study was unpalatable after all the work he had put into it. *I have been thorough!*

He surveyed the paper piles filling his apartment. The longer he considered his options the clearer it became. He would write the report Finnegan wanted. The outbreak of sleeping sickness had been a godsend. He almost believed Finnegan had done a deal with the devil; damning his soul in return for earthly glory, however transient it might be.

Sleeping sickness conveniently explained why animals were dying. No one would look for any other reason. The consequences of an epidemic were frightening enough. Recriminations would abound with people asking why hadn't the politicians maintained the preventative programmes or invested in genetic engineering; creating infertile male tsetse flies. He could see the debate resulting in funding and research because if successful, the outcome would be hugely beneficial. By choosing to hide GG42/OO was he in fact ensuring more effort went into finding ways to eradicate sleeping sickness? This perverse logic made him feel better. *I'd be vindicated.*

And if other problems emerged, there was a long list of other possible candidates. This had always been part of Finnegan's plan; put the spotlight on issues that were highly sensitive and opposed by groups around the world. Who knew what would be uncovered if environmentalists received funding to investigate what was happening in Africa? He was confident no one would stumble across a chemical no one knew about. And because no one knew about GG42/OO, why mention it in his documentation? He wrote his report for Finnegan.

♦

An envelope marked PRIVATE arrived. It was from that bitch at Ham Farm. He re-read the letter before tearing it into small pieces. *How dare she accuse me of betraying Tomas? It's not true. I loved him.*

♦

Eliot pushed the buzzer. Professor Li walked into Finnegan's office. He was standing by the window, his whiskey glass half-empty in his hand.

'What do you want?' Finnegan said without looking at him.

'It's finished.' He held out the report. 'You can launch Bucephalus.'

Finnegan didn't move for several minutes, before downing the remains of the whiskey in one gulp. 'Excellent it's about time.' Finnegan snatched the report; his breathing laboured. He appeared flabby. His usual domineering stance seemed less upright. He looked his age and his face was florid from one too many whiskeys.

For once Professor Li didn't mind that Finnegan failed to congratulate him on his efforts. He was savouring the moment, watching the man who had taunted him accept without question the report. He sat down, something he never normally did unless invited to do so.

Finnegan didn't make eye contact. He was too focussed on skimming through the report. He glanced up. 'What do you want?'

'Now I have completed the field study, what do you want me to do about the facilities we have out there?'

Finnegan considered the question before answering, 'My wife has a fondness for Africa. We'll keep the concession. I'd rather she shot lions than me.'

It was the first time Finnegan had joked with him. It was unexpected. He assumed it was all down to the report's contents.

'As to the others, they are part of our new trust. It's time the Finnegan name was more widely known.'

Professor Li hid his expression. *What vanity! He believes he'll be feted, acclaimed, a true hero, yet it will be my work, my name everyone will know.*

'Close the door on your way out.'

Professor Li continued to sit, forcing Finnegan to look

at him. 'What are you going to do about that girl from Ham Farm?' he asked, 'she's alive, and she's the only one left who knows about Bucephalus.'

Finnegan stared at him, 'Nothing.'

Inside Professor Li boiled with rage; dismissed like a servant! He regretted writing his report. He imagined the *Schadenfreude* of exposing him. But he knew how thorough Finnegan was in destroying people and their reputations. Besides he doubted he'd succeed; one voice against Finnegan, the resources of LCC and even those of the president. His courage collapsed. He remembered. He'd insisted Tomas's work was only the first stage, a false start and that he would finish it. Finnegan would blame him. Slowly he rose, angry at his impotency.

But what was he going to do about the bitch? He'd meet her, as she suggested. Finnegan might have overlooked her. He wouldn't make the same mistake. Her letter forced him to remember the last time they had spoken on the phone. She had described herself as "Tomas's fiancée". He didn't believe her, it wasn't true! She had lied. Perhaps she was lying now, trying to blackmail him. He wasn't going to let her spoil his dreams.

♦

Josie walked up to reception. 'I'm meeting one of your guests, Professor Li.' She'd chosen Shindwalla because it was a public space, somewhere she felt safe and she was sure the luxury would appeal to his tastes. She wanted him to feel relaxed, comfortable in his surroundings, albeit it was in Africa.

He walked towards her, as effete as always; his cream fedora-styled Panama hat held in his right hand, the left mopping his brow. She noticed his pale silk suit was immaculate. His aftershave wafted towards her; a long forgotten memory of the first time they'd met. Even without heels she towered above him. They didn't shake hands.

'You had the temerity to write to me. What do you want?'

'We have Bucephalus in common, and Tomas. I think we have a lot to discuss.' She indicated they should sit. The generous tub chairs were covered in impala hide. The waiter took their order.

'I saw him die.' She watched him closely. She looked for any telltale ticks. There was nothing. It was as if Tomas had never existed. 'What if I tell Finnegan you stole Mike's laptop to get your hands on his drawings?'

'Why would I do that?'

'Because you needed them,' Josie said.

'I don't know what you are talking about.' His voice was a little too shrill.

'Finnegan was so paranoid about Bucephalus, he didn't even trust you.' She looked at his eyes, looking for a flicker of doubt. 'How does that make you feel?' She noticed he was flipping his talisman. 'What will Finnegan do if he finds out?' She stopped to gauge his reaction. He had a slight film of perspiration on his face. 'Now that Finnegan has his report, are you safe I wonder? Everyone involved in the Bucephalus project has been disposed of, are you next I wonder?'

She saw the expression on the professor's face change. He looked afraid and nervous. It confirmed two things:

Finnegan had the report and secondly he'd been given the green light to launch Bucephalus.

'I know about GG42/OO.' She wanted him to fully grasp the significance. She handed him Dr Holloway's report and a copy of Jon Maguire's death certificate. 'Cause and effect so neatly summarised in those two documents.'

He scanned them rapidly. 'How did you get hold of these?' He spoke in a low voice, glancing round quickly, before putting them on the table in front of him, implying they were of no consequence.

'You don't deny the terrible consequences GG42/OO has on humans.' She let her words register. She focussed her grey eyes on him. 'It's killing people, like it did Jon Maguire.'

Professor Li stared at her through his tortoiseshell glasses, before taking them off to slowly clean them. 'How much do you want?'

She laughed. 'Did he order you to prove Bucephalus is EPA compliant?' She wanted to shame him. 'So you rolled over and did exactly as he wanted, taking his dirty money to buy another pretty boy to fuck; all the time keeping your job, your position and whatever else Finnegan funds.' She didn't hold back. 'You know everyone laughs at you behind your back.'

Unexpectedly Professor Li smiled at her. It wasn't the reaction she was expecting. She hoped she'd insulted him enough to unnerve him, get him to admit to something she could use against Finnegan.

'You silly bitch, you don't know what you're doing.' He picked up one of the documents and waved it in her face. 'What does this prove? Only that you are a thief.' He leaned back into the chair. 'You are still bound by LCC's confidentially agreement. You think he'll let you speak out?' He was growing in confidence. 'Who will believe you? I have document after document proving all that we need.' With a self-satisfied expression on his face he added, 'You against all the power Finnegan can muster as well as LCC's reputation and my own.' He lowered his voice, 'Who will believe you? You aren't even a scientist, just a grubby tart.' He took out his cheque book and Mont Blanc fountain pen. 'How much do you want?'

'Does he know?' she asked.

'Know what?' He looked up at her, less sure.

She smelt his aftershave. 'About the existence of GG42/OO or have you lied to him in the report. It tells only part of the story doesn't it?' She stared at him. 'What do you think he'll do to you once he knows the truth?'

'Bitch.' The people sat closest to them turned, surprised by his high pitched voice and the venom behind the word. Embarrassed, they looked away before resuming their own conversations, still fascinated by the unlikely couple.

'Call yourself a scientist. You've betrayed Tomas.' She stood up. 'He was a genius, you are nothing. You'll never find a solution.'

As she walked past him he grabbed her arm. 'Be careful. This is a dangerous place.'

♦

The sweat under his arms had darkened the silk. He wiped his brow. Professor Li remained seated. He needed to think. She didn't ask him for money. He was disappointed. He began to consider his options, when a disturbing thought entered his mind. What if she approached Finnegan, told him about GG42/OO? Did she have enough evidence to convince him? He had not referred to it in his report. He must act quickly. He made his decision. He would tell Zhou it was no longer safe for him to remain at LCC.

He got up. He'd warned her. His conscience was clear.

CHAPTER 27

PAVILION

Professor Li sat in the Pavilion in Beijing. The chair was uncomfortably low, even for him. In contrast the two chairs on the dais were intricately carved with imperial five-clawed dragons. A large circular window behind the dais elegantly framed the water and foliage beyond. The ancient trees were like old women, their trunks thick and bent over, reliant on t-shaped poles to support their branches. Light from the window shone across an exquisite vermillion lacquer screen. On it the life-size tiger shimmered, the gold's intensity reinforcing the sense of living flesh. The powerful creature, rather than leaping forward, lay beside the river intent on licking one of its paws. Looking more closely he saw the embedded jade thorn. He flipped his own talisman; a movement so familiar he barely registered it. He looked to the other side of the screen. A large mother-of-pearl horse, its head down, was drinking calmly from the lapis lazuli river, unconcerned by the proximity of the tiger. Above these symbols of good fortune and intelligence swooped iridescent long-tailed birds.

'Do you remember the story?' A thin, high voice broke the silence.

He nodded.

'Welcome Professor Li, it has been many years.'

Unsure of the protocol of an audience with Chen Jia and Wen Zhimou, he nodded again. He assumed these two elderly men must be in their nineties. They were soldiers on the Long March, part of Mao Zedong's Cultural Revolution and somehow had survived as respected members of the Chinese Communist Party; this achievement testament to their political skills and their continued influence.

'You still have it?' Chen Jia asked.

Professor Li opened the palm of his hand so they could see.

'We gave one to all our young men, reminding them of their duty and purpose. You did well rising to an important position in America.'

He was pleased his efforts were recognised. It boded well and gave him confidence he would be suitably rewarded. 'I wish to come home.' He hoped the words were enough and that they didn't ask him why now. The strain of the last few weeks left him drained. *I haven't run away*, he told himself. His stomach disagreed. He looked down, his palms were sweating.

Professor Li had been one of the many exchange students sent abroad. From time to time he had reasons to visit the Chinese Embassy in Washington. When he loaned objects from his ceramic collection to special cultural exhibitions or attended business delegations representing LCC's interests. These were the only contacts he had with his homeland. And because he never spoke about his early life, everyone soon assumed he was an American who had become a collector and fluent linguist. Surrounded by his luxuries and the sexual and personal freedoms of America, he'd found it easy to forget why he had been sent there. Bucephalus changed everything.

Chen Jia and Wen Zhimou had waited patiently, hoping one day one of their students would bring them something like Bucephalus; giving them a way to distract the tiger so they could correct a miscalculation on their part, arising from the one-child policy. Chen Jia and Wen Zhimou were concerned about the adverse social consequences and unrest that might arise when families preferred boys to girls. Their fears had materialised, there was an alarming imbalance that needed to be rectified.

In the silence Professor Li concentrated on his talisman, as if seeing it for the first time. He looked from his hand to the screen; such a small object. He now understood. He felt immensely proud. He was the thorn in the tiger's paw.

'We were pleased when you told us about Bucephalus.'

'It needs further work,' Professor Li said, anxious that he had spoken too quickly, too eagerly. He had grown accustomed to Finnegan's aggressive manner but these fragile men frightened him more. He wasn't sure why. Was it the location? He was far from home, where other people acted on his instructions, where he felt in control. Here he was insignificant; one man in a billion. He acknowledged too, he'd been away a long time and lost his ability to detect nuances and subtlety in conversations. He'd got used to high-intensity testosterone. He felt queasy and uncomfortable, aware of his balls tightening, knowing his homosexuality was not tolerated here. He wondered if he'd made a terrible mistake.

'You can make it work?' Chen Jia asked.

He breathed in slowly to suppress his nervousness. He should answer but his mouth was dry. He looked to his side, hoping to see a glass of water. There was nothing. Its absence suggesting it was deliberate, all part of the stage set surrounding him. Despite the location, he didn't feel he was an honoured guest.

'I cannot finish the work at LCC.' Had his words been too direct, too insistent? He tried to soften them by saying, 'The secret would come out,' giving them a sense of urgency and a reason to act in his interests – their interests. He assumed they wanted to launch their own version of the car and fuel, ahead of America or in direct competition. Or why else had they acted as they had done? *What will Finnegan do when he finds out?* He looked at their faces, hoping to read their intentions. He thought how much Bucephalus had cost him. It wasn't just Tomas. It was all the day-to-day pressures, constantly devising ways to lose it within other projects. It required an enormous amount of resilience and many hours of work. He had to be thorough, meticulously vigilant, looking over everyone's shoulder, careful that only he saw the bigger picture, afraid something would slip out, or he'd make a mistake and the edifice would come tumbling down. It had nearly happened. It was such a small thing; a spike Tomas called GG42/OO. He felt frightened, like a child waiting to be punished.

'If I have my own laboratory…' His words trailed off when he saw Wen Zhimou lean in to whisper to Chen Jia.

'Who else knows about it?' Chen Jia asked.

He didn't hesitate. 'Josie Ryland, she's living in Matsane. She was at Ham Farm.' The words out; he was relieved. She was no longer his problem.

A man came up to Wen Zhou, listened and left. Professor Li watched fascinated and horrified. Was it that easy? Had he just witnessed the power of these two men? It was a power not even Finnegan had at his disposal. He felt his stomach squeeze tighter.

Zhou had promised him; he would have his own laboratory. A niggling doubt rose up. *What if I fail? What if I cannot deliver it?* A drop of sweat began to trickle down his forehead. He quickly put his hand into his pocket to take out his silk handkerchief; in his haste the talisman tumbled out and onto the dark polished wooden floor. It was the first time he'd dropped it, and it felt like an omen; his good fortune slipping out of his grasp. He struggled awkwardly out of the chair, aware he looked ungainly. *I must appear foolish to them.*

'There is no reason to worry Professor Li. Whether you succeed or not, it does not matter. Bucephalus has given us the opportunity we needed.'

He was relieved but confused. Surely they realised the potential of Bucephalus. Yet they seemed unconcerned. He was at a loss. 'Will I have my own laboratory?' His voice sounded desperate.

Wen Zhou again spoke to his comrade. Chen Jia replied, 'A place where no one will find you. Is that what you want?'

Professor Li felt sick. This didn't sound like the prestigious appointment he'd hoped for. What had they planned for him? He imagined being sent to some distant province to work on his own; his work no longer useful to them. For the first time he wondered if Bucephalus had been worth it. He saw his apartment, his lifestyle and his position gone. *I've made a dreadful mistake.*

Chen Jia clapped his hands. The suddenness of the sound made him jump, imagining in his febrile brain the sound of a bullet. Unexpectedly six young, beautiful women came into the Pavilion. They were dressed as vividly as the song birds. They darted in and out and around the elderly men, each one vying to outshine the other, their lilting voices cooing in admiration. It was an exquisite performance. Professor Li was the only member in the audience. One by one they left the dais in a tumbling cascade reminding him of the birds on the vermillion screen; fortune and intelligence gone.

It was a message for him.

♦

Professor Li walked into the lobby of the Peninsula Hotel. He needed a drink. The rooftop terrace with its view of the city didn't appeal, despite the attraction of the night-time neon skyline. The air was heavy with grey-yellow smog. He chose instead one of the other bars. A sultry Eurasian chanteuse, with straight black hair, full red lips and thigh-high slit cheongsam was singing in a smoky voice, sat on the high stool by the piano. The songs were chosen to appeal to the international guests. He ordered a bottle of Margaux, letting it breathe as he surveyed the other guests. Solitary travellers like him sat in silence with their glass as a companion. Dotted around were couples who looked bored, only speaking occasionally before familiarity reduced them to silence. Large groups ignored the other guests, talking loudly and laughing; while waiters nimbly weaved between chairs carrying drinks. He noticed someone looking at him, a very attractive black man. He seemed familiar. He smiled back; it was a fleeting movement on his lips. He needed to be careful and discreet as always. His thoughts returned to his list of uncertainties. But swung back to the man looking at him; was he being followed? Unsettled by his audience in the Pavilion he couldn't focus. Where had he seen him before – or was he imagining it? He cleaned his glasses to get a better look. But his eyes were tired. Had he seen him in Africa or was it on the flight to China?

In the dimly lit atmosphere he thought of Finnegan and how he'd react to his betrayal, even though he'd given him the legacy he craved. He remembered Chen Jia's last words: "a place where no one will find you." He shivered. He rose from the chair unsteadily, his hand reaching out to grip the chair's arm, unconcerned if the other guests thought he was drunk. He straightened up feeling lightheaded and disconnected from his body. As if in a trance he walked over to where the young man was sat and dropped his talisman as he passed by. He didn't need it anymore. He had done what they wanted. Up in his room he rang for room service, ordering champagne and waited for the door to open. "One more pretty boy to fuck," he said, using her words not his. The door bell rang.

PART FOUR

ATTACKS ON US SOIL

CHAPTER 28

SUNSHINE CLEANING

'Mr President.' William shook his shoulder, 'Wake up Sir.'

'What time is it?'

'It's five-thirty Sir; you are needed in the Situation Room.'

The Sit Room is in the basement of the West Wing. From here the president and his advisers can run the country. It has satellite feeds coming in from across the world and secure communication links to NORAD. It's where the president makes secure phone calls to Heads of State.

His chief of staff walked in. 'Jim, what's going on?' Montgomery was out of bed and dressing hurriedly.

'We've got live action. Everyone is waiting for you.'

At the table already seated were Douglas Dennison, the vice-president; Andy Clarkson, Secretary of State; Jason Gillet, Secretary of Defence; the National Security Adviser, David Sharp; Ralf Sneider, Director of National Intelligence and CIA and Admiral John Curry, Chairman of the Joint Chiefs of Staff.

'Good morning gentlemen, what are we watching?'

♦

It was three o'clock in the afternoon. The Sunshine Cleaning van pulled up at the service entrance. 'You're late today.' The American guard looked into the van.

'Sorry boss.' Thabo smiled apologetically, peering through the open window at the man with the gun.

'Different vehicle I see.' The guard wrote down the number plate details. The barrier rose. 'I'll let housekeeping know you're on your way.'

The American Embassy on Pretorius Street was an undistinguished modern concrete and glass building. Its position on a slight rise gave it extra presence; the ten-foot-high security fencing equivalent to a moat. The service entrance was at the rear in the underground car park. It ran the length of the building. Around 800 people worked at the Embassy. Even before Feed Africa, America was South Africa's third-largest trading partner.

Thabo sat sweating; everything inside was sticky. He picked up the clipboard looking for the paperwork for this delivery, accidentally ripping it in half. Today was not going well. He'd been late getting to the depot to collect his bakkie. The white boss refused to believe him when he said the bus had broken down, docking his pay instead. How would he tell Judith, his daughter, she couldn't have a new school uniform?

He'd gone to start loading his usual bakkie when he discovered it hadn't come back from the garage. He swore.

He was going to be in very big trouble now; afraid any excuse and his boss would fire him.

'Thabo take mine,' Junior threw him the keys. Junior nodded his head in the direction of the boss, gesturing crudely with his hand. In a loud voice he said, 'Thinks he's a big man.' Junior grabbed his manhood provocatively. Sat watching Junior were a group of young girls on their break. They were whispering to each other before one of them cried out indignantly, and they all started laughing. Junior sauntered over to the girls, fooling around – showing off his dance moves; trying to get one of them to come for a ride.

The Afrikaner boss stood by the open door and shouted *'Voetsek kaffir'* angrily at Junior.

Junior grabbed his balls again, a broad grin on his face. 'Yes boss.'

'Get back to work,' the boss yelled at the girls, 'or I'll fire you too!'

Junior scooped up his jacket nonchalantly and sauntered off towards Sunshine Cleaning's automatic gates and his shiny new black BMW car.

The boss man glared at Thabo, 'You still here?'

Thabo hurriedly climbed into the driver's seat. It was hard to keep a job. Someone else would always do it for less money.

He parked up in the Embassy's car park and jumped out; going round to the back he lowered the tailgate. The Embassy's metal cart was at the far end, stacked with linen wrapped in brown paper parcels. He unhooked the cart from the floor to push it forward. Suddenly the bakkie exploded. Thabo's body vaporised. The boom, shockingly loud, created a deep chasm, scattering tiny twisted metal fragments; clues to be later collected and analysed.

The explosion triggered a secondary reaction, igniting the fuel tanks of parked cars as one after the other, the devastation rolled like thunder along the length of the building. The shock waves ruptured the structure's internal strength as it buckled from the upward force; deforming the reinforcing rods in the concrete pillars and bringing down the building.

People died surprised; blown apart like sacks of watermelons. The rubble covered in scattered chunks of red and fatty flesh and dismembered body parts. It would be up to specialist police officers to begin collecting these pieces; trying to find enough so families had at least parts of a body to bury. Others were trapped, calling out – hoping someone would hear. Rescue dogs searched for the living and the dead.

The survivors wandered around, confused and numb. Their silence now a cacophony of alarm bells, sirens and screams. People in the park across the street rushed away from the sound or stood frozen, unable to comprehend what was happening. Outside on the road, cars screeched to a halt crashing into each other, adding to the chaos. Drivers abandoned their vehicles, leaving car doors open as they fled, and making Pretorius Street look like a billiard table after the opening break. Miles away people stopped and looked up as the dust plume filled the cloudless blue sky.

The president sat horrified watching the screens; video feeds, mobile camera footage and reports coming in from TV crews on the ground. 'What the hell just happened?' he asked, hoping for answers. 'Do we have any numbers on the casualties?' He was aware of peripheral people talking into phones. Everyone was mesmerised by the real time satellite images. 'Jesus Christ, who saw this coming?' He felt his stomach tighten.

Ralf Sneider spoke first, 'We don't know how many yet, but it's not looking good. There were three hundred and ten Americans at our Embassy in Pretoria.'

The Secretary of State stared at Sneider. 'Should we raise the threat level at our other Embassies?'

Montgomery pre-empted Sneider's reply, 'I'd hope we'd done that by now.' He turned away from the mesmerising images on the screens. 'Give me your ideas.' As Commander-in-Chief he had one role to perform inside the Sit Room; defending America's interests, but he had another as spokesperson for the American people. He needed Vernon (his speech writer) to find the right words. He had to look as if he was in control. His felt his hand start to shake. He glanced down at it trembling. Immediately he hid it under the table. 'I need answers and quickly.'

Sneider spoke again, 'This is regarded as a safe, friendly nation. We don't have listening stations in the country.' He looked around the room. 'We have been monitoring a rise in chatter coming out from other parts of Africa; but as yet no one has claimed responsibility.' He turned to face the president. 'Sir, we're watching this live.' He broke eye contact. 'I'm sorry, but we don't have anything useful to add at this juncture.'

'We're not leaving here, until you tell me why after all my support with Feed Africa, Africans would want to blow up our Embassy. It makes no sense.' He felt his ulcer grumble. 'Get Elizabeth in here.'

Admiral Curry spoke next, 'Sir, there is something else you need to know.' Everyone turned towards him. 'We have been monitoring increased activity on the Chinese and Vietnam borders.'

The president stared at him, his right eyebrow raised, before standing up. He waved his arms at the screens like a man high on drugs at a rock concert. 'I hope you're not suggesting they're linked, and this,' he said pointing at the images coming from Pretoria, 'is just the warm-up act?'

The room felt chillier. Elizabeth came in. POTUS whispered something to her. He sat down. 'Gentlemen, I think we need to focus.' He began allocating roles, 'Ralf, I want you to stay on the Pretoria incident. Jason as Secretary of Defence and Admiral Curry take a look at China, and Ralf make sure you have someone sit in – who understands the region.' He looked at Douglas Dennison. 'I want you to chair the meeting, remember I want a considered response.' He gave him a hard stare. 'I'll speak to President Abyoie. Andy, as Secretary of State, sound out our allies. Finally David, you and Jim handle the media and foreign press.' He looked at his chief of staff. 'Jim, I need a statement expressing our condolences to the families who've suffered a loss, etc. Ask Vernon, he'll know the form. We reconvene in sixty minutes.'

He grabbed Douglas Dennison's arm as he passed him. 'None of your "send in the boys," China is important to this administration. I don't want us ruffling their feathers, if all they are doing is playing springtime war games with each other. We've got enough on our hands.' He stared at him, seeking confirmation he'd understood. Montgomery didn't like Dennison; his mother had picked him as his running mate.

It was going to be a long day and with the extra pounds he'd put on, his trousers felt too tight to be comfortable.

He'd have a word with William. In front of the cameras, his appearance needed to convey strength whilst looking sombre. The shirt and tie had to be right. It was the sort of thing his mother usually sorted out. But since the incident at Shindwalla she'd taken herself off. It flooded back, *Jesus Christ I've got a daughter!* He was surprised how many times during the day he thought of her. He remembered how much she looked like him. It unnerved him. She was like an earworm, constantly in the background. *It's all I need right now; a bastard being paraded in front of the TV cameras.* Just for a moment, he wondered if he'd said the words out loud. He quickly glanced around. No one was looking at him. He had to be more careful. It wouldn't do for the secret to come out, not until he knew what he was going to do about her. His anger at his mother's actions twisted his stomach. He needed to forget about both of them and concentrate. He must talk with President Abyoie – find out what he knew. Right now he needed to be the president, not someone's papa. Feed Africa made him feel differently about himself. It created a sense of paternal responsibility. Individuals looked up to him, grateful for his initiative; if not quite a hero, certainly the statesman he longed to be. He'd given ordinary Americans pride in what America stood for, only to have this morning's images shatter his newly-found confidence.

At 7.05 they reconvened. He started, 'I've just taken a phone call from Andy Malone, owner of AMOIL. He's pretty upset. He's lost ten fuel tankers in the last fortnight. Is this connected to this morning's bombing?' He looked at his Director of National Intelligence.

Sneider leant back to say something to the aide behind him. The aide got up and left. 'The attacks are coming from groups of young people, mostly teenagers. They've arrested several dozen. It appears they are being paid to cause trouble.'

Montgomery repeated Sneider's word "paid" his intonation rising, 'Who by and more to the point – why?'

Sneider didn't answer the question but added, 'You can reassure Andy Malone the South African government is taking the problem very seriously. They've deployed army units to key Feed Africa sites and AMOIL petrol stations.' He looked up at the president. 'The police are now instigating a "shoot to kill" policy against the mobs attacking AMOIL.'

'Jesus Christ, that's the last thing I need on prime time TV, more black teenagers being shot.' He looked round the room. 'Let's get a grip and not panic.' His words sounded like they were said for his benefit as much as for the others in the room, 'I'll remind President Abyoie we need to take a more measured response. Malone can easily afford to lose the odd tanker.'

The aide came back and passed over a note. Sneider skimmed the sheet. 'Mr President, good news; the South Africans have intelligence on this morning's bomber. The police in Pretoria say they have checked CCTV. Just before the bomb went off a delivery vehicle arrived. Our guard noted its registration number. Officers are on their way to the company and will be interviewing the staff. They think this is how the bomb was delivered.'

'At last!' He relaxed. His pills were working too. 'Ralf, is the FBI on its way out there? American citizens died.'

'Yes sir, as we speak. I've sent Paul Barr.'

'Then I also want you to take a look at the AMOIL situation. This is a major American company. I want your FBI agents to investigate it and the bombing. I want to know what's going on and quickly.' Next he turned his attention to the Chinese.

Douglas Dennison picked up one of the handsets. 'You'll want to see this.'

The satellite image zoomed down. It showed lines of armoured tanks and army trucks in convoy. The picture changed. This time it showed an airfield, two lines of fighter aircraft and tugs towing others into position.

'What the hell is this?' the president asked.

Everyone focussed their attention on the high resolution images. Douglas Dennison pushed the handset button again. This time the screen was filled with the face of a female Chinese news reporter. In the background it showed an honour guard, an aircraft landing, a man stepping out and waving, as the Chinese Premier stepped forward to greet him.

'Is that—?'

Dennison interrupted, 'Yes it's Trurong An, Vietnam's head of state, I met him at the ASEAN conference.'

Tetchily POTUS looked at the vice-president. 'Is this painting by numbers? I get it, a state visit followed by a show of military co-operation. Admiral Curry said they were carrying out joint military manoeuvres, so what's your point?'

He noticed the other Joint Chiefs of Staff had joined the meeting. Army General Jones addressed the room, 'Gentlemen, we believe the invitation to "play war games" in Vietnam,' he stressed the words, 'has more to do with China's expansionist desires in the region, than this friendly co-operation portrayed by the state's media. Put crudely, we believe China is planning to turn an independent country into a vassal state.'

‘That’s a pretty big assumption. I hope you can back it up.’

The vice-president added, ‘Tensions are rising in the region. I’ve spoken in private to a couple of my friends who are members of ASEAN.’

The Secretary of State bridled; spheres of influence, demarcation lines and toes were metaphorically being stepped on. Dennison continued, ignoring anything Andy Clarkson might have to say. ‘They view China’s actions as a violation of their mutual aid declaration. And given China is now a member,’ he looked at everyone individually, ‘I think we need to be greatly concerned.’

Smug bastard! He’s implying his tank manoeuvres trump my bombing. It felt like a direct attempt to undermine his authority. In his mind Douglas Dennison had overstepped the mark; he needed to remind him who the president was. He felt the weight of expectation in the room. Montgomery took his time; he let the minutes tick by before he posed a question, ‘Is this,’ he nodded towards the screens, ‘nothing more than a PR message, China reminding us it has muscle?’

‘And how do we respond?’ the uniformed men asked almost in unison.

He was looking not at them but at Douglas Dennison. ‘We need to send back a strong message of our own, but one that doesn’t escalate the situation further. Tell your ASEAN friends, America is ready to stand by them. Admiral Curry, send one of our *Nimitz*-class aircraft carriers on a goodwill visit.’ A gentle sound of approval echoed round the room. ‘For the time being I think we need to focus our attention on whomever it was that killed Americans and destroyed our Embassy, and not worry about being the world’s policeman.’

He had reminded his cabinet he was still in charge. The FBI would be on the ground in Africa carrying out their investigation, and the United States had sent a clear but measured response back to China. Perhaps now he could relax for a moment. He'd speak to the nation later. Before that he rang Andy Malone.

'Andy, rest assured President Abyoie and I agree it's a bit like the frontier towns in the Old West. You just need to show them the strong arm of the law and let things settle down. I've asked the FBI to follow up any leads and find out what's going on.'

His day ended with him feeling like Slow-Hand Joe was back in the saddle riding high. *I've got a daughter.* There it was again. How the hell was the hero expected to ride into the closing credits with that back story unresolved? It was unsettling. His ulcer agreed with him.

CHAPTER 29
MOVING FORWARD

The White House and government agencies were all focussed on one objective: how to explain the attack. The media were told it was too soon to speculate on who was behind it. But in order to fill the news channels, experts and politicians, retired military men and university professors were asked for their opinions. There was no consensus. It was either the actions of a lone bomber with a grievance or some dissident faction targeting American interests. There was a long list to draw from.

It was 8am on Tuesday morning. Ralf Sneider sat waiting for the president, alongside him Paul Barr from the FBI. They made small talk but without much enthusiasm.

The president came in looking haggard. 'I assume by your expression and timing, this is more bad news.'

Sneider spoke first, 'We've had a breakthrough. We thought you needed to know before we went any further.'

The FBI man added, 'As you know we sent one of our teams to Africa to investigate. We recovered fragments from the bomb and found traces of military-grade explosive.' He looked at the president. 'The chemical signature matches that used by the Chinese military.'

'Are you certain?' Montgomery said, shocked.

Sneider answered, 'Metaphorically, their fingerprints are all over it.'

Barr opened his file. 'We found something else. As you know the agitators targeting AMOIL's tankers are being paid to cause trouble. We were following up on the physical evidence, mobile phones and shop receipts. Before our teams arrived on the scene, the local police had interviewed several of the troublemakers.' He stopped before adding, 'We'd advise you not to ask President Abyoie about their methods.'

There was a long pause. 'Are you saying they tortured them?' It was a question neither man answered. 'The last thing I need right now is some inquisitive journalist out to make their reputation with a Pulitzer Prize.'

'Rest assured our hands are clean, sir.' Sneider looked at the president.

'I hope so.' He rose and walked towards the window. He thought about his daughter, how long before a journalist discovered her? He turned and sat down again. 'So what leads do you have?'

'That's what's so unusual. They made it easy for us to find out,' Barr said.

'Who the hell are *they*?' he asked, annoyed by their apparent reluctance to explain.

'The Chinese sir, we can link both incidents back to them.' Sneider looked grim.

'Jesus Christ, why the hell would they want to do that?'

'We're not sure,' Sneider replied, 'but we thought you needed to know as soon as possible.' He waited. 'How do you want us to proceed?'

He now understood why they had come to him. A foreign government actively supporting violence against another, it went beyond a diplomatic row. It could so easily escalate. He was afraid of war; it required a strength he knew he didn't have. His mother had emasculated him. She was the one with the balls in his family.

Montgomery had other problems; this was his second term. He felt the jackals circling. It was always the same, no sooner had you been sworn in than the manoeuvring began, as politicians started vying for position in the nomination game ahead. Friends became less honest as they looked to align themselves, assuming they were re-elected, with the candidate they thought most likely to succeed, leaving the president alone and isolated. It was like the children's game of musical chairs; no one wanted to be left standing and without a job in the next administration. He was all too aware Douglas Dennison was looking for any opportunity to raise his profile. This wasn't going to be one of them. 'Sit on the report for a while.'

♦

The president invited Ambassador Zhou to the White House. After the usual formalities the two men sat down; unusually the president had insisted it was a private meeting with none of their advisers present. He needed Zhou to feel he could speak more freely.

'My administration is concerned China is behind the increasing anti American actions in Africa.' He'd gone straight in, wanting to see how Zhou would respond.

Zhou took a moment, as if surprised by the frankness of his opening remarks. 'Our partners in Africa mistrust America's motives.'

That's rich, Montgomery thought. 'America believes in the right to self-determination, economic free trade and building mutually supportive alliances.' It sounded trite but he wasn't about to have Zhou lecture him on foreign policy.

'We have built roads, railways and other important infrastructure. While you send them goods you cannot sell elsewhere.' Zhou didn't actually use the words GMO, but they both knew what he was referring to.

Zhou's words were surprisingly provocative. He needed to lower the temperature and keep the discussions focussed. He tried again, 'We're not here to scrap over the continent like the old colonial powers.' He forced a thin smile. 'We are here to find a way to defuse the situation we both find ourselves in.'

Zhou looked on without comment, giving nothing away by his demeanour. Montgomery wondered if Ambassador Zhou was the right person to be talking to; but anyone higher up the food chain would have raised questions from people like Douglas Dennison and the Secretary of State Andy Clarkson, who'd have insisted on being present. He wanted to handle this on his own. 'My understanding of the situation is this. You think we have stepped on your toes in Africa, whereas Feed Africa has no other agenda other than a humanitarian one. It's not about building a power base out there. Yet we have evidence you are behind the recent attacks on an American company.'

Zhou considered the accusation. 'Young people have nothing to lose and unfortunately it sometimes leads to violence.' He began listing possible causes, 'Corporate America taking over, ignoring native traditions, gang rivalry, and local grievances.' He paused. 'Change is too fast – too slow, everything and anything is possible.' Zhou looked at him, the slightest of smiles on his otherwise neutral face. 'If you had children, you'd know they become headstrong teenagers.'

Montgomery tried to ignore the remark, whilst inwardly regretting he'd not seen his daughter grow up. Instead he said, 'You left a trail we could find.'

Zhou shrugged. 'How our aid is spent is not under our control.'

'But why target AMOIL?' the president asked.

'Focus on AMOIL, not on a few phones.'

The president was surprised by the directness of the ambassador's words. Perhaps he was being offered something. 'If we accept the mob's violence is linked to say, some local frustrations – will it now disappear?' His right eyebrow rose.

The ambassador nodded.

'Good, but the bombing of our Embassy is a different matter. It is an act of aggression we cannot ignore; they will want someone to blame.' He didn't clarify who "they" might be, but the hawks in his administration and the media wanted action and answers.

'My government will deny any involvement.' Zhou remained impassive. His candour of a moment ago gone.

It was time for the president to remind Zhou who had the bigger dick in the room. 'If we publish our findings, our partners will arrive at the same conclusion as we did; China had a hand in the attack on the United States.'

'Explosives are sadly readily available internationally, even ours, and the first point of sale might not be the end user.'

The president knew China would deny any knowledge. But he needed something. 'You'd risk our trade agreement?'

Zhou looked at him, surprised. 'You are not happy with Finnegan's deal?'

Montgomery didn't say anything. He didn't know the specifics. But he sensed Finnegan had set him up. Whatever it was, the politician in him knew it wouldn't be good news. It felt like Zhou and Finnegan had their hands on his balls. He needed something. 'There must be a way forward.'

Zhou took his time. 'There is always a scapegoat.' He waited. 'I expect you'll find it will be a labyrinthine trail of money, sadly ending up in untraceable accounts.'

Montgomery felt uneasy. Zhou was dictating terms, telling him to cover it up. The ambassador carried on speaking, 'China considers the deployment of the warship *Nimitz* in our region as an act of aggression.'

'You'd bombed our Embassy. What did you expect?' He knew Dennison and the others wanted stronger action, arguing the United States had a duty to protect its assets and react forcibly. He breathed deeply. He favoured a more considered approach. He tried again to be reasonable, leave the door open to diplomacy. 'If we withdraw our warship, what will you offer in return?'

'We can move forward.'

'Meaning what exactly?' The president needed it to be clear.

Zhou kept his gaze steady. 'Let us concentrate on the economic benefits of our trade agreements,' before adding in a low confidential whisper, 'you have done well out of our partnership with LCC.'

Montgomery sat upright, fully aware their conversation was being taped. He had to stop Zhou from saying anything more about the arrangement in case it incriminated him. He felt uncomfortable in his own office. Dennison was constantly asking about the funding of Feed Africa. He needed to be careful. He didn't want the deal with Finnegan to come out. It would lead to some very awkward questions. Besides, Feed Africa brought him kudos on the world stage. He wanted it to continue.

He felt the bile rise, burning its way into his mouth. He reached for the water carafe and poured himself a glass. He drank, coughing as he did so. His throat eased. He believed "humanitarian" was a more powerful sobriquet than "warmonger". *Let China strong-arm its way into Vietnam*, he thought. People remembered the last time the United States had gone into Southeast Asia. He knew there'd be no American appetite for another intervention. In a strong loud voice he said, 'I take it we are agreed. This has been an unfortunate misunderstanding.'

Ambassador Zhou nodded.

He rose, indicating their meeting was over.

By the door Zhou leaned in very close as they shook hands, so that only he heard the words, 'We all want to see our sons and daughters grow up safe and happy.'

Montgomery looked back at him open-mouthed, afraid as another wave of bile rushed up his throat.

♦

After the bombing in Pretoria and the last of the funerals back in the States, he made a promise to the nation in his State of the Union address, 'To rebuild America's commitment to Africa and not let a few disgruntled dissidents disrupt the progress of Feed Africa.'

Privately he told Sneider and Barr to keep looking. Zhou had indicated there was more to find out. He wanted to know what it might be before he spoke to Finnegan and Malone.

♦

The number of incidents in southern Africa appeared to reduce. Sneider and Barr reported they'd identified a young African, but he'd been shot. They'd found traces of the explosive in his black BMW. They had no other leads.

Yet it still seemed he spent more time in the Sit Room than in the Oval Office. It felt like the White House was under siege; normal business pushed to one side.

Admiral Curry pointed to the monitors. 'They are building military outposts and satellite stations on any tiny rock, claiming it as part of their legitimate territory. It's all part of this expansionist agenda.' A number of heads nodded. 'It's bully-boy tactics. We need to remind them the Pacific is our backyard, not theirs.' The order to have the *Nimitz* return to base still rankled with him and the other hawks.

Douglas Dennison agreed, 'ASEAN is worried. They don't want to get swallowed up by China.' His comment suggested the president's decision had been premature and ill considered.

'Is there any likelihood of that happening?' the president said, exasperated. He needed to keep everyone on board and make sure they didn't agree to a course of action that would upset the understanding he and Zhou had arrived at.

'We need to show them America is a world power,' the Secretary of Defence said, aligning himself with the vice-president.

It made Montgomery nervous, watching their manoeuvrings. Dennison was building a consensus around him, favouring his position. 'Where are we exactly with the situation in Vietnam?' he asked.

The Secretary of Defence spoke first, 'The Vietnam regime is only nominally in control. The Chinese have stationed soldiers at all the key installations: power, water, transport and they have control over the media.'

Was he hearing this correctly? He felt uneasy. Perhaps he hadn't been as clever as he thought; the familiar pain making him wince.

'Our satellite surveillance shows a build-up of troops along the Cambodian and Laos borders. It looks like a similar manoeuvre.'

Montgomery felt every one of his fifty-six years. He hated to admit it, but perhaps Dennison and the others had a point. This was more than posturing; it looked like a planned campaign. He took in each man in turn. 'I don't hear anyone telling me – why they are doing this? He directed his remarks to Dennison, 'As I see it, if we'd left our *Nimitz* out there, it would have been exposed and we'd have risked looking impotent.' He raised his voice, 'I'm not prepared to send the Pacific fleet in to defend some rocky outcrop.' He stared at the men wearing braid. 'Let me be clear, no one is to fire a missile, not even a fourth of July rocket on my watch.' He had their attention. 'We are not going into Vietnam, or any other damn country, only to get our arses kicked out again.'

There was silence.

'Gentlemen, let's see if we can get through the next twenty-four hours without there being another crisis.'

He pulled Dennison aside. 'Ask your buddies in ASEAN to raise it with the United Nations.' At least then Zhou couldn't blame him for sabre rattling. Calls for action would come from others. He could continue to act as the statesman. *He wanted her to be proud of him.*

CHAPTER 30

'YOU'RE FIRED!'

'When is Dr Wedderburn going to see Martha Lintel Montgomery?' Kate asked.

Josie avoided answering Kate. They both knew once Dr Wedderburn went their situation would be even more critical. But Kate had to see Dr Wedderburn before he left for America. She wasn't convinced he'd make the case for Matsane, whatever Josie might say. She thought it more likely he'd further his own career. She was also worried he'd tell Martha about TJ. Kate was afraid of losing her grandson and Josie; lured away by what Martha Lintel Montgomery might offer them.

Both women were anxious. Josie because she wasn't ready to confront Finnegan and was unsure of her father's involvement; Kate terrified Martha would stop their funding completely and her life's work would be over. She hated to admit it but she didn't know how much longer she could continue. The long hours and the unremitting deluge were overwhelming her. She still hadn't fully recovered. But she had no choice. Kate asked Josie to drive her into the hospital in the Land Cruiser.

She walked in, stopping every few feet to say hello to staff and patients, reassuring them she'd be back soon. Her office door opened and a smartly-dressed woman in her thirties appeared; fair shoulder-length hair and made up like a sales assistant at a cosmetic counter. She was carrying a hefty medical briefcase. Kate smelt her perfume. It wasn't a smell she associated with the hospital.

'I'll see you next month.' She smiled at Dr Wedderburn, shaking his hand.

Kate saw him hold on to her hand for a fraction longer than was necessary. He must have caught sight of Kate approaching because he immediately dropped it.

'Who's this?' Kate asked.

'This is Elaine Wagner. She works for Carlyle, the American pharmaceutical company.'

The woman's smile was wide. She had perfect teeth. She seemed over eager. 'I'm hoping Dr Wedderburn will try our new Aids drug. We are very excited by its potential.'

'Really, and do you have other samples for us?' Kate could feel her pulse quickening.

'Why yes, Carlyle's a keen supporter of Feed Africa. We have several new products we think you'll be interested in. They are—' she bent down to open her bag.

Kate stopped her. 'And you want us to be your guinea pigs.'

Elaine Wagner stood upright, her smile fading.

Kate gave her no time to deny it. 'I'm sure, if they are as good as you hope Carlyle will retail them at prices we cannot afford,' her ire rising, 'and whoosh, all the free samples will disappear.' Elaine Wagner looked uncomfortable. 'And if they don't work? Well – we will have saved your company millions.'

Dr Wedderburn stepped in between the two women. He propelled Ms Wagner along the corridor, his hand in the small of her back.

Kate walked through into her office. She sat down, feeling drained. 'How long has this being going on?'

'I don't see a problem.' Dr Wedderburn stood in front of the desk. 'We struggle to get drugs and if they want to hand them out for free; I'm sure they don't care.' He half turned and gestured towards the wards.

'They're our patients, not lab monkeys.' She stared at him. 'You've never liked working here.'

Dr Wedderburn was on the verge of retaliating but stopped as the door opened.

'Dr Kate, you're back!' Dr Mokaba stood in the doorway beaming. He must have sensed the tension in the room because he began to retreat, pulling the door closed behind him.

'No, wait,' Kate called out. She turned to face Dr Wedderburn. 'You're fired.'

Dr Wedderburn looked at Dr Mokaba then Kate. 'You think this native can run your precious hospital well let him try, and see what happens.' Stony-faced, he collected his framed diploma from the wall. He looked down at Kate. 'Does Martha Lintel Montgomery know about the little black bastard?'

Kate rose from the chair. 'GET OUT.'

Josie arrived as Dr Wedderburn pushed past her and strode down the corridor, navigating his way through the interested onlookers. The drama over they slowly dispersed, everyone keen to spread the news.

'We have to speak to Martha Lintel Montgomery before he does.' Kate looked up at Josie. She knew how much she depended on her now; all too aware that once again her temper and outburst had got them into this precarious position.

♦

Driving them home, Josie was concentrating on what to do next. She barely registered the number of people milling around beside the road. Subconsciously she slowed down, almost to a stop, instinctively glancing down at the new gun sticking out of her open handbag. Suddenly an amorphous mass blocked the light. Youths surrounded the 4x4 banging on it, their fists thundering down and shouting; the sound worse than any hailstorm she'd experienced. It filled the vehicle. The low boom resonated in the pit of her stomach, her heart pounding faster.

'What the hell is happening?'

'Josie – just keep driving,' Kate screamed at her.

The low thud of beating fists changed to the sharper tinnier sound of rocks hammering against the metal body of the car. The front windscreen cracked like forked lightning, turning the glass opaque. Both women cried out. Josie's head spun to her right, aware of someone attacking her driver's window. For a moment she froze, mesmerized by the repeated blows; as if it was happening to someone else and all in slow motion.

'Josie what are you doing?'

Her mother's voice broke her inertia. She reached for

the gun and fired it above her head, hoping no one was on the roof of the vehicle. The gunshot deafened them. It had the desired effect. The mob pulled back momentarily. Josie floored the accelerator pedal. The vehicle leapt forward. She heard the thud of rolling bodies and felt the forks rise and fall as they drove over one of the attackers.

Kate shouted at her, 'Don't stop.'

She looked at her mother. She was white. Josie knew she had no choice. Someone in the mob might have a gun. They'd certainly have machetes.

Clear of the rabble, she slowed the vehicle as her heart's rhythm tried to return to normal. She could barely see through her windscreen. She pulled up and got out emptying her stomach, leaving traces of vomit in her hair. She grabbed it and pulled it back with one hand, before another bout of retching. She immediately thought of TJ. Thank God he wasn't in the car with her.

'Mom, are you okay?'

Kate was out of the car and shaking. 'I thought we were going to die.'

Josie found a rock and hit the windscreen, creating a hole to see through, sweeping the shards off the seat. Both women got back in.

'I could do with a drink,' Kate said.

On the way back to Tugela Josie tried to understand what had just happened. Was it a deliberate attack aimed at her? She couldn't decide. But her heart and mind focussed on one outcome. She was going to destroy Finnegan, and her father – if he was involved. Bucephalus would be their nemesis.

♦

Kate looked through Josie's paperwork. As a doctor she knew the ramifications of Bucephalus were devastating. They had raw data but it needed a professional team to make the case. It wasn't something she could do. 'If Finnegan goes ahead with it, you can tell them about the fuel.'

Josie snorted in disgust. 'Annie and I talked about this. The financial potential is huge; it's an opportunity, someone else will risk it.'

'But it's too dangerous.'

'They'll deny it just like Finnegan will, besides who will believe me? I need a plan.' How many times had a whistle blower been believed? Josie remembered what Tomas had told her, everyone would blame the scientist who'd discovered it. No one would know or care about his sacrifice. She wanted Finnegan to face the consequences; feel her pain and horror at what he'd sanctioned.

Of course there was another scenario. What if Bucephalus was launched and eventually Finnegan's competitors came up with a different/better solution like hydrogen cells? Would Bucephalus have been worth it – if it helped to avert the consequences of climate change? Was it a price worth paying? Out loud she said to Kate, 'Some zealots might even welcome Bucephalus, saying it's all part of God's plan to reduce the population, before we run out of land, food and water.'

'You don't seriously believe that, do you?'

Josie sat with her head in her hands. 'Mom, I don't know how to stop Finnegan.'

Kate looked at her daughter. 'Do you want TJ growing up knowing you could have done something to stop it, but didn't?'

'That's grossly unfair.'

'I face the same dilemma each day. What can I do to stop HIV and Aids? Nothing, but I treat each person one by one; hoping someone else is looking for an answer that will help me and them. It's the same for you. What would Tomas want you to do?' Kate asked.

Josie hesitated. 'Not abandon TJ. I wish Johannes was here. He'd tell me a story, and it would be obvious what I should do.'

'You know what to do.' Kate said it quietly, her voice full of certainty.

Josie looked at her mother. 'I suppose I'll have to accept, I am the dung beetle after all; and I so wanted to be the lioness.'

Kate laughed. 'Just remember, you're strong, determined, with a sense of purpose and can overcome any obstacle put in your way.'

'While you just roar at people, scaring the hell out of them; Martha Lintel Montgomery won't stand a chance if she comes out here.'

'So you think we should invite her out here?' Kate asked.

'Yes, before Dr Wedderburn does his worst.'

CHAPTER 31
MARTHA

'I'd better apologise to Martha Lintel Montgomery.' Kate hated the thought of it.

'You don't have a choice. Now that you've fired Dr Wedderburn, and you're still not well enough to return full time; simply replacing him isn't going to be enough.'

Kate looked at her daughter. 'Dr Holloway rang me.'

Josie smiled at the mention of his name. 'I need to apologise to him too for leading him on and stealing the information. What did he want?'

'Isaac won't be going to school for a while.' Kate took a deep breath. 'He's confirmed it. He has leukaemia.'

Josie cried out, shaking her head in disbelief.

'More and more of the samples we send over show abnormal cell structure. He called in a pathologist from Joburg, just before LCC fired him. The numbers were frightening. He'd never seen anything like it before.'

'Can you treat him here?'

Kate looked at Josie. 'Cancer requires specialist equipment, trained staff and more space than we've got.'

'He has to go to Joburg,' Kate added, 'but the others won't be able to afford treatment. What will happen to them?'

'Finnegan ought to fund it. He's the one who caused it.' Josie said, tears in her eyes, 'I thought we were safe out here, away from the worst of the traffic. What if TJ is affected? I couldn't bear it.' She began to cry.

Kate got up to put her arm around her daughter, aware of the fear in the pit of her own stomach. 'We need Martha Lintel Montgomery and the president on our side.' Kate refused to call him Josie's father. 'He's the only person powerful enough to defeat Finnegan.'

♦

The number of holidaymakers flying into Matsane to view wildlife decreased; once attracted by the smaller intimate private game parks, these were now struggling. In the past they prided themselves on herds of twenty or thirty antelope, now it was down to groups of four to six. The eco system was changing and rapidly; affected by something unseen and deadly.

The charm of Matsane had disappeared under the boom and blandness of more shopping malls, franchised diners, AMOIL petrol stations and Feed Africa warehouses. Patrol cars were replaced by armoured vehicles; one permanently at the township crossroads. A new township had gone up for the construction workers. These modest cream-coloured houses stretched row upon row, blighted by the rubbish, standing water pipes and trailing power wires. The old ways of guns, gangs and dagga flourished. People died. This was Africa, what did people expect.

♦

The black bullet-proof limousine and accompanying vehicle stood out as it sped along the road. The driver wanted to get clear of the town and into the countryside as quickly as possible. A few curious people looked up, but most were by now blasé to the arrival of another dignitary.

Approaching Tugela the limousine slowed down, cautiously negotiating the boulder-strewn road. As it came to a halt four secret service agents jumped out, one opening the door for Martha Lintel Montgomery. She stepped out; her eyes hidden behind huge sunglasses, her hair held in place by a Hermes scarf. Christina Fairfield walked round to stand one pace behind her. The president's mother walked towards the welcoming party lined up to greet her. Mary and Winnie curtseyed, Moses and Brown stood in a line in their white freshly-ironed school uniforms. Precious was hiding behind Winnie. Kate took her hand and bent down to whisper in her ear. Precious came round and thrust out a roughly tied bunch of Tugela flowers. The president's mother took it and with the briefest flash of a smile, passed it back to her assistant.

'Thank you Precious,' Kate said pointedly, 'I thought we could sit on the stoep.' Kate looked at the men in suits, their bulky bodies more like comic book heroes than the gaunt ones she was used to. 'I think we are safe here.' The men moved off.

Martha Lintel Montgomery sat down. 'I thought you were having a lot of trouble out here.' She looked around. There was an awkward silence.

Kate heard the criticism. She couldn't help herself. 'No worse than the rioting America is experiencing. Your son seems unable to stop it from spreading.'

Martha Lintel Montgomery's neck coloured.

Kate reminded herself of what Josie had said, "Don't scare her off like the last time." Kate apologised, 'I'm too used to speaking my mind,' then ruefully added, 'you're right, I would never have fitted in.'

Christina Fairfield got up to help Mary as she came out carrying in the tea tray. Mary ignored her. Christina turned to Martha Lintel Montgomery, 'I'll have mine with the others,' and followed Mary out.

'I understand the hospital has lost more doctors.' Her tone loaded with disapproval, somehow implying Kate was negligent.

Kate forced herself not to react. 'That's not why I invited you out here.' Kate didn't want her to think it was just a matter of a salary or two. 'There's another more serious reason.' She wondered what words to use. 'We're facing a catastrophe.' Kate watched, hoping for a curious even positive reaction. After all, she had flown out here.

Martha Lintel Montgomery sipped her tea, before setting it down and taking off her sunglasses. Her stare was intense. Her eyebrow went up reminding Kate she was Josie's grandmother. Her face showed an exasperated expression, making Kate feel like she was an annoying child seeking attention. Kate felt her temper rise quickly. She took a deep breath, which turned into a rattling painful cough.

Martha Lintel Montgomery looked on unconcerned; as if it was part of a performance, put on to elicit her sympathy. She replaced her sunglasses.

'I battle on a daily basis with HIV and Aids, TB and now sleeping sickness,' Kate gathered herself. 'Sleeping sickness has pushed our ability to respond over the edge. Yes, we need more doctors, nurses, space and medicines.'

'I hardly think describing sleeping sickness as a catastrophe is justified. This is Africa, it's hardly unexpected.'

'That's not the only catastrophe I want to tell you about.' She was fighting hard not to shout at the woman opposite, 'I realise you might not believe me, that's why I've invited Dr Holloway and Coetzer our chief vet to meet you.'

'Do they want money as well?'

Kate rose out of her chair, on the point of throwing her guest out.

Imperiously Martha Lintel Montgomery called out, 'Christina, this was not part of my itinerary,' her head turning, expecting her PA to arrive immediately and explain.

Kate's tone made her turn back. 'The little girl who gave you the flowers, she has Non Hodgkin's lymphoma. It's not a problem I've seen before in Matsane. One or two cases maybe, but I've been here over thirty years; we are seeing more people each day with blood-related problems, and most of those are related to cancer. Her oldest brother needs to go to Joburg for specialist treatment.'

Martha Lintel Montgomery said nothing.

She's a hard bitch, Kate thought. *How the hell are we going to get through to her?* In the distance a cloud of dust appeared; the line following the road. The Hilux stopped. A young woman and a tall African climbed out. Kate wished

Martha Lintel Montgomery wasn't wearing her sunglasses. She couldn't see her eyes, to see if she recognised her granddaughter.

From the back of the house, a little boy came running out. 'This is TJ.'

'The African's boy, I assume?' Martha Lintel Montgomery asked.

At that moment Josie swept TJ up into her arms.

'No, this bundle of energy – he's your great grandson.' Josie kissed him. 'His father was Swedish, a chemist. He died before TJ was born.'

Christina Fairfield appeared, accompanied by the secret service men. 'Is everything all right?' she asked.

Martha Lintel Montgomery's mouth was thin and narrow. Her neck flushed pink. She turned towards Kate. 'Do you think you can get away with this? I came here in good faith. I was prepared to listen to you, even after that dreadful scene, when you embarrassed me and my son.' She caught Christina listening. 'I might have helped you with your current dilemma but…' her voice was rising, as she stood up.

Josie was standing in front of Martha Lintel Montgomery, blocking her exit as TJ tumbled out of her arms. 'TJ, shake the lady's hand.'

TJ looked unsure. She nodded encouragingly. He took a step forward. 'Do you want to see my dumper truck?' he said, before running off to get it.

Josie and Kate laughed. 'He's obsessed by it.' Josie turned. 'Don't go on my account. We passed the other two, they're on their way.'

Everyone looked at the snaking trails heading towards them.

Martha Lintel Montgomery remained standing, 'If you think I'm going to spend another minute in your company.' She turned to Kate, 'I thought I'd fired you.' Next she turned towards her granddaughter, 'The last thing my son needs is you and your no doubt illegitimate coloured baby.'

Josie intervened by grabbing Kate's arm. 'Mrs Clarkson won't help us to change her mind!'

Christina Fairfield and the two bodyguards looked on bemused.

'It's what I call our revolver.'

At that moment TJ emerged, pushing his yellow truck along the ground; his voice making the sounds of its engine revving hard and with its gears crashing. TJ encircled Martha's legs like the Indians and the wagon train; oblivious to everyone watching him. In an instant he deflated the situation.

Josie smiled, 'I promise you, what you are about to hear is hugely important. If you rush away now you'll regret it. It affects your son and my son.' Josie stopped. 'In fact everyone's son.'

Martha Lintel Montgomery sat back down; Christina Fairfield passed her a glass of water and backed away into the shadows of the stoep.

'Please, don't fire Mom. You'll see why you need her when you hear what the others have to say.'

At that moment the two vehicles arrived. As their doors opened the secret service men were waiting. Coetzer was clearly unhappy at being frisked. Josie called over to him, 'Do you want a Castle lager?'

He nodded, glaring at the Americans.

She turned towards their other visitor, 'How about you?'

Dr Holloway nodded.

'Sorry to hear you've been fired.' Josie looked at Martha Lintel Montgomery. 'He used to work for LCC at the blood clinic Finnegan and Lady Alice set up in Matsane. Philanthropy, he called it,' Josie harrumphed, 'all done so he could carry out his field study.' Josie sat down next to her grandmother.

Her demeanour was untouched by the warmth of the sun or the closeness of her newly discovered extended family.

'The Finnegans have used you, and your name. Your fortune won't save you now. No one will believe your son when he says he knew nothing about what was going on. It's not the legacy you wanted.' Josie stopped. 'I don't expect you to believe me, but perhaps you will believe these two men.'

CHAPTER 32

TYRELL

Seven-forty: he was going to be late for the change-over shift at LCC. He wound down the window. Jeez – it was going to be a hot one today. He could feel the heat already. He honked, not that it made any difference but he felt better. The driver of the car in front gesticulated through his open window; seemed like he was having a bad day too.

'Chill man,' Moose said as he rocked backwards and forwards listening to WMFZ-95. 'We ain't going to be late.' Moose got his name in school, on account of the size of his head and long, lugubrious face.

'I don't need your chill man vibe. Everything ain't going to be fine if I lose my job. You know how WhiteBitch wants me gone.'

'He needs you, needs us all; factory's as busy as a man chasing chickens on speed.'

Tyrell shook his head. Moose didn't get it. He was late because Dixie was expecting their third. She'd taken it into her head at six o'clock in the morning that she must have gherkins. "And don't you come back, saying they had none! I know you Tyrell." He had enough grief in his life without a woman screaming in his face.

The traffic began to move. 'See told you man – chill.' Moose laughed.

WhiteBitch – his actual name was Mitch Chalk, but the African-American workers preferred their name, knowing he had no idea they were talking about him. He and Tyrell had had a run-in last week. It was over the length of their lunch break. The union negotiated forty minutes but WhiteBitch wanted them back on the line in twenty; production targets were up. LCC was anticipating an increase in sales and they needed more cars coming off the line.

Tyrell had taken the union time. No one pushed him around; he was a proud man. He argued with the others, if WhiteBitch gets his way on this, then who knows – it would only get worse. It was important to stick with the union. Not that the other workers felt much sympathy. In good times no one needed the union and besides they wanted to keep their jobs. LCC paid well and they knew there weren't that many other places in the city; not for black Americans with poor grades.

Tyrell thought they were fools, like Moose thinking only about today and not worrying about tomorrow. He was afraid of the future, where technology and robots made men redundant. What then? No pride, no money, back on the streets looking for handouts and who'd care? Not WhiteBitch and the other white folks. They'd get the jobs first, if there were any jobs going. Wasn't it always the same? Look after your own kind. Tyrell knew things don't change – you have to make them change, any way you can. And standing up to people like WhiteBitch was a start; besides Tyrell had the responsibilities of a family. He wanted them to have a better chance, get out of this neighbourhood, away from the drugs and gangs. A part of him believed in the American dream; above all he was a union man.

Dixie didn't understand why he paid his dues. 'You taking money out of their mouths, baby.'

Tyrell reminded her, 'At least I'm around, looking out for my kids.'

♦

At the LCC dealership, the salesman shook the hands of Mr and Mrs Brinson. He handed over the keys, the paperwork for the loan agreement and smiling said, 'Don't you forget to use this.' He gave them the voucher: a tour of the LCC factory where their car was being made.

They parked in the vast car park in the area designated for the visitor reception. The factory occupied a huge site; running alongside the highway, it had its own exit. There was also a railway junction shipping out new vehicles from the 24/7 production line. The Brinsons walked into the visitor reception. The souvenir shop looked more like a duty free airport, with bright lighting and glass and chrome display stands. The merchandise was extensive: from primary coloured gewgaws aimed at children, areas for women with travel rugs and mugs to men's gadgets like signs and beer dispensers for man caves, along with the usual T-shirts, caps, sweat shirts and bags for sports gear. In the centre was the aspirational Genco stand with its leather luggage, platinum cufflinks, cocktail shakers and Hermes silk scarves. The marketing department at LCC worked on the assumption, once you bought one of their cars, you became part of the LCC family. As you grew up and your lifestyle changed, the next model was waiting for you, with the Genco being the apogee.

'Wouldn't you love one of those?' Mrs Brinson nudged her husband, pointing to the revolving stand lit by stage lighting. The Genco looked sleek, dangerously fast as well as hand crafted.

The guide gave them each a headset, so in the factory they would be able to hear her commentary. They put on their high visibility jackets and were told to leave phones and cameras in the lockers provided. They boarded the coach and drove to another part of the site.

Everyone stopped, mesmerized. In the low, dull light of the factory metal cages housed giant robots. They stretched far into the distance, above their heads a continuous line of moving parts like some labyrinthine lair. The robots stood like metal dinosaurs yet in their swift, precise, repetitive movements they seemed gently balletic. Each creature, because it was hard not to see them as caged animals, evoked feelings of empathy. Following yellow lines, driverless trucks swished past, powering down if anyone stepped out in front of them; sat down as if on their haunches. Once the obstruction passed, they powered up moving off to their programmed destination.

'Where are all the workers?' Mrs Brinson asked her husband. She wasn't sure she liked the factory. It seemed inhuman, too alien. There was no pleasant background music, no daylight, no voices calling out to others; just the machines that looked like prisoners unable to escape from mindless tasks. Mrs Brinson thought this is what hell must be like, and at her age it wasn't reassuring.

The tour continued. It became easier to identify the different body shapes on the continuously moving lines. The guide explained, 'Each vehicle is specified at the car showroom by the new owner. In effect we build your car to your design.'

Mr Brinson asked, 'I expected to see just one type of car being built in this factory.'

The guide smiled. 'In the past maybe, now we need to be flexible.'

Mrs Brinson was getting tired. They must have been on the tour for nearly forty minutes and inside only one building. They'd only seen about ten workers and they were at workstations in small groups, looking at computer screens. Occasionally a worker filled up a robot's cage with more widgets; feeding time at the zoo was how Mrs Brinson thought of it.

The guide explained, 'These people can see if there is a problem and step in to rectify it. Nothing must hold up the line. However, if there is a problem the computer running the system can regulate the workflow. A certain amount of delay is built in. The line can close down for twenty minutes.'

By now the cars looked nearly complete; finally they saw gangs of people. Each person had beside them a moving line of parts like wheels or seats. Their job was to attach the part to the car as it passed, the line never stopping.

'You can see how it all comes together here; the car and part arriving at the same time. The worker turns round confident the right part is waiting to be fitted to the right car. The computer makes this possible.'

At the end of the line someone jumped into the car and drove it off to be tested. 'Every thirty seconds a car drives off this line.'

♦

Tyrell persisted in taking his forty minutes. It was a matter of principle. He had the union behind him. Why didn't the others see it? How long before the gang was replaced by a robot?

Moose shook his head, 'You asking to get fired, brother.' Moose sauntered back, joking and fooling around with the others. He was part of a gang of six men at their workstation. The line didn't work if Tyrell was late and no one had time to cover for him.

WhiteBitch came over. He looked at the gang of five men, 'Plenty more negroes where you come from.'

Finishing their shift, Moose and the others surrounded Tyrell, pushing and shoving him.

'Get off me, what's up with you?' Tyrell asked.

One of them used his shoulder, knocking him hard, unbalancing him and propelling him forward and at the same time someone else stuck out a leg, tripping him up. He fell to the ground; the other workers nearby jeered. Tyrell was mortified. His pride hurt, it reminded him of the schoolyard. Suddenly the mood changed, they weren't laughing at him.

One of them bent down and spat in his face. 'WhiteBitch says you work like the rest of us or he's going to fire all of us; you straight?'

Tyrell felt a boot in his groin. He curled up in pain.

Moose came to his rescue. 'He's cool,' pushing the others away before it got ugly. He helped Tyrell up. 'See, these are your brothers, we stick together, union ain't going to help you.'

Driving home they didn't speak. Moose got out of the car as Tyrell drove off, his foot hard down on the accelerator. The office was on the second floor. The brass plate the only sign it was the union's headquarters; the last occupant in a building about to be condemned. Full employment made the union an anachronism; gone were the glory days when they'd put politicians into the White House.

A large, yellowing, dog-eared map of the United States dominated one wall. The furniture looked second-hand. The blind hung down at an angle. One hard yank and the last screw holding it up would give way and the whole thing would rattle to the floor, sending years of dust up like choking smog.

'Tyrell,' Eugene gave him a brief hug and fist pump. 'You should have called.'

Tyrell felt aggrieved; suddenly he wasn't welcome? He looked around bemused; people on phones, tapping keyboards, heads down, ignoring their fag-end environment. He saw through the open door, across the corridor into the normally vacant office, more people sat at computer screens, with the sound of a printing press clattering in the background. He couldn't figure it out. Where had all these new people come from? The whole place felt energised, purposeful, not like the union he'd defended, whilst fearing its demise.

'What's up?' he asked.

Eugene didn't say anything, as if sizing him up.

Tyrell felt uncomfortable, like he didn't belong. But he had to tell someone. 'We've been told to double production targets. The factory already works 24/7.'

Eugene's expression changed. 'That's good news, brother.'

'No, not when they take our breaks away.' He was still smarting about what his friends had done. 'They're blind and too stupid to understand; it ain't going to last.'

Eugene slapped Tyrell good-naturedly on his shoulder. 'You the only one who's smart, but you need to keep working. We've got plans.' He looked around the busy office.

Tyrell wasn't done. 'Heard a conversation I shouldn't have.'

Suddenly Eugene appeared interested. 'What you hear, brother?'

Tyrell's stance was challenging. 'You planning a strike I don't know about?' He had family responsibilities.

Eugene asked the question again.

'Everyone was back on the line – I heard two men talking, something about LCC and lighting a fire across America.' Tyrell didn't move. 'What's up?'

'Come into my office,' Eugene's hand firmly on his back, pushing Tyrell in front of him.

Tyrell didn't know Eugene had an office. He was beginning to wonder who was paying for all these people, and equipment; no one at LCC wanted to join the union, so it wasn't union dues.

Eugene sat down behind a brown timber desk. It was old like all the other furniture. The computer was new. 'It's like this. We see the president helping our brothers in Africa, but what does he do at home for us? It's still as bad as when segregation was the law down south. When did you last see a white boy shot by a black policeman? And when it happens to us, no one bothers to ask questions. They're happy to leave us in the ghettos.' He looked at Tyrell. 'Working the line but not supervising.' He paused. 'You know I'm speaking the truth, brother.'

Tyrell nodded; knowing how his skin colour prejudiced his opportunities.

'We've got to look out for each other. We're angry, we've had enough. It's time we woke up. We've got support.' He stopped; there was some hesitation. 'Raise the consciousness by lighting the fires across America. They will hear our voices.' He looked like the minister at Tyrell's church. Then in a lower cadence he said, 'This is our fight, our purpose now.' Eugene pushed back his chair and got up; he steered Tyrell towards another room. In it printing machines were spitting out posters in the thousands. Eugene took one from a stacked pile. 'The union needs you to put these up.' Eugene waited while Tyrell read the poster.

Tyrell hesitated, he thought about Dixie and what she'd say if he lost his job. 'We're expecting.'

'The union takes care of its own, brother.' He grabbed a box and passed it over. 'We're starting at LCC.'

Tyrell nodded his head slowly, taking in the words. It was like he'd always imagined. He was going to be part of something important. He was a man. His back straightened; Dixie would be proud of him. He looked at the words on the poster. 'Ain't that the truth,' he said.

By the time Tyrell got home, Dixie's temper had simmered dry like a boiling saucepan. Her eyes didn't leave the television screen. 'Dinner's in the trash can.'

'Why'd you do that?' he asked. 'I had business down the union.' Tyrell knew what he had to do. He started to massage her feet; working his way up and into her good books. 'You watching this babe,' Tyrell asked, leaning forward to give her a kiss. The President of the United States was on their screens every night.

'Don't think I've forgiven you, running off like that,' she laughed. 'Looks like this president can whistle the blackbirds out of the trees, just like you.' She put his hand on her belly. 'Times are going to be good for this one, I know it.'

Tyrell didn't believe life was going to get better for black people just because the president was promising to help the brothers in Africa. What about the brothers in his neighbourhood? He looked at Dixie. 'I promise you, it's going to change.'

The next day he swallowed his pride. Tyrell took twenty minutes for lunch. He had a new fight. Posters began appearing, stuck on notice boards and lockers. They all said the same thing; "Black Lives: White Lies". WhiteBitch and the other supervisors interrogated the black workers. No one claimed to know anything.

Moose maintained, 'It's just a new band. They'll be on WMFZ-95 or at some festival.'

♦

Of course it never happened; but the posters spread like a super efficient marketing company with a limitless budget. Posters covered walls like wallpaper, moving through the neighbourhood, colonising not just lampposts but derelict hoardings and eventually paid-for billboards; moving closer into the city centre. It transmogrified overnight into a fashion item, worn first by skateboarders before hip young urbanites claimed it. The political statement lost in the commercialisation.

Six Degrees, the new social media network picked it up and spun it out again, this time finding fertile ground in urban decay and social housing projects. Journalists and professors at black universities took an interest, calling it an awakening in the consciousness of the black mind; refuelling the arguments from the sixties and seventies, arguing little had changed. Black people were still being ignored; their rights and lives less valued.

Moose grew an Afro.

Like a forest flame it spread underground, rumbling below the surface, only to reignite. The sparks lighting tensions, as Black Lives: White Lies took hold in white working-class and immigrant suburbs. Tyrell noticed Dixie stopped visiting friends from work who were white; girls she had gone to school with. It was as if invisible boundaries had been painted and no one was going to cross them.

As the weather heated up, tempers started to frazzle. At first there were just little incidents, fights with fists, knives; white on black, black on white – everyone was starting to take it personally. Police sirens became the constant backdrop day and night.

No one knew for sure who was stirring things up.

It sat uncomfortably alongside Feed Africa with its daily news stories, advertisements and the president's sound bites and speeches. Politicians wanting to dampen unrest in their neighbourhoods began questioning who were more important, black people in Africa or those in America. The president came under pressure to do something.

♦

At LCC people weren't happy in their old cross-racial gangs; they now insisted on segregation. The black workers felt empowered, no longer enjoying the joke between themselves, they shouted out clearly whenever Mitch Chalk walked by, "WhiteBitch". It was obvious who they were referring to. Quality control was failing more vehicles.

A workers' meeting was called at lunchtime in the car park. Tyrell stood up on the platform, speaking on behalf of the union, 'We're working harder, but we ain't robots.' A cheer went up. 'You cut the breaks, but we still gotta pee.' There was another loud cheer and laughing. 'Do you see as many black supervisors as white?' Tyrell asked. The response was loud but not unanimous, 'We need a union.' Another voice called out, 'We want our rights.'

Tyrell put the megaphone down and began clapping, shouting out, 'Black lives,' and before he could finish a thunderous response went up, 'White lies.' The shout became a chant, over and over again, the volume deafening as feet and hands provided the bass rhythm. Around the edges opposing voices tried to drown it out by booing. Slowly the crowd began to part and regroup into two tribes lining up to oppose each other.

Moose climbed onto the platform, stomping his feet like a festival goer wanting an encore from the band.

A single gunshot, the sound so distinctive it silenced the crowd. For a brief moment people looked round to see where it had come from. Then a second sent them immediately running and screaming, some fell to the ground, trampled on by others; everyone desperate to escape the shooter.

Within minutes police cars arrived, blue lights and sirens adding fear to the already panicked crowd. The sirens faded as officers took cover behind their vehicles, their guns out. A third shot was fired. One section of the crowd ran towards the nearest building. A group of officers followed them in. Adrenalin coursing through their veins they attacked the only machines they could – the computer terminals. The whole site shut down as the tsunami rolled through.

Moose and WhiteBitch found themselves standing opposite each other, glaring.

'N*****.'

Moose ran at him blinded by his rage, his left and right fists pummelling into the supervisor's chest and face like a boxer working out. It wasn't pretty or skilful, merely brutal; splattered blood and spittle made the floor slippery. Tyrell came up behind Moose and grabbed him.

'Stop, enough.' He dragged him away, hugging him to his chest to stop his flaying arms. They looked transfixed at the motionless body on the ground. WhiteBitch no longer seemed like an appropriate description; Red Meat a better one.

'Moose, you'd better run.'

Moose turned, 'Where you going Tyrell?'

He knew there was only one place he could go.

♦

Outside, dog units, the FBI and SWAT teams arrived. Some men tried to climb over the car park barrier but were attacked by police dogs and those on the ground hit with batons, as others fought back. It had been simmering for months. The violence stoked by resentment, past injustices and old scores needing to be settled on both sides. Before officers formed a line behind their shields, batons out ready and with gas masks on, tear gas bullets exploded.

The whole drama was captured by cameras in helicopters circling above, feeding live pictures back into studios. The president sat in the Sit Room watching. More and more TV crews arrived. Vehicles on the highway stopped, people got out to watch. People further back, caught up in the traffic jam turned on their radios to listen. Images of bloodied bodies, ambulances and the sight of men being arrested were caught on camera. By the end of the day, ten people had died. The factory was a crime scene.

Moose hammered on Dixie's door. 'Let me in,' he shouted.

She opened it expecting to see Tyrell. Moose stood there; Dixie cried out, seeing the blood. Moose grabbed her to stop her from falling. The television was on.

'Where's Tyrell?' she screamed at him.

Moose, his eyes dancing around along with his body, was muttering, 'No one calls me that.'

Dixie grabbed hold of him, trying to calm him. 'Where's Tyrell?'

'He told me to run.'

'You'd better wash. I'll get some of Tyrell's clothes.' She propelled him down the corridor towards the bathroom. 'How much trouble you in Moose?'

Tears were running down his face and hers.

♦

Tyrell sought sanctuary in the union building.

'Shouldn't have come here Tyrell,' Eugene looked at him and threw over a clean T-shirt, 'Better lose yours.'

The next day Eugene told Tyrell, 'The FBI is looking for you. Best you keep out of sight.'

'What I gonna say? I put up posters? I spoke up at the factory?' He looked and sounded aggrieved. 'You know – that's all I did.' He didn't mention WhiteBitch or Moose. Tyrell was restless, anxious about Dixie.

Eugene insisted he mustn't contact her. If she knew nothing – then she couldn't help the police.

'If she comes knocking, what you gonna tell her?'

'You're gone.'

Tyrell wasn't happy with that but what choice did he have? He was innocent. Who'd believe a black man – when there was a dead white body lying on the ground?

♦

Eugene had him working during the day loading the delivery vans but at night he locked him up. He reminded him, 'You ring Dixie and tell her where you are and the police are going to charge her too. Then what's going happen to your children, with no one looking out for them?'

He had time to think. He walked into Eugene's office. 'I reckon there was more than one union brother working at LCC.' He paused; 'working to set the fires raging?' He remembered the overheard conversation. 'Who fired the gun?'

'He's smoke.' Eugene grabbed Tyrell's upper arm, propelling him towards the door.

Tyrell struggled free. 'Time you treated me with respect.' Tyrell stared at Eugene. 'I'm going home. What you going to do?'

Eugene opened his desk and threw down a plastic bag. In it was his bloodied T-shirt. They both stared at it. He'd always spoken up for the union. He felt betrayed.

'You walked right in, remember.' He looked at Tyrell. 'Maybe you're smart. Tell me, what do you think we are doing?'

'Black people are rising up demanding justice.' It was what he wanted. Then he remembered Moose and the trouble he was in. His hands were clean; he'd tried to stop Moose.

Eugene laughed. 'The union's long gone, you know it. We've got a new purpose. We are part of a revolution. This is war and you are a foot soldier.' He patted Tyrell on his upper arm. 'We'll take care of you.' Tyrell saw him pick up the T-shirt packet and lock it back up in the desk drawer. 'Get back to work.'

He missed Dixie and the children. He worried about them. What was happening to Moose and his other friends? He felt like a prisoner, not a soldier. He wondered about the other people working here. They came and went, what made him different? It was like Eugene said, "We are planning a revolution." But he wasn't part of it. He'd not signed up for that. He'd done nothing wrong; he didn't want to spend time in jail for something he didn't do. He wanted to see his children grow up. He wanted them to be proud of their father. That's all he'd ever wanted. He decided Eugene was hiding him not because he cared, but because he didn't want the FBI to come sniffing around, see what they were doing here. If he got out, he'd bring them here. Yet he just couldn't walk out. Eugene had made sure of that. He needed to find another way.

He couldn't set fire to the building alone at night. The fire department would let it burn to the ground with him locked inside; it looked derelict anyway and they were too busy saving public buildings, shopping malls and people's houses, to bother with this one. He needed a daytime distraction, so he could slip out undetected.

Tyrell knew about car wheels. No one noticed the knife gash in the two front tyres or the missing spare. As usual Tyrell loaded the delivery van. The garage doors rolled back and as the van drove forward, Tyrell thumped on the passenger's door. 'Stop – you've got a flat!'

The driver braked, swearing as Tyrell came round to his side, shaking his head. 'You got two flats brother, never seen that before, going to need another spare.' Tyrell went back into the back of the garage and scrambled underneath another van, releasing its spare. While he was there he punctured the van's fuel line. He stood up slowly, wiping the grease and dirt off his hands. He threw the cloth on the floor, absorbing the thin line of fuel. Unobserved Tyrell lit the match and dropped it on the cloth. It took a few moments to burn strongly before gathering speed towards the van. The van caught fire and for a brief second everyone stood looking confused. Tyrell slipped out rounding the corner – before he began running.

CHAPTER 33
STORM CLOUDS

It was the start of a summer of rioting. During the day protesters marched demanding change. Black Lives: White Lies T-shirts were this time worn as a uniform; proclaiming solidarity to the cause. On radio stations one song played, the sounds of voices chanting Black Lives: White Lies fulfilling Moose's prediction. Only those singing were frustrated, disenchanted, angry people; voices fragmented into the many different social issues, causes and grievances. Cracks wallpapered over for decades now ripped apart – exposed and ugly. Factories, business, shops, colleges and schools, nowhere escaped the sporadic violence; buildings were burned and looted, police vehicles set alight. They responded with tear gas, rubber bullets and batons in rolling street battles. Each time it appeared under control, it burst out, fanned by the resentments and injustices of decades; not helped by the brutality of beleaguered police departments. Curfews were ordered in thirty cities across America; state governors declaring a state of emergency and calling in the National Guard.

Ordinary Americans flocked to gun shops, clearing them out as they created personal arsenals. Even Mr and Mrs Brinson bought a gun, telling their friends, "It's my right." They no longer believed the authorities had the capacity to stop the attacks. Cartoonists lampooned the president using the imagery of the lawlessness of the Old West frontier towns; only these frightened townsfolk lived in leafy suburbs. Outside commentators portrayed America on the verge of collapse. Black Lives: White Lies had taken root in fertile disturbed soil.

The FBI followed up hundreds of leads across the country, pulling in their sources, targeting criminal gangs, liaising with the CIA to monitor dissidents. It was contradictory. Some outbreaks were characterised by low-key violence focussed on local issues, wanton vandalism and organised criminal gangs settling old scores, carving out new territories. Others appeared to be led by political agitators feeding on the mistrust ordinary Americans had of federal and state government. The courts and prisons were full.

No matter how many times it was analysed, discussed or spoken about, it was clear no one knew who had started it or why. The only aspect everyone agreed upon was America was in trouble; some pessimists called it America's Second Civil War. And like the flame on the credits of *Bonanza*, an old 1960s cowboy serial on TV, it burned, branding America; leaving it with a seeping wound. Slow-Hand Joe no longer looked like a safe pair of hands; he looked impotent, holed up in his White House office.

♦

Dorothy unlocked the shutters and turned on the fluorescent lights; it was five-thirty in the morning. The routine was the same. She put on her AMOIL fleece and cap, took the money from the safe to the cash register, opened up the shutters in the shop, checked the fridge temperatures and quickly noted what items needed restocking. She turned on the oven to bake the muffins, brownies, chocolate chip cookies and cinnamon rolls. Little Linda arrived, bringing in with her the stack of newspapers and magazines left outside. The two women gossiped for a few moments in the windowless back space, before she started on cleaning the floors and toilets. Jimmy arrived next. He checked the pumps, swept the forecourt and opened up the shuttered bins outside selling car and BBQ items. As the clock turned 6am the first van pulled in. The driver got out, nodded and pointed to the toilets. Jimmy nodded back from his vantage point at the till and carried on filling up the cigarette dispenser behind him. Little Linda had finished one toilet, her galvanised bucket and mop outside the other. She was lighting a cigarette, when a man ran past her – clattering into the bucket. It sent him sprawling. Quickly he got up and ran off. Little Linda stood open-mouthed; the cigarette burning away in her hand. Out front the white van exploded. The underground storage tanks went off like bombs, flames shooting out, burning fiercely, engulfing the petrol station within minutes; the conflagration raging out of control before the fire department arrived.

♦

AMOIL was hit by compensation claims as their loyal customer base disappeared; terrified of being caught up in the next incident and incinerated. A group of vocal demonstrators barricaded Malone's oil refineries and storage facilities, the ones now full of Bucephalus fuel. The situation became tense; more security people with dogs were drafted in. Malone rang the state governor and insisted he had to protect AMOIL, in words that were crude and forthright. But the person he really wanted to shout at was Gene Finnegan; in his mind the frigging bastard who'd sold him the Bucephalus concept in the first place. He didn't ring because he assumed his phones were being monitored and besides he wanted to look Finnegan in the eye and punch him hard in the face. This wasn't the legacy he'd been promised. Andy 'Lucky' Malone bitterly regretted his nickname now, as people looked to blame someone. He was constantly reassuring AMOIL's board and shareholders, speaking to old friends and other manufacturers afraid they would be next, fending off the media and having to open up his business to federal officials who were crawling all over him and his operation – all demanding one thing; to explain what the hell was going on. 'Lucky' could only lie. He had no idea, he told them. He woke most nights in a cold sweat; afraid some diligent investigator would ask about a one-off, clandestine shipment to England and the secret would begin to unravel. He kept silent because the only thing that would save him now (his reputation and his company) was Finnegan launching his emissions-free vehicles.

♦

Ralf Sneider and Paul Barr were sat with the president.

'A man walked into one of our FBI offices with an

interesting story. It appears the Black Lives: White Lies propaganda is coming from one source,' Barr began.

The president sat forward, fearing the worst. His ulcer rumbled ominously. He opened his drawer. 'And the source is?'

'China.' They had spoken in unison.

He could barely focus; his left hand trembling as he grabbed it, hiding it under the desk. Slowly with deliberate concentration he popped two pills into his mouth. Normally they eased the pain. Not this time. He felt a bead of sweat appear on his forehead.

Sneider and Barr looked at each other. 'Are you all right, Sir?'

He nodded his voice unsteady. 'How do you know?'

'The man was known to have connections with the union. Our agent interviewed the head of the union at the bureau. He said, our man had come in looking for help and they'd given him a change of clothes and told him to give himself up. They didn't know anything more. Later someone from the union brought round his clothes. The blood on them matched one of our victims.' He paused. 'We had someone else in custody for the same murder; though he was claiming he'd acted alone.'

'I'm still waiting for the Chinese connection.'

'After hearing his story, we went to the building to check it out. It's going to take weeks to go through it all. It's just as before, the Chinese haven't hidden their payments. They've been bank rolling the Black Lives: White Lies campaign.'

'Jesus Christ, so arrest them.'

Barr asked, 'Who do you suggest? We don't have the resources or the authority to lock up everyone in the nation with a grievance.'

Sneider added, 'The Black Lives: White Lies started at LCC, now it's nationwide.'

'So what you are saying is – we are helpless.' He held his head in his hands; looking not like the President of the United States but an ordinary man floundering under the weight of his problems.

As the minutes ticked by Sneider looked at the president. 'Sir, America is a deeply divided nation, now at war with itself. All they needed to do was light the touch paper. We did the rest to ourselves.'

His mother and the Lintel name wouldn't save him now. 'Is there more?' he asked nervously.

'They supplied the lone shooter at LCC,' Sneider added, 'He's back in China.'

He'd been duped, made to look like a fool by Zhou.

'Sir, you might want to take some time and consider your position,' Sneider said.

He looked up, then back and forth. 'What are you saying?' he asked, afraid of the answer. He felt the perspiration on his upper lip. 'You think the trouble here has something to do with Feed Africa?' He needed to remain calm. He noticed Sneider's steady gaze. 'Malone and Finnegan supported it, along with many other American companies, it's all I know.' He wanted to get up and pace, instead he tried to laugh lightly. 'Jesus Christ, Feed Africa – it's a small overseas aid programme.'

'There is one possibility, and that's why we wanted to speak to you in private.' Sneider looked at the president. 'Maybe all of this is a smokescreen as the vice-president claims and we're missing the bigger picture.'

The president glowered at him.

'Remember the satellite images we saw,' Sneider said.

The president groaned. 'Are you saying China deliberately wanted to weaken America, simply in order to follow its own territorial expansion?' It was hard to concentrate with the pain. His ulcer was getting worse. He swallowed two more pills.

Sneider shifted in his chair. 'We believe they bombed the Embassy to test our resolve, see how we would react to the provocation.'

'See how this administration would respond,' Barr added for extra emphasis.

'And I failed? Is that what you are saying?' He stared at both of them. 'I chose diplomacy over war.' He stood up. 'I need to speak to Ambassador Zhou immediately.'

He wondered if he could trust them. Was their loyalty to the office of the President of the United States or to him? 'I hope I don't need to remind you, this remains between us for the time being.' He stared at them. 'This is absolutely top secret.' He raised his eyebrow, seeking confirmation. 'If it leaks – you will bear the burden of escalating the situation into a possible nuclear war. And with our current situation we'd find ourselves fighting on two fronts.'

'Yes Sir.' They rose and left the meeting together.

He knew it was impossible to keep anything secret in the White House, eventually someone would leak it.

Sneider and Barr walked down the corridor together, their voices low. 'At what point do we take action?' Barr asked.

Sneider took his time. 'We still don't know how involved he is. And if we get it wrong – it could blow up in our faces.'

'We need to find a way to cover our asses. I don't want to be fired because of this.'

'Let's take a closer look at Finnegan and Malone. Also I don't like the way Stagecoach' – he used the president's code name – 'keeps meeting up with Ambassador Zhou on a one-to-one basis.'

'Do you think he's been compromised in some way?' Barr asked.

'That's one God almighty accusation.' Both men walked on deep in thought. 'I suggest we review the Oval Office tapes.'

'Investigate our own president?' Barr whistled.

'Leave it with me.'

♦

Their dinner over, the president suggested they sit outside where the air was cooler, taking their whiskey glasses with them and in Zhou's case a Cuban cigar.

'The nights remind me I'm getting older,' Montgomery said, 'Each night I pray, and ask God to spare me; let me wake to greet the next morning.' He looked across at his guest. 'How many children do you have?' He'd been unable to forget Zhou's closing remark the last time they'd met.

'It has been the policy in China for many years, to limit families to one child. We did not foresee the problem it would cause. Families chose sons. We have far too few women in China. It is of great social concern.' Zhou paused. 'I have one son but he is not married, like too many of our sons.' He sensed Zhou had spoken personally and not as his government's representative. 'You have a daughter.' It wasn't a question.

'I…' Words failed him. He was aware of Zhou watching his reaction. In a level voice he said, 'Yes, I have only recently discovered I have a daughter.' It was the first time he had acknowledged her. It felt like a huge burden taken off his shoulders.

'She lives in southern Africa,' Zhou said, surprising him further. 'We wondered why you chose it for the Feed Africa project.'

He hadn't chosen the location. Finnegan had. Thinking about it now he assumed Finnegan had known all along about his daughter. But he didn't want to discuss her. They had more pressing matters. 'Ambassador Zhou, I want us to understand each other clearly. When we last met I thought we had solved our misunderstanding over Africa, but now you are funding agitators in America.' He hoped Zhou had good news for him. The buzzards in his administration were circling, getting more vocal. He didn't want to be the president who started a nuclear war.

Zhou looked into the night. 'The world is watching what is happening here, afraid it could so easily jump continents. Britain, your oldest ally, is not immune. It is holding its breath.' He turned to look back at the president; his implication being China would use the same tactics elsewhere, if they wanted to.

He was horrified. 'So how do we stop it?' He lifted the whiskey decanter, needing another drink.

'I would advise against a military option,' Zhou said.

The whiskey decanter slipped out of his grasp, rattling as it landed on the table. He grabbed at it to stop it toppling over, as he looked down at his shaking hands. Zhou ignored his actions, it only added to his embarrassment. He refocused his mind on Zhou's words. Had China's military actions overstretched its resources, leaving them vulnerable? He assumed his military advisers and the vice-president had arrived at a similar conclusion, strengthening their call for action.

He considered Zhou's remarks about Britain; all too aware his actions could have serious consequences not only for the United States but its allies. Tomorrow he'd tell Dennison, "We cannot use the Security Council as a way to condemn China's actions", however much Dennison wanted to. Instead he would talk to the British Prime Minister in London, seeking his help to apply economic and trade sanctions; without Russia's support he knew its effectiveness would be limited. But what alternatives did he have?

'Men in uniform have one role, we have another. We have to be more cautious.' Zhou was looking at him.

He felt the weight of responsibility. 'I cannot ignore our situation, especially as it seems you are responsible and we can prove it.' Zhou was his conduit to China's leadership. 'The media and some of my closest advisers are demanding action; I need your help or we will find ourselves on the brink of a nuclear war.' He hoped he'd been clear enough.

A moment's look of self-satisfaction crossed Zhou's normally immobile expression. He inhaled deeply, drawing the cigar smoke into his lungs as both men sat in silence. Zhou blew the billowing cloud away. 'We are both parents. We want grandchildren to comfort us in our old age.' His words drifted into the scented night air. 'We must be left to pursue our own destiny.'

'And in return, you will cease your operations against the United States?'

Without answering him, Zhou got up and went inside, returning with a box. 'A friend gave this to me for my help.'

He opened it. Inside was a beautiful celadon-glazed

porcelain horse. It was exquisite. The president looked at the gift, not sure what to make of it.

'The Tang period was one of great prosperity and peace in China.' Zhou had spoken the words slowly, giving them added emphasis.

The president repeated the word "peace", looking directly at Zhou.

The ambassador nodded. 'We have what we want.'

Montgomery relaxed. He now felt able to admire the horse; turning it in his hands he asked, 'What does it represent in Chinese culture?'

'Many things, today it is the unyielding spirit of the Chinese people and our belief we cannot be conquered.' Zhou looked beyond into the night sky. 'Ask Gene Finnegan about his horse, Bucephalus.' Zhou took several quick draws on his cigar. 'Consider it as another gift.'

Montgomery felt conflicting emotions. On the one hand a bond of friendship, and on the other a sense of foreboding rising from the pit of his stomach at the mention of Finnegan's name.

'We are no longer supplying LCC with vehicles.'

The candour of Zhou's words shocked him. The president clutched his hand to stop it shaking as his ulcer rumbled. Finnegan hadn't told him the deal was over. Where did that leave his funding for Feed Africa? With all the trouble at home, no one was interested in it anymore. It had become an embarrassment. His statesman-like speeches now played as sound bites over the images of civil unrest at home. He realised the legacy he'd longed for had come to an abrupt end. He could hear his mother's voice mocking him, reminding him she'd been right all along.

Zhou rose. He took something out of his breast pocket. 'Give this to your daughter.'

Before Zhou could pass over the small object, the president's ulcer burst. The sharp pain twisted his body. He called out, groaning in agony, falling forward onto his knees.

'Josie.' It was the only word he said before collapsing prone on the ground.

CHAPTER 34

BID FOR POWER

Douglas Dennison was in the Oval Office, having been sworn in as acting president while Montgomery underwent surgery.

Sneider knocked and entered unannounced. 'Well what have you got for me?' Dennison asked.

'None of their meetings suggest anything underhand. The president appeared to agree to not interfere with China's move on Vietnam, in return for continued trade and peace in southern Africa.'

'So we've got nothing.' Dennison sounded disappointed.

'I don't agree Sir, China is behind all of it; though they'll deny it of course. Nonetheless I believe their message was clear – take a closer look at AMOIL and LCC.'

'And what have you found?'

'We started with AMOIL. Fuel tankers make an easy and spectacular target; hard to ignore. We tracked their movements and found an anomaly. One consignment was sent to a rural location in England. We are following that up. As to the trouble at home, we assume China is funding the demonstrators. It would fit in with their actions out in Africa.'

'And LCC, where are you with them?'

'Finnegan and Malone are old friends. The Oval Office tapes make it clear they sold the concept of Feed Africa to the president.'

'I never thought it was his idea,' Dennison laughed.

Sneider carried on, 'Both companies have profited from Feed Africa. Both have been targeted – our attention has been drawn to them.'

Dennison nodded. 'I agree, go on.'

'LCC's deal with China means all their vehicles are shipped to Africa and nowhere else, and AMOIL is the sole distributor of fuel. Finnegan, Malone and the president are all tied together by Feed Africa, along with China.'

Dennison said, 'I knew he was up to something. Tell me about the money.'

'The federal support is smaller than you'd expect; you could say it's because the president and his mother did a fantastic job, in bringing on board corporate America. But that's when we discovered Finnegan has made a considerable personal contribution. And the money doesn't appear to have come via LCC. That's when we discovered he's receiving payments from China and laundering it through the Finnegan Trust.'

Dennison looked eager. 'Can we tie Montgomery into any of this?'

'We're looking to see if Finnegan has redirected any of the Chinese money into the Lintel Foundation.' Sneider looked directly at Dennison.

Dennison whistled through his teeth. 'There has to be a link – find it.'

'It would be highly damaging if he has. And as you know Finnegan's wife and the president's mother are close confidantes, so it's possible. It could bring down the presidency,' Sneider said starkly.

There was a moment of silence.

Dennison's mood changed, his facial expression went from an eager child to a worried man. 'The media will have a field day; the United States portrayed as no better than a banana republic. We'll be a laughing stock; China paying for our aid programme – do you see how bad this could be? Jesus Christ this is a disaster.'

'That's why we are treading very cautiously.' Sneider kept Dennison in his gaze. 'Sir, you are a personal friend of Martha Lintel Montgomery and the president. It places you in a delicate situation too.'

'You mean guilty by association?'

'If it is made public where would that leave you? You'd be tainted, being part of the Montgomery administration. And if you denied all knowledge, you'd appear incompetent, lacking judgement or simply considered to be a liar. If you fail to expose it knowing what you do now, you'd become part of a cover-up. You would certainly lose the party's nomination.'

Dennison stared at Sneider. 'Don't threaten me, I could fire you.'

Sneider didn't react. He knew he was the gatekeeper of too many secrets. He knew Dennison was lashing out, fighting for his career. 'There's more Sir, the head of LCC's research and development Professor Li, visited China and has not returned.' Sneider closed his file. He could almost see Dennison's political mind working through his options. He gave him some time. 'Given the situation, we cannot expose our findings to the scrutiny of a Congressional committee. I'd also suggest it limits what we can do to China. I think we have to accept there's been a shift in the balance of power.'

Dennison looked at him; dark emotions increased his breathing and heightened his colour. 'If China thinks it can act with impunity, I'll show them.' His eyes narrowed. 'Those bastards have brought the United States to its knees. I want them to pay for it.'

Sneider paused. 'Is shining a light on this farrago the way to do it?' They both smelt the word impeachment in the room. Sneider continued, 'I don't see how turning a spotlight on this as the best option for you, or the country. Do you?'

'Are you suggesting we look at a more bespoke solution?'

Sneider paused, then said, 'It's the only way.'

♦

The Belmont Hotel's top floor had become an annexe to the White House; from here Martha Lintel Montgomery set up her court in exile. It was how the gossip columnists referred to it. Her explanation was simple. She could hardly carry on living in the White House with her son temporarily no longer the president. However, she carried on with business as normal. Today's visitor was her old friend Douglas Dennison, now the interim president.

'Martha, you somehow manage to never change.' Dennison kissed her on the proffered cheek.

'I would return the compliment, if I wasn't so sure you were being ironic.' She waved away his show of mock indignation. 'We know each other too well. I heard you took the oath the moment he went into hospital for the operation.'

Dennison coughed. 'It is good news, he's recovering, albeit slowly. I understand there is some concern.'

'Why the caveat, it was a simple operation.' Her gaze was uncompromising. She motioned for him to sit down opposite her. 'We might be old friends but this isn't a social call, is it?'

Dennison looked uncomfortable. 'I've had a report that suggests Gene Finnegan, Andy Malone and your son have…' He hesitated as if searching for the right words.

Martha Lintel Montgomery didn't wait for him to find them. 'My son is a stupid fool.' She looked at Dennison, her grey eyes piercing his. 'Remember only I can say that.' Her tone reminded him of being chided as a child. She held up her hand preventing him from saying more. 'There's something you need to hear; unless you know already – hence the reason for your visit.'

Dennison looked surprised, then relieved.

She ignored his reaction. 'I won't let Finnegan destroy all I've worked for, all the sacrifices I've made, letting him ruin the Lintel name and all it stands for.' For a moment her imperious façade cracked and she glanced away. 'Lady Alice was my oldest friend.'

It lasted only a moment. Her spine straightened as if corseted in steel. 'All I can hear now is them laughing at me and my son.' Her face was thunderous. 'No one does that to a Lintel and expects to get away with it. I don't forgive…' she hesitated and then added, 'easily.'

He felt his balls contract; as if her bony hands had cupped them both.

'You and I will destroy that man, his reputation and his company.'

He imagined her hands squeezing his genitals harder with each word.

'What is he after all – nothing but a jumped-up car salesman?'

Dennison's mouth was dry. He moved in the chair, easing himself.

'Sorry, you came to me and here I've interrupted you.' She caught him glancing down at the plastic toy hidden behind the sofa. Their eyes met. Martha Lintel Montgomery called out, 'Josie, come here.'

A young woman in her thirties with black hair and grey eyes walked in. She looked self-assured. 'Yes grandmother?'

Martha ignored her visitor's surprised expression. 'If you want my help, and I expect that is why you are here, there are two conditions. The first is Josie. She and her son are my future. She is not to be harmed in any way. In return my son will be exonerated. The Lintel name is to continue, unaffected by any scandal. Are we clear?'

At that moment a little boy ran into the room, only to be scooped up by the young woman and carried out squealing. By the door she handed him over to Christina and came back and sat down.

Martha Lintel Montgomery, clearly displeased by the interruption said, 'Listen to what she has to say.'

Josie began telling Douglas Dennison all she knew about Tomas and Finnegan's refusal to listen to his concerns and how she was the only person alive who knew about

Bucephalus. She didn't mention Annie; afraid she'd become a target. She told them about Professor Li and his failure to find GG42/OO and how damaging it was. Then she explained what was happening in southern Africa, ending with a simple statement, 'If Finnegan launches Bucephalus, millions will be exposed to it and die. He has to be stopped.'

'God almighty, what a mess,' Dennison looked at the old woman, sat with her back rigid and her lips tightly drawn. 'How the hell do you expect me to save your son and the Lintel name?'

'There must be a way. Release the data, rescind the EPA approval; explain the situation.'

'What, and admit there is genuine substance to Black Lives: White Lies; as we kill black people with impunity in Africa? Admit the president's Feed Africa programme was a smokescreen to test a dangerous chemical and tell everyone it was paid for by the Chinese?'

Martha Lintel Montgomery and Josie stared at him.

'You didn't know?' he scoffed, 'I hope for your sake, we don't discover the Lintel Foundation is involved in laundering Chinese money.' He sat back. 'They wanted us compromised, weakened and unable to interfere in their foreign policy.'

'Did my father know about this?' Josie asked.

He didn't look at her; he concentrated on Martha Lintel Montgomery. 'Your son has been in regular contact with the Chinese ambassador.' He paused. 'We cannot risk exposing the truth. It would be too damaging.'

Josie looked on, horrified. 'And what about the Africans and what's happened to them?'

Neither of them answered her.

'Leave us.' Martha Lintel Montgomery ordered her out.

Josie got up and stormed out.

'My son will be out of hospital soon, what are you proposing we do?'

Dennison waited a moment, until he was certain no one was listening. He was about to suggest the unthinkable.

CHAPTER 35
BUCEPHALUS

Finnegan sat on his sofa looking up at the Jasper Johns painting; a slow smile grew until he began to laugh, a loud, full-bellied roar. He saluted the image of the US flag and gulped down one more whiskey. Inside his head he heard his wife's voice admonishing him for his drinking, reminding him what the doctor had said: "he must cut down." But today was not the day! He'd open several bottles of Bollinger tonight and they'd celebrate. Bucephalus was his gift to her. She had become the wife of Gene Finnegan from Detroit; now he'd give her a name to be proud of and immortality alongside him. He continued to let his thoughts flow freely. All those difficult decisions, far reaching calculations, meticulous planning and billions of dollars of investment had been worth it; he'd succeeded, he'd pulled it off. Bucephalus was about to be launched.

He pressed the intercom. 'Eliot, invite Ambassador Zhou to a meeting here. Insist he comes immediately.' He had one message for Zhou – "Build me more factories". The trouble at his LCC plant meant they'd missed his production targets. He wouldn't have the same problem in China, and if Zhou objected, he'd sweeten the deal by offering a second launch at the Beijing Motor Show. He knew China and the Far East were important markets. But then he was going to have no trouble selling the Bucephalus range. He laughed once more. He had already decided that without Feed Africa to fund, he'd hold on to the licence fee, thereby increasing his fortune even further. He felt magnificent, the equal to Alexander. His ego pumped up with pride at what he had achieved.

♦

Ambassador Zhou made a point of ignoring the sofa, choosing instead the firmness of the leather armchair. He sat down with the suppleness of a man who did tai chi each morning.

Finnegan was prepared for Zhou's foreplay. 'Are you pleased with the Genco?' he asked.

Zhou's answer didn't disappoint him. 'A fine car, but will it hold its value?'

'A Genco will always be a collector's item.'

'So you think it has rarity value?' Finnegan caught Zhou's slight mocking intonation; implying he understood how Finnegan used them to bribe people. 'I had it shipped back to China.'

Finnegan wondered if the Communist Party would allow Zhou to keep the expensive gift. It would raise doubts about his length of tenure in Washington. They would assume he'd been seduced, exposed to Western values and had developed an unhealthy love of personal luxury. He'd had enough of this. 'I have the report.'

'Professor Li delivered.' Zhou glanced up at the Jasper Johns painting. 'So where is he?' Zhou looked around pointedly, as if seeking him out.

Finnegan's temper rose but he held it in check and ignored Zhou's enquiry. Finnegan forced a smile. 'I don't need him here. We both know you speak perfect English. In my office we play by my rules.' He wanted to get down to the business. 'I need you to increase the volume of cars and trucks coming off the assembly line. It will require two more factories built immediately, with a further four to follow.'

'Yes with all the trouble in America, I can see how you might need us.'

Finnegan felt his heart rate increase, his insinuation wiping away the pleasure Finnegan felt. He walked over to his desk. He returned with a file. 'This will show how many more units we need.'

Zhou didn't look at the paperwork, instead he placed it face down on the table in front of him.

Finnegan was getting annoyed with Zhou's reluctance to agree to his demands. Did he have to remind him how much foreign currency China would earn?

'Do you remember when you gave me the keys to the Genco I made a little joke about being wary of Americans bearing gifts?'

'How is that relevant?

Zhou looked at Finnegan. 'You still intend to launch Bucephalus?'

'Why the hell wouldn't I?'

Finnegan's anger was simmering, the large vein thumping

on his forehead. 'Who told you about Bucephalus? Up till now it's not a word I've used in my dealings with you.'

The ambassador shrugged. 'It seems the president has forgotten my story too. How Troy was destroyed by a horse. You should remind him,' Zhou chuckled. Then his demeanour changed in an instant. The blank neutral mask returned. 'Without Bucephalus we might never have been able to achieve our goal.'

'What are you talking about?'

'I have a message from my government. We have ceased production of all LCC vehicles.'

Finnegan's heart rate shot up, his vision blurred for an instant as he yelled, 'You motherfucker.' He rose to his full height, towering over Zhou. 'What are you saying?' His voice was threatening and loud. He was aware of a tightening pain in his chest and sweat on his forehead. His breathing became more rapid with rage rolling up from the pit of his stomach. No one, especially not some slit-eyed yellow bastard was going to interfere with his plans; not now. He yelled at him, 'Do you know why Professor Li hasn't returned from Beijing?'

Zhou remained calm. 'His report, it doesn't mention GG42/OO – such a pity. It seems you have a problem with Bucephalus that Professor Li kept to himself.' Zhou dusted an imaginary flake of dust off his suit. 'He gave you the report you wanted and we have another.'

Finnegan was dumbstruck.

'I expect once the world knows about GG42/OO, we'll be able to buy LCC very cheaply.' Zhou actually laughed, 'because your company will be worthless.'

Finnegan couldn't move.

'Of course with all the help Professor Li gave us and the engineering design drawings we stole from Ham Farm, there is nothing to stop us producing our own version.' He smiled up at Finnegan.

Finnegan went white, feeling as if he was about to be sick, 'You fucking bastards!'

'Ah-ha the bastard; it's a pity she escaped. Like you we wanted it kept secret. Did you never wonder about the explosion on the boat? No, I see, it suited you too.' Zhou had risen out of the chair. 'How does it feel, knowing your legacy will be destroyed by the girl you chose?'

A torrent of actions and questions filled his mind, but the excruciating pain stopped them from forming into a coherent thought.

Zhou rose, bowed and walked out.

As the lift doors closed behind Zhou, he shouted at Eliot, 'Get me the president now!' He gripped his chest, his heart thumping hard, in time with the pulsating vein on his temple. He grasped his left arm as the pain shot down it.

At that moment the lift doors opened. Andy Malone strode in yelling, 'You frigging son of a bitch, what have you done to my company?'

Finnegan collapsed to the floor.

♦

Lady Alice opened the door. 'Andy how nice to see you, he's through there.' She pointed. 'No talking about business and don't stay too long.' She added quickly, 'Those are my orders. It's been a warning.'

Gene Finnegan was dressed, a rug over his knees, sitting

in a wheelchair looking out across the green paddocks and white fencing, to the grazing stud mares. He sat down on the chair beside him, putting his hand on Finnegan's forearm and leaving it there for a moment; a sign of their long friendship.

'How are you?' Andy had never seen him looking as vulnerable.

'I'm fine.' There was a slight slur. 'They pulled out of the deal.'

'No business talk, I've had my orders.' He winked. Inside he felt nervous.

Finnegan leaned towards him. 'Alice doesn't know about Bucephalus. I was going to tell her, when this happened.' He waved one hand around, the other inert on his thigh. 'They've used me.'

Andy looked round the room. There was no TV screen, computer or phone. 'Right now Gene I've got my own frigging problems.'

Lady Alice walked in with coffee. 'No business talk, remember. I don't want him worried about anything, other than getting better.'

'We're being good.' Alone, he leaned in inches away from Finnegan's face. 'Have you heard?'

Finnegan looked blankly at him.

'First they targeted my tankers in Africa and now I've got all these protesters barricading my refineries down south. The Governor's had to call in the National Guard. What if they impound my fuel and have it analysed? I've got the FBI asking me what's going on. What am I supposed to say?' He glared at Finnegan. 'The report – you said we had the green light?'

Finnegan nodded.

'There isn't a problem with it is there?' He remembered

an early meeting. 'You son of a bitch, you'd better not be lying to me.' He stared at the man in the wheelchair, wondering if he could trust him.

'Bucephalus, Zhou used the word. He knows. Li betrayed me.' Finnegan grabbed Andy's arm, his grip surprisingly strong. 'When I find him, I'll cut off his balls.'

'Damn the Chinese bastard. Gene, remember our plan. We can still do it.' He paused. 'I need to recoup my investment. AMOIL is haemorrhaging.' He looked out of the window. 'I don't want to lose my company.'

'They said they'd take over LCC.' Finnegan appeared to be in his own world.

'You need to get back to work, and sort this out.' Andy had got up and was standing by the window. 'You hate horses.' He turned. 'Unless they are made of metal and have an engine – remember.' It had the echo of their former bravado. Andy sat down beside Finnegan. 'Does anyone else know about Bucephalus?'

Finnegan didn't answer him for a long time. Then he said, 'The president's daughter.'

Andy stared across at him in disbelief. Who the hell was the president's daughter! He was going to say something then changed his mind. 'Make sure she doesn't speak to the president. You have to stop her. Do you hear what I'm saying?' He was gripping Finnegan's forearm tightly.

Lady Alice walked in. 'You've got visitors.'

♦

Sneider and Barr entered the room. 'We'd like to interview you both.' Sneider looked at Lady Alice, as she tried to interrupt him. 'As you said, your husband is making a good recovery, I'm sure he's up to answering our questions.'

Barr indicated to Malone and Lady Alice that they should step out of the room. He closed the door and sat down.

Sneider began, 'We are giving you the courtesy of interviewing you privately, away from the media or the public humiliation of an enquiry. In return we'd appreciate your total honesty. As you know the United States is going through a very difficult time and as an American patriot, I'm sure you will want to help our investigation.'

Finnegan nodded.

Barr began by asking him to explain what he knew about Feed Africa.

'It was my idea. LCC is always looking for new opportunities and markets. Africa has potential. I needed a way to test the market. The president saw the benefits and invited other American corporations to join in. The Lintels are well respected for their humanitarian work. It seemed a perfect fit. It was a way for me to sell more cars and for my old friend Andy and me to work together, as we've done before on many occasions.'

'As a true patriot and bona fide supporter,' Sneider's tone made the words and the sentiment sound disingenuous.

Barr spoke next, 'Why do you think AMOIL was targeted?'

'AMOIL's tactics are ruthless. They moved in, took over and upset the locals.' He paused. 'I expect they were getting their own back. A fuel tanker is an easy target.'

'Tell us about your deal with China?' Barr asked.

Finnegan didn't hesitate, as if his answers were well rehearsed. 'Their labour costs and raw materials are lower.

LCC supplied the engines and other parts to guarantee LCC quality.'

'Were there any other benefits?' Barr looked up from his notepad.

Finnegan asked for a glass of water. He drank some of it and passed the glass back to the FBI officer, treating him like a manservant. 'You know nothing about business do you? LCC is about innovation, quality and profit. I had a licensing deal with them. I had to recoup my investment costs.'

'And we'll be able to find the financial trail, will we?' Barr snapped back.

'Are you suggesting you'll find a problem?'

'We haven't seen any payments going into the company's accounts.'

'Because the money was paid into my charitable trust fund,' He looked amused. 'How I choose to spend my money is my decision.'

Barr wrote something down. 'We understand China has stopped producing LCC vehicles, why is that?'

Sneider added in quickly, 'It must have come as a shock, a bitter blow given all the benefits you've described, and coming on top of the trouble back here in America, not the best of timing.'

Finnegan looked at Sneider. 'You're the spook – you tell me. Who do you think is behind this unrest? Black Lives: White Lies, it was around long before my factory was hit.' Finnegan laughed. 'You must be desperate. You're not planning on making me your scapegoat are you? I'm an old man in a wheelchair and you think I'm responsible.' He laughed.

'Tell us about Bucephalus?' Barr sat waiting.

Finnegan took his time. 'It was an LCC project.'

'And…' Sneider leaned in, 'we can find no evidence of it at your laboratory. No one there has heard of it. But it exists, we know it does.'

Finnegan remained mute.

Barr asked, 'Let's leave that for the moment. Does the name Ham Farm mean anything?'

Finnegan's pupils reacted, before he slowly nodded his head. 'It's one of the farms on my wife's family estate in England. I visited it once. We toyed with the idea of establishing a stud farm on it. The Leals have always had an interest in horses; in fact there's a public racecourse on their estate.'

'So you never used it for Bucephalus?' Barr looked at Sneider.

'Why do you keep going on about Bucephalus?'

Sneider sat back. 'Now that's what we find very interesting. We thought your head of R&D could tell us, but he seems to have disappeared.'

Finnegan's right hand thumped the arm of his wheelchair. He looked at the two men. 'I'm the victim here. He's defected to China.' Finnegan continued to look affronted. 'He's the man you need to find and interrogate.'

Sneider leaned in. 'Again China.'

Finnegan didn't hesitate. 'I never trusted the Chinese. It was just a business deal. But you know what they are like. They've probably had a go at re-engineering my components. So if there's a problem, blame them.' He stared back at Sneider.

'So there's nothing troubling you?' Barr asked.

'The EPA gave me the go ahead.' Finnegan looked beyond the room. 'Ask Malone, it's his refineries that are under siege. I don't know what he's done to upset these protestors.'

'Do you think there is a problem?' Sneider asked innocently, 'We understand people are dying in southern Africa. President Abyoie has ordered an investigation. We believe China is supporting his enquiry. They are behind the African Union's request for the matter to be brought up at the UN. Do you want to add anything?'

'Find Professor Li,' Finnegan bellowed, 'Do your job; don't you see China wants to bring America to its knees, take us over; and you're helping them by focussing on me. They will launch their own version of my car!' He waved his hand at a blister pack on a nearby tray. 'Give me two pills.' Barr got them. 'We have to get in first before China dominates the market.' He stared at the two men. 'You don't realise how important this is. Financially it will save the US, allow us to rebuild our economy.' He breathed deeply. 'I am a patriot. I've only ever wanted to put America back on top. I'm innocent of whatever it is you think I've done. This interview is over.'

Neither of them moved. 'GG42/OO means nothing to you?'

'I build and sell cars.' Finnegan was flushed, a light sweat on his face. 'Get out.'

This time they did rise. 'We'll be in touch.'

Lady Alice was waiting for them. 'I heard shouting. I hope you'll leave him alone now. By the way Andy Malone has gone. He gave me a message to pass on. He'll talk to you, but only with his lawyer present.'

CHAPTER 36

ACT NOW "OR ELSE"

Montgomery was feeling tender but a whole lot better than he had done in years as he recovered in hospital. 'Jesus Christ who the hell let you in?' Finnegan was the last person he expected to see, and in a wheelchair. 'What happened to you?'

Finnegan ignored the question. 'I've got fantastic news. I've developed a completely green, emissions-free vehicle.' Despite being in a wheelchair, Finnegan still looked powerful. 'Do you realise what this means? How significant it will be?'

He remembered the last time Finnegan had sold him an idea. Feed Africa had been a glorious defining moment in his presidency. But now it was like ash in his mouth; the machinations of China, the threat to America's stability and the resulting deaths of so many of its citizens. It was no wonder he'd ended up in hospital. He didn't feel like listening to what Finnegan had to say; figuratively speaking his inbox was full.

Finnegan beamed. 'I'll be hailed as the world's saviour.'

Montgomery stifled a laugh. He knew he shouldn't trust Finnegan. There was always a price to pay. He was wiser. Yet the idea tumbled around in his head; an emissions-free car. As things were now, this could save his presidency. The news would go global. He could see it now; the world's media clamouring to know more. He put his hand up to shield his eyes from the late afternoon sun; at the same moment the light transmogrified into flashlights, TV crews and journalists calling out his name in his imagination. Currently the world tuned in each night to see America on its knees, struggling to contain the violence destroying its cities. This news was transformational. He felt a bubble of excitement burst. It would put America and the dollar back where they belonged. *This is how I'll be remembered.* He thought.

Finnegan was watching him.

Previously Montgomery thought Finnegan cared only about making money, until now when he realised he was like everyone else, afraid of his mortality. He felt sorry for him; he didn't have a child to pass his legacy onto. 'How long have you known about her?' he asked; a part of him felt jealous.

Finnegan merely shrugged. 'Do you want me to tell the media about your bastard?'

Montgomery's former compassion evaporated. 'Why are you here?'

Finnegan was by the window, the bright sunlight like a halo around a dark, breathing Mephistopheles. 'I know what you want.' Finnegan wheeled himself round to face Montgomery. 'You felt it with Feed Africa – all that adulation.'

Finnegan's words transported him back to those

wonderful days, the warmth and rapturous joy that greeted him.

'Imagine what this will be like.' Finnegan conjured up a dream with Montgomery centre stage, basking once again in the triumph and glory of being a world statesman.

He wavered, the desire to be acclaimed and admired rose up. He blamed his mother and her overbearing control. He hated to admit it, but Finnegan understood him. He wanted to be that man; a man who made his own decisions. He wanted his daughter to be proud of him. He couldn't stop the feeling of joy, as the automatic pump released another dose of morphine. At a stroke he would give the United States its pre-eminence back; not this mockery they were enduring. 'Why was Feed Africa so important to you?'

'I needed somewhere to carry out the field testing, without anyone suspecting.'

'You used me.' His euphoria evaporated. 'I'm not some tart you can pimp out for your own benefit.'

Finnegan turned on him. 'A bit late for your moral indignation, you were happy to take the bribe when it paid for Feed Africa.' Finnegan stared down at him. 'Look I don't give a damn about Africa. What I do care about is being an American. Every government across the globe will have to sanction these vehicles. Our economy will boom. As President of the United Sates, you'll have all the trillions of dollars you need to rebuild our country.' Finnegan looked at him. He laughed. 'Let's stop kidding ourselves. I know you Joe. You'd do anything to be free of your mother. It's why you jumped at Feed Africa, when we pitched it to you.'

'I didn't know you were setting me up.'

'Does it matter now?' Finnegan looked sanguine. 'For all I care, you can pull the plug on the whole damn lot.'

He stared at Finnegan, disgusted. 'Why do you want me to announce it? Don't you crave the glory? What was it you just said? "Hailed as a saviour"?' They glared at each other.

'Mr President, I don't care what you think of me. You need to do this for our country. We need to believe again. The Chicago Motor Show is in five days time. Make sure it is your first official visit.'

Montgomery hesitated. It was all too easy. He tried to see how Finnegan might be setting him up again. Where was the catch?

'You'll go down in history as one of the most remarkable presidents; turning America's fortunes around, bringing in a new era of unprecedented prosperity.'

It sounded like a voiceover to a hagiography of his life. It was flannel and he knew it. But from his inner being he knew too, he craved it as an epitaph. Everyone would remember him and what he had done. It would be his enduring legacy.

'Show them Slow-Hand Joe's back in the saddle and riding high.' Finnegan started to laugh. 'Or I can always ask Douglas Dennison to make the announcement.'

Montgomery pushed himself up in the bed. 'What is Bucephalus?'

Finnegan looked at him momentarily surprised. 'It was the name I gave to the project. Rather appropriate, don't you think? Alexander's horse, horse power; look at what he achieved on the back of Bucephalus.' His sustained laughter echoed in the room.

'I'm not sure,' he wavered, 'you've not explained why

the Chinese tried so hard to point the finger at you and Malone?'

'You put their noses out of joint by focussing on Africa. They considered it their backyard. They were simply out to make trouble.' Finnegan looked at him. 'You know your mother visited your daughter. Has she told you that you have a grandson?'

His right eyebrow rose as his mouth fell open.

'No, I'm not surprised.' Finnegan looked at him with pity. 'You know what that means. She has her legacy – a great grandson. I'm afraid she's given up on you. What can you offer her now? Your presidency is coming to an end and Dennison won't want his name associated with Feed Africa.' Finnegan leaned in close. 'Do you have the guts or has she finally eviscerated you?' Montgomery stared back at him. 'Remember what I've said – Chicago in five days.'

By the door he wheeled himself round, giving Montgomery one final look. 'Dennison's looking everywhere for dirt. How are you going to explain the Chinese laundry?' He laughed. It was a deeply unpleasant sound. 'I'd say you are facing an impeachment hearing. What will Josie think of you then?' He waited a moment. 'You don't have much time or many options. This really is your last chance, act now or else!' The shaft of yellow afternoon light surrounding Finnegan disappeared as the door slammed shut behind him.

CHAPTER 37

SHOWTIME

Martha Lintel Montgomery, Dennison, Sneider and Barr were together at the Belmont. No one else was present. This meeting was definitely off the record.

Barr began, 'We've found no evidence that Finnegan contacted Josie Ryland while she was out of the country, working at Ham Farm. Eliot Finnegan's secretary is a hundred per cent loyal. She'll never divulge anything. Whatever happened in England will end up being her word against his.'

'So no further forward then,' Dennison said.

'We do have one piece of evidence, a shipment of AMOIL fuel. It is more promising than it sounds. I think we can use it to drive a wedge between the two of them.'

'I very much doubt it. They've been close friends for nearly fifty years,' Martha Lintel Montgomery said.

Dennison looked at her, 'Even the oldest and closest of friends can fall out.'

Martha Lintel Montgomery looked stony faced.

Barr picked up the thread, 'Malone would only talk to us with his legal team present. He was at pains to point out the fuel used in Africa was a formula LCC provided. The deal was exclusivity; in return for AMOIL agreeing not to re-engineer it.'

Sneider added, 'He's denying any culpability.'

Dennison was looking more interested. 'You think he might give evidence against Finnegan in return for immunity?'

Sneider immediately stepped in, 'No, you cannot risk it. Exposing what went on raises the stakes in an already volatile situation.'

'What do you suggest we do?' Dennison asked abruptly.

'Offer President Abyoie something he wants. Buy him off – to keep him quiet.'

'Fine, but I still want to bloody the nose of the Chinese; make them pay for what they've done. What are my options?' Dennison looked at Sneider.

'You won't like it, Sir. Expand the Feed Africa programme.'

'No never!' Dennison exploded.

Sneider wasn't finished explaining, 'In essence it was a sound and successful programme.' He looked at Martha Lintel Montgomery. 'You succeeded in attracting all the major American corporations, so why stop now? Trade is what we Americans do best. Throw in a new black Peace Corp for Africa,' he paused, 'and the noise surrounding LCC and AMOIL will be yesterday's news.'

Martha Lintel Montgomery looked to be in agreement.

Sneider needed Dennison to see the bigger picture. 'With China supporting the AU, we're going to find ourselves constantly rubbing up against China. Who is to say they won't agitate and sponsor violence as before? Africa will become a breeding ground for militants; with the United States as their primary target?' He hoped Dennison was bright enough to understand. 'Nor do we want to expose the US to further internal scrutiny. What I'm saying is offer friendly African countries investment, trade deals; don't let China walk away with the whole continent unopposed.'

'You want me to cover it up.'

'Yes,' the two men said in unison.

'It's not enough.'

'There's one more thing you need to consider. We cannot assume the Chinese aren't about to produce their version of an emissions-free car.' He looked at Dennison. 'Do you want to give them that opportunity?'

'You said you wanted to get even,' Barr added. 'Launch Bucephalus and make the agenda all about climate change.'

'China will oppose it because it undermines their economic growth. But you'll have the rest of the world on your side, supporting the US position.' Sneider briefly smiled at Dennison. 'You'll have outflanked and out-manoeuvred the Chinese, Sir.'

'But what if they release the data? We know Bucephalus is dangerous.' Dennison still wasn't sure.

'If they publish or leak any damaging reports, it will look like sour grapes,' Barr said, reassuring him. 'We have our findings too. They show how China stirred up trouble, targeted American companies and blew up our embassy.'

The room fell silent.

'Where does that leave my granddaughter and her accusations?' Martha Lintel Montgomery asked. 'She's unlikely to walk away.'

‘Can she be trusted?’ Dennison looked at his old friend.

‘What do you mean?’ Martha Lintel Montgomery’s neck coloured instantly.

Sneider didn’t hesitate. ‘We know Dr Holloway was fired, so he’s like any employee with a grievance and nothing to lose. If Finnegan pulls out of Africa having got what he wanted, Coetzer will be looking for someone else to pick up the tab. And as for Dr Ryland, she has her own agenda. I imagine she’s always desperate for more doctors, nurses, equipment and medicines; it all comes down to money.’

Barr chipped in, ‘We’ve found a South African government lab report, saying there was no evidence of sleeping sickness in the sample provided.’

‘Will your granddaughter’s evidence stand up to scrutiny?’ Sneider posed the question. ‘We know how reports can be written to support a particular argument. Has she done the same?’ He paused letting the idea take root. ‘Is her plan simple: designed to extract millions from the Lintel Foundation by ruining the president’s name and blackmailing the administration?’

‘No, that’s not true!’

‘Your granddaughter is a bright, resourceful young woman. She’s seen an opportunity, offering you the one thing you want – the continuance of the Lintel dynasty. And you’ve accepted everything she says.’

Martha Lintel Montgomery got up and left the room.

Dennison looked at Sneider. ‘You may come to regret that.’

Sneider shrugged. ‘The granddaughter has inherited more than the Lintel raised eyebrow and those piercing grey eyes.’ Everyone chuckled. ‘She appears to have the same single-minded focus to get what she wants. Besides it wouldn't surprise me if Martha hasn't already done a deal with her.'

'So she's not going to be a problem?' Dennison asked. It sounded like a decision not a question.

Sneider and Barr both nodded.

'We haven't got much time Sir,' Sneider stood up. 'There's one more thing.' Sneider looked towards the closed bedroom door. 'Has she agreed to it?'

'If it saves the Lintel name she'll swallow it, especially if you sugar the pill. You remember we spoke about that previously.' Dennison rose slowly like a man carrying a heavy weight. 'Make it happen.'

They shook hands.

♦

Josie slammed the door, 'Bastards.' TJ heard and in his sing-song voice he stomped around the room mimicking her.

Christina heard the door open and shut as Martha Lintel Montgomery went in to see Josie. She couldn't quite hear what they were saying to each other. But at one point she heard Josie's voice shouting, 'Your hands will be dripping with even more blood.' Martha must have said something to her because Josie's next words were quite clear, 'I'll never let you get your hands on my son.'

The bedroom door opened and Martha Lintel Montgomery called out to Christina, 'Take the boy for a walk. His mother's being hysterical.' She turned and looked back into the room. 'You need to calm down. We all have to make sacrifices. I've made more than most.'

♦

'Annie, it's me – have you got a moment?'

'Hi you, yes; you sound angry by the way. What's happening? Is TJ fine?'

'He's getting bigger by the day.' She paused, 'They're going ahead despite all I've told them.'

There was a long pause, 'Did you really think you could stop it?'

'I suppose I did.'

'What can you do now?'

'You've still got all Jon's records haven't you? If anything happens to me, you know what to do.'

'I take it you've not given up then,' Annie laughed, 'you really are that determined dung beetle.'

Josie smiled at the memory of Johannes. It reminded her of what was at stake.

'Josie, are you in any danger?'

♦

The cavalcade of twenty cars drove down Martin Luther King Drive to the McCormick Place convention centre in Chicago. Alone in the car President Montgomery was able to question Jim on what had happened in his absence. He'd already been briefed officially. This was the chance for Jim to give him the nuances, shifts in power and trouble that might be heading his way. He was particularly interested to know what Douglas Dennison and his mother had been up to.

'In your absence your mother's court moved to the Presidential Suite at the Belmont. I think you could say her feathers were ruffled. No one asked her to be the president while you were in hospital.'

They both laughed.

'She and Lady Alice have not seen each other since her return.'

He raised an eyebrow. 'Perhaps she took umbrage that Finnegan came to visit me rather than her.' He paused. 'Do you know she never contacted me while I was in hospital?' It made him sound like a spoilt child, but then she had an uncanny ability to get under his skin.

'There may have been another reason. She was spotted with a little boy.' Jim carried on, 'The gossip is it has something to do with Feed Africa, an orphan or—'

'More like a photo opportunity,' he interjected quickly remembering Finnegan's conversation.

'There are rumours about an important announcement.'

He didn't trust her. Somehow – whatever it was, it would be about promoting the Lintel name; it always was. He could never remember a time when it wasn't. As he settled back into the leather of the limousine he waved the speech in his hand. 'Has it been checked?'

Jim nodded. 'It is as Finnegan claims, an emissions-free car. Don't worry this is going to be great for you.' He paused. 'Dennison however, is more of a problem.'

Montgomery's political antennae lit up. 'Why, what's up?' He tried to appear calm. 'Has he met with Ambassador Zhou?'

'Zhou's been recalled.'

He was surprised. He hoped China wasn't about to change its position. He had only been back a few days and already the stress of the office returned. His skin tones were unhealthily pale. Should he get William to dye his hair again?

'Don't worry. Dennison is on a fishing expedition. He's been asking about something called Bucephalus? I said you had no knowledge of it.' Jim looked at him for confirmation.

It was his turn to nod his head in silence.

Jim carried on but Montgomery wasn't listening. What if Dennison found out about the Feed Africa payments? It might have been filtered through Finnegan, but it was the source of the money that mattered. How would he explain to the American people and his fellow politicians that communist China was paying for his humanitarian programme? It diminished America further. He imagined the feeding frenzy his opponents would have. His hands felt sweaty. He never should have trusted Finnegan again.

He glanced outside at the huge crowds now lining either side of the road. He relaxed. This was more like it. The White House had done its job; leaking that POTUS was about to make an important statement.

'Did my daughter accept the invitation?' he asked Jim, hoping she'd be there to see his moment of triumph.

'Yes, she's travelling with your mother and Sneider.'

The crowds grew thicker, waving placards. He noticed the placards had the now familiar Black Lives: White Lies words; reminding him how much work was needed to heal the rifts. 'Jim, why are these protesters here?'

Jim leaned forward slightly and pressed the communications link to the secret service. He asked for an update on the situation outside.

He could now hear quite clearly what they were chanting. He looked on in disbelief. He shouted at Jim, 'Jesus Christ what the hell is going on?' His face was flushed and shiny. Had the situation escalated in his absence? 'I'm about to make a major statement on climate change!'

The crowd surged forward, rattling the metal barriers; shouting and jeering as the line of cars drove towards the entrance. The police raised their shields, their batons ready. The crowd kept on pressing forward, not intimidated but angry; the chanting increasing in volume. He saw people wearing face masks daubed in red paint; the same colour dripping down placards covering the Feed Africa logo.

He looked on, incredulous.

Jim shouted, 'Abort, abort, Stagecoach is leaving now.' The whole cavalcade suddenly sped up, driving past the official party waiting on the steps.

He craned his head round, looking back. 'Who gave the order to abort?' He went puce. 'You've made me look like a coward!' Suddenly he doubted everyone around him; had there been a *coup d'état* in his absence?

'Sir, there was a warning – a lone shooter. The secret service called it in. We had to leave.' Jim was shocked. 'What do you want to do?' he asked.

'Get me into that convention centre now! I intend to deliver my speech.' He looked at Jim, his closest adviser and political fixer. 'You can explain to the media and the reception party why we didn't use the front entrance, and you'd better make it sound good.' He was boiling over with anger. 'And Jim, I want confirmation before I step outside of this vehicle that those protestors haven't infiltrated security, and are waiting inside to hijack my speech.' He hoped he could trust Jim. 'Do you think you can manage that?'

It had been a routine operation, and even if he had come

back sooner than his doctor advised, he shouldn't be feeling this bad. His medical team didn't understand politics. In the vacuum created by his absence the White House, far from running smoothly, opened itself up to intrigue like a medieval city state. Keep your enemies close; wasn't that the mantra all powerful men operated by? He felt certain Douglas Dennison was behind this. Why wouldn't he? He'd tasted executive power and no doubt wanted more. The president knew how intoxicating it was.

'Is the vice-president here?'

'Yes, he insisted.'

I bet he did, Montgomery thought. 'Once we're inside and before I go on stage, tell him I want to see him.'

They arrived safely underground using a service entrance as the cavalcade regurgitated secret service agents. They fanned out clearing and securing a safe passage. The reception party had gathered backstage. He greeted them with a relaxed smile and firm handshake; giving the impression the situation was under control. He saw Jim Morgan apologising for the sudden change, the threat of the lone shooter as the reason. Looking at Jim, the words created a mental picture of a deserted, dusty Western street with Slow-Hand Joe walking down it, his duster coat tucked behind the gun rig, his hand ready.

'Are you all right?' Douglas Dennison was suddenly in front of him.

His hand twitched. They shook hands for the cameras. 'After I've given my speech, I want you to explain to me what the hell was going on out there.'

He didn't want to see his mother. This time he would show her. He looked around for Josie and saw his mother in animated conversation with her. He caught sight of Sneider and Barr standing nearby. He didn't have time to talk to Josie. He was being called onto the stage. Walking towards the podium, he hoped Vernon had done a good job. He felt his anger drain out, replaced by rising anticipation. He was about to surprise them all and especially his mother. *Stride out there confidently*, he told himself, *make sure everyone sees I'm fully recovered and back in charge.*

The speech was short and powerful. It outlined the global catastrophe represented by car exhaust emissions, saying it was one of the greatest threats to mankind as well as the planet's eco system. 'Today I can announce the Lexington Car Company is unveiling the first ever emissions-free – green car.' Suddenly there was rapturous applause with people screaming and whistling. He held his hand up, grinning broadly. 'LCC in partnership with AMOIL, two great iconic American brands have changed the future of the petrol-driven engine.' He then took everyone by surprise. 'As of now the United States will reverse its position and sign up to the Kyoto Protocol. We will halt climate change; just as we put a man on the moon, the United States of America will lead the way to a new dawn of hope for mankind.'

It was as he'd imagined it. The stunned gasp and then the immediate furore as wild applause and cheering rang out from the Green Peace activists. The White House had done a good job; they were here in numbers. The crowd's delight enveloped him; flashlights exploded from every direction, giant American flags unfurled to the sound of the Star Spangled Banner and green balloons in their hundreds descended. Centre stage, flashing lights on a spindle lit up the revolving stands. Three iconic vehicles: a sleek red

Genco, in the middle a white LCC 4x4 utility truck, and beside it in blue an urban family saloon. Gene Finnegan sat alone in the back of the 4x4 waving at the crowds, his wheelchair cleverly disguised. There was no sign of Malone.

Back stage it was bedlam. The president was surrounded by the press and people wanting to shake his hand. He was jostled, shaking outstretched hands, enjoying every moment. Slowly the suited bulky shapes of his secret service agents surrounded him, moving him imperceptibly away and into a private reception suite where Douglas Dennison, his mother and Josie were waiting for him.

Still euphoric, he went to kiss his mother on her cheek. 'So what do you think of me now?'

She slapped his face. 'You were always such a disappointment, just like your father.' They glared at each other.

'What the hell do you mean?' He was flabbergasted. She'd done what she always did – taken away anything he valued and replaced it with her disapproval.

'For once, be the son I can be proud of.' Martha looked at him with tears in her eyes. She grasped him to her bosom briefly, her long fingernails digging into him, before pushing him away from her.

Sneider stepped forward, accompanied by two secret service agents. 'You need to leave now using the underground exit.' The agents stood either side of him with Barr behind him.

'I thought this time I'd leave by the front door,' he said. He looked around. 'Where's my daughter?'

Douglas Dennison stepped forward, blocking his way. 'Either you follow our orders, or you can answer questions before the Senate at your impeachment trial. This is about saving America, not a president.' Dennison gave the order, 'Get him out now.'

♦

All the photographers, journalists, TV crews and crowds were gathered at the front of the building waiting for the emergence of the president, who had been delayed by the reception inside. The police were lined up behind the barriers, preventing the now familiar protestors from rushing forward, when out came a flood of Green Peace activists from the convention centre. The police were caught between the two excited, baying groups. The commander on the ground immediately knew he needed more men and quickly.

He radioed the command centre, 'Who ordered the release of the crowd out the front? They were to exit at the rear.'

The radio crackled, 'Stagecoach is using the rear exit.'

The commander swore. The FBI had been spooked earlier by the threat of a lone shooter. Was the threat still live, hence the change of plan? He didn't have time to find out. He needed the officers stationed at the rear to come to the front of the building and help keep the two groups apart. The secret service inside could handle the presidential party. Everyone's attention was focussed on the front with TV news cameras poised, ready to capture the rapidly disintegrating scene; outside the service entrance and waiting, the line of black limousines with their engines running.

♦

Finnegan's gait was unsteady, relying on the walking-stick in his right hand. Lady Alice was poised, ready to grab his upper arm should he fall. They walked slowly towards the president. Lady Alice caught Martha's eye. She very deliberately turned her back on Lady Alice; her imperious features cast in cold marble.

Finnegan hadn't seen the exchange. 'I wonder how comfortable she feels having a coloured great-grandson.'

'Gene, I'm not interested.'

Her voice had an edge to it. What did it matter now; today he was Alexander. His testosterone running high, he kissed her full on the mouth. Nothing was going to ruin his day. 'Let me walk over to him by myself. I want to shake the president's hand and see our photograph on every front page tomorrow.' He'd achieved everything he'd dreamed of, this was the apogee of his career, the culmination of his dream – Bucephalus launched.

'Mr President,' he called out.

The president turned and saw Finnegan. He looked at Sneider. 'Give them a moment,' Sneider said.

The agents moved discreetly forward standing either side of the passageway, with their arms by their sides, continuously scanning up and down the corridor.

Finnegan reached Montgomery. 'Didn't I tell you it'd be like this? Together we've saved America.' Finnegan looked round. 'Where's the White House photographer? I want him to capture this moment.' He grasped the president's hand, partly to steady himself though his grip was firm.

Sneider pressed himself up against the wall and called out a name. A slight, bespectacled man ran forward; as he drew level he pulled out a gun and fired two shots. The secret service men reacted immediately, drawing their SIG –Sauer P220 pistols. They fired in unison. The gunman fell at their feet. One agent checked him as the other moved towards the president and Finnegan. Both lay dead.

The corridor looked like an abattoir; crimson-red fresh blood and brains, contained in the small space, splattered up the walls, ceilings and onto the floor making it slippery. Sneider looked down at his feet, smelling piss and cordite. He moved his arm to his mouth to shout into his radio, 'Stagecoach is down.' A tiny fragment of skull and hair dropped to the floor from his raised arm.

The sound of gunshots brought people running from the service entrance and reception room. Lady Alice screamed. Two secret service agents grabbed her, holding her back. Martha Lintel Montgomery rushed forward. She collapsed onto her knees, grasping her son's body to her chest and rocking it backwards and forwards, as cameras flashed capturing Slow-Hand Joe in his final moment; the narrative of her Lintel legacy secured. He'd died a hero, gunned down at his moment of triumph; his mother as always by his side.

Josie stood open-mouthed with shock. Everyone around her moved as if in slow motion, their screams muffled. She looked down the corridor, knowing she'd witnessed the assassination of the President of the United States and Gene Finnegan. She was unable to move. Then time accelerated, as secret service agents arrived shouting, ordering people to move, herding them away from the scene; the cacophony confusing already terrified people. Suddenly she was aware of someone grabbing her, as she watched Sneider take hold of Douglas Dennison, propelling him towards the line of waiting limousines outside.

'Come with me.' Barr gripped her upper arm.

She tried to wrestle her arm free, to loosen his hold on her. His grip tightened. She stopped struggling and looked directly into his eyes. 'Am I next on your list?' As he began to drag her away, she peered over her shoulder yelling, 'Martha!'

Suddenly a tall, well-muscled black man stood in front of them, blocking their way.

'Move your ass.' Barr went to get his gun, when the black man swiftly grabbed his hand, crushing it before he could reach inside his jacket. Pinned up against the wall, he couldn't reach for his radio either.

'Let go of her,' the man said, 'she's coming with me.' He had a strong South African accent.

Josie pulled herself free and stood looking at the black man, not sure who he was.

'President Abyoie sent me. He wants to meet you.' He gave her a reassuring smile. 'I'm to escort you home. You are a very important lady apparently.'

The black bodyguard turned to Barr. 'Don't try and stop us. There is a diplomatic car waiting outside to take us to O'Hare airport.'

♦

In the car on their way to the airport, TJ beside her, the bodyguard passed over a small package. She opened it carefully; surprised to see a jade thorn. 'Who gave you this?'

'I was told it has very strong muti,' he said grinning at her, 'it'll protect you from bad men.'

Josie looked at the talisman; images of Ham Farm, Prof Li, *Grey Goose* exploding and Tomas flooded her mind's eye.

She was having trouble processing all that had happened in the last forty minutes. She was intrigued by the thorn. Slowly it dawned on her. She'd become a pawn in another game. This time the game was being played by China and America. The one wanted her alive because of the threat she represented to the other. The talisman was their message to her. They would protect her. The other player wanted her out of the game and silenced because of what she knew and could reveal about their actions. She flipped the talisman repeatedly like an experienced poker player. *This is not over yet*, she thought.

♦

The little dung beetle turned around and with its back legs, pushing hard it eventually manoeuvred the ball out of the bowl in the dusty road. Its task far from over, it turned around and carried on.

Matador